MISTLETOE AT THE MANOR

Teresa F. Morgan

SAPERE
BOOKS

MISTLETOE AT THE MANOR

Published by Sapere Books.

20 Windermere Drive, Leeds, England, LS17 7UZ,
United Kingdom

saperebooks.com

ISBN: 978-1-80055-477-1

For Fi,
Long may our prosecco (and cake) fuelled adventures continue!
Thank you for being a truly fabulous friend who always makes me
laugh, and will always go that extra mile.
This story is for you.
Kapu!
Love Patsy Xx

ACKNOWLEDGEMENTS

Back in September 2018, I joined a business networking group for women now called Weston Business Women. I initially went along as a lonely author but have since then gained so many new friends and experiences from this group of empowering women.

One friend I met was Jane Dare, who, at the time, owned a network marketing business called Captain Tortue. It was a pop-up boutique. For research, I went along to Jane's house and saw all the wonderful clothes — and came home with a few too! Jane's business was the inspiration behind Beth's pop-up boutique, and she even helped me with the idea of the fashion show as a charity event, although we sadly never got to actually run one. So, this is a big thank you to Jane for all her help and encouragement with the research for this book, and for being a lovely friend who has improved my wardrobe! I'm never short of an outfit now.

During writing this series, I also got to attend a writing workshop organised by Alison Knight and Jenny Kane. It was held at Northmoor, on the border of Somerset and Devon. Although it was only a one-day event, it was a truly inspiring and relaxing day. The house and the grounds became the inspiration behind Trenouth Manor, which had a little walk on part in *Cocktails at Kittiwake Cove* but featured more prominently in this novel. At the time of attending, it was late spring and Northmoor was in full bloom with Wisteria. Luckily, regular visits to Tyntesfield at Christmas helped with adding the seasonal touch to the manor. Jenny and Alison hold regular writing retreats at Northmoor, and I intend to return (one day!) to one of their weeklong writing retreats.

My regular National Trust adventures also feature in this book. I love all the houses that I visit locally, but one is Knightshayes in Devon. The Stables at Trenouth Manor, the home of Beth's Boutique, are based a little on the old stables at Knightshayes — which is the entrance and coffee shop. If you've not visited, you must!

I cannot write acknowledgements without giving my RNA Chapter — Weston to Wells — a mention. It's been a tough 18 months, and some of us were finally able to meet in September 2021 face-to-face. However, Fay Keenan has kept me going regularly over zoom! So, thank you to all in my Chapter, and especially Fay who is my writer-y best friend.

Thank you to Sara Keane, my agent, for always helping to add flavour to my books. Thank you to Amy Durant at Sapere Books for bringing my books to life in the publishing world.

There have been many more people involved in this book's journey and I am grateful to you all. And my biggest thanks always goes to you, the reader. I love writing, and creating the escapism, so without you, well, I just wouldn't have the excuse to do it.

CHAPTER 1: PINGU

October

"Really? You're going to do this to me now, Pingu?"

Frustrated, Beth Sterling slammed her hands down on the steering wheel, then jumped at the sudden sound of her car horn blasting.

Although hindered by a flat tyre, she'd managed to steer the small car into a side turning on the Cornish country lane. Stepping out of her Fiat 500c convertible, she slammed the baby blue door and kicked the deflated front wheel for good measure.

"Bugger you!"

She tucked a strand of her bobbed red hair behind her ear as she fought down the urge to scream. She didn't have time to wait for the recovery services. She would have to call them later. Even though her brother was a mechanic, she refused to call him out. Jason did enough for her as it was. He'd found her the car a couple of years ago, and it suited her perfectly. Fun, cheap to run, and practical-ish — until she had decided to open a pop-up boutique.

Needing to abandon ship if she were to make her appointment, she ducked back inside the car, pressed the roof button, and with a mechanical whirring sound, it rolled back up. It was that time of year where it was chilly in the morning, but by the afternoon the sun's warmth made you want to strip off your jumper and wish you were still in flip-flops rather than boots. Today was proving to be one of those days.

Praying she had enough signal, Beth fired up Google Maps on her phone and entered the postcode of her destination. It was now twenty minutes away on foot. Luckily, she'd set off early this morning, never liking to be late, so she would just about make her appointment in time.

Fifteen minutes later, her calves aching because she was walking fast in the wrong footwear for hiking along a narrow country lane — ankle boots with heels — she neared her destination: Trenouth Manor.

Out of nowhere, a small tractor came hurtling around the corner of the lane. The man driving it, a blur, swore at her. She jumped out of her skin and out of the way, just in time.

"Look where you're going!" he shouted over the rumble of the engine, as Beth thrust herself deep into the hedgerow lining the grassy verge, her heart pounding at such a near miss. The driver hit the brakes, his tyres skidding on wet leaves, then he carried on, shouting something about bloody tourists and mobile phones.

Yes, she'd had her eyes on her phone, but why the hell had he been driving so fast on such a narrow road? Beth swore back at him, but he was long gone.

And she wasn't a tourist, thank you very much. She'd lived in Cornwall her whole life.

As her heartrate normalised and her fury abated, Beth reached the entrance to Trenouth Manor. She walked along the gravelled drive, trying to scrape the mud from the grass verge off her heels. She really should have worn flats. It wasn't as if she was attending a job interview. *They* needed to impress *her*.

Part way down, the drive forked; left for The Stables, right for the house. She'd been asked to call in at the office in the main house first, so she picked up her pace, her calves complaining, and took the right-hand fork.

As she rounded a corner, Trenouth Manor came into view before her. It was a breathtakingly beautiful Victorian mansion, possibly not as large as some of the National Trust properties she'd been dragged around as a child with her brother and her parents, but just as impressive. She followed a path to the back of the house, from where the building's L shape was revealed. At the far end, a wisteria clung to the walls, only the leaves remaining, but Beth could imagine it would look spectacular in late spring with its lavender-blue blossom. She spotted a small sign which read, 'The Office', pointing to the left. Glancing at the time on her phone, she picked up her pace, jogging around to the left of the house before at last finding the office. She arrived red-faced from the exertion. "Sorry I'm late," she said breathlessly, holding her hand out. "I'm Beth Sterling. I'm here about leasing your available unit in The Stables."

"Oh, yes," the young woman shook her hand. "Welcome to Trenouth Manor. I'm Anya; we spoke on the phone. I'm the events coordinator and general dogsbody, but don't tell my boss I said that." She chuckled. The two women were about the same age, and Beth admired Anya's welcoming smile and pretty features accentuated by her short, dark hair, which was tucked behind her ears. Her eyes were a warm, welcoming brown.

"My car broke down, so I had to walk the last mile," Beth puffed, feeling the need to justify why she looked anything but calm and fresh. She'd wrapped her jumper inelegantly around her waist. "And then to make matters worse, I was nearly run over by a bloody tractor!"

"Oh, you poor thing," Anya said sympathetically. "Would you like a drink? Coffee?"

"I could murder a cup of tea."

"Take a seat for a minute." Anya pointed to a couple of office chairs lined up against the wall.

Beth was relieved to sit down. In the corner, behind another desk which was clearly not Anya's — it was messier with paperwork — was a large dog bed. Snoozing inside lay a Border Collie, which lifted its chin and looked briefly up at her, before settling back to sleep.

There was a table in the corner of the office, where a kettle stood with ceramic jars marked tea, coffee, and sugar. Anya fetched a clean mug and made the tea.

"Sugar?"

"No thanks."

While Beth drank, Anya explained that although her official title was events coordinator, she was also the office manager. She had an assistant called Cathy who worked mornings, to help with the administration.

Anya then escorted Beth to The Stables. They strolled along a path lined with clipped square yew hedges, the gravel crunching beneath their feet. It led to a modest archway, through which was a huge, cobbled courtyard, surrounded on all four sides by the original Victorian stables which had been built with red-flecked bricks. Perfectly symmetrical, on each side of the courtyard were four large stable doors, painted a deep glossy red to match the bricks. Beth assumed that each of these former stables were now rental units.

Opposite them was a tall archway, which would have once had carriages and horses trundling through. In the middle of the courtyard was an old fountain, now empty. Beth imagined it had once been the drinking trough for the horses.

Anya unlocked the door to the unit and gestured for Beth to enter first. Beth was pleased to see that it was painted a gloss white on the inside and, being a stable door, the top half could be opened without the bottom. Inside, it looked as if an office-based business had previously used the unit. There were still a couple of desks and a filing cabinet.

"Oh, I thought those had been removed." Anya tutted. "And I'll get our local decorator in to touch up the paintwork before you take it over." Anya gestured to a few marks on the walls and some grubby fingerprints around the light switch. "If you take it, that is."

Looking past the unwanted furniture and the scuffs on the walls, Beth could see the area was perfect for what she needed. She could imagine rails installed to hang the clothes and a small corner sofa for her customers to sit at if she had a small group in. She would have white or beech wooden box shelves for displaying folded T-shirts and the odd accessory, like a hat, purse or shoes. She'd turn the compact space into the perfect boutique, with full-length mirrors dotted around and a changing corner, shielded by a screen.

The upstairs, which was not as large as the ground floor, had a small kitchenette area, including a small fridge, and would be perfect as her office and for storage of additional clothing and orders, as well as her upright garment steamer.

She was pleased to find a toilet on the ground floor, too. Apparently, each unit had had plumbing installed in the renovation a few years ago. This would work for her less abled or older customers, who might find stairs difficult. Even though her clothing range was casual to contemporary, there were more formal outfits in the spring/summer range that would work for the mother of the bride, and this was a market Beth wanted to tap into. And being situated near a venue used for parties and weddings might help her pick up some trade.

"What is it you do?" Anya asked as Beth snapped photos on her phone and jotted measurements down in her notepad.

"I own a pop-up boutique."

"A what?"

"A sort of travelling boutique. I visit people's houses or attend charity events, workplaces or even salons or gyms. Wherever customers are, I can bring my clothing range and pop up!" Beth said. "The brand is Vivienne Rémy, and it's not found on the high street."

"Oh, right. That sounds intriguing." Anya nodded with interest as she continued to show Beth around.

"Basically, I've outgrown the spare room at home, and would love to create an environment for my customers to come and enjoy their shopping experience."

'Outgrown the spare room' was an understatement. And having to clear George's toys away and keep the house spick and span was tiresome. Her brother Jason shared his house with Beth and her young son George, and he'd insisted that she needed to build her business before taking on the expense of a premises, so that's what she'd done. She now wanted to take her business to the next level, by offering the full one-to-one boutique experience or hosting small personal styling parties.

Moving her business out of the family home would also make more room in the house for the three of them to live comfortably again. Especially as George was growing so fast. The spare room would become George's bedroom. She would have a room to herself, at last, and Jason wouldn't have to put up with women's clothing lying around his house. She might still have to visit customers in their homes and other venues, but she wanted this to be her new base.

However, attempting to do this two months before Christmas was possibly not the brightest of ideas. But when she'd spotted this unit being advertised, she felt she should snap it up. She knew a workspace like this would go quickly. And everything else she'd seen was either out of her budget or too small.

"Oh, so this space would be perfect," Anya said, her smile brightening further.

"Yes, I think it will be. It would be a lovely place for customers to come."

Once Beth had finished measuring and getting a feel for the space, Anya gave Beth a tour of The Stables, to introduce her to the other occupants of the units. There was a florist called Poppy, which Beth considered an apt name given her profession. Then she met Lisa, who made pottery and ran workshops. Her workspace was slightly larger. She was busy at her pottery wheel so waved a wet, red clay-covered hand. There was also a wood carver, a sugar crafter, someone who made jewellery and someone else who blew glass.

The introductions over, Anya walked Beth back towards the house.

"The business owners organise a Christmas fayre at The Stables, so this might be something that would appeal to you, too, with people buying their Christmas presents," Anya said eagerly.

"And last-minute Christmas party outfits."

"Oh, I might have to take a look!" Anya said with a smile. Beth was already feeling she'd made a new friend today. "If you're interested in the unit, I can give you the date."

Beth nodded enthusiastically. "Yes, yes, I'm definitely interested. It's ideal. But I'd like to run it by my brother first."

"I understand. As you can see, it's empty, so you can move in as soon as you like really," Anya explained, holding the door open to the office so Beth could enter first. "Let's make another cuppa."

While Anya ran through the terms for renting the unit with Beth, a man popped his head around the door. In his mid-thirties, tanned and very handsome with dark wavy hair, he was casually dressed in a surfing T-shirt and khaki shorts. He was clearly a man who didn't want to see the summer disappear just yet and was ignoring the fact that autumn had arrived.

"Hello! Is Tristan about?" he asked Anya. He glanced at Beth, giving her a friendly, apologetic smile for butting in.

"No, sorry, he had to head over to the glamping field," Anya replied.

"I was just popping in as I was passing. I've got a quick question for him." Looking relaxed, he pushed his hands into his pockets. "Do you know how long he'll be?"

Anya shrugged. "Sorry, Joe. I'll let him know you called in. Or you can call him on his mobile."

Joe nodded. "Yeah, I'll do that."

As he turned to leave, Anya called after him. "Hey, Joe, you couldn't help a woman in distress, could you?"

"Yeah, sure," Joe frowned questioningly. "Who's the woman in distress?"

"Beth here. She's got a flat tyre."

"Oh, there's no bother. I'll ring the AA in a minute." Beth shook her head.

"But you'll be waiting ages. Joe can change a wheel." Anya looked pleadingly at Joe. "Can't you?"

"Yes, of course." Joe shrugged nonchalantly. "I'll wait until you're ready, if you two have business to attend to."

Anya looked at Beth with a warm smile. "No, I think we've gone through everything we need to. You can give me a call if you have any questions." Beth noticed she'd popped her business card in with the paperwork for her to look over.

16

"Yes, I'm fairly certain I want it, but I'll sleep on it. Don't want to make a hasty decision." Story of her life, hasty decisions. However, she could never regret having George, even if it had meant giving up her dream of studying fashion design at university.

"I understand. I'll hold it for you for a couple of days."

"Thank you."

Beth stood up, finishing her tea. She always liked to run things by Jason first. He was her trusted advisor and she wouldn't make a decision like this without consulting him. Once, she'd had loads of confidence, but it had soon disappeared with the birth of her child. And the disapproval of her parents. She'd started to question everything, including her ability to raise her son.

"Are you sure you don't mind helping me?" Beth asked Joe, gathering up her bag.

"Of course not, come along." He opened the door and let Beth walk through it first, then he followed.

Out in the gravelled courtyard, where Joe's vehicle was parked, Anya and Beth shook hands, and then she found herself clambering into an old, green Range Rover with a surfboard strapped to the roof rack. At least Beth had no fear of being run off the road in this monstrous thing. It was twice the size of her own car.

She directed Joe to where she'd left her car parked. As they rumbled slowly along the road in his Range Rover, being sat up so high gave her a great view of the Cornish landscape, as far as Kittiwake Cove. Everything was changing from the summer greens to the reds, oranges and yellows of autumn. She hadn't appreciated her surroundings earlier, but now she admired the different colours of the leaves still clinging to the branches of the various trees. She could see the inspiration behind the autumn range of her collection that had come in at the end of August, with its warm colours and leafy prints.

Joe seemed nice; a very laid-back guy who made her feel at ease. As he was unloading the spare wheel and the tools he needed to change the flat, he chatted easily with Beth. She slung the paperwork and her notebook onto the back seat of her car to free up her hands in case he needed her help.

"Do you need to be anywhere this afternoon? Got to get back to work?" Joe asked, cranking up the Fiat 500c with the jack.

"No, not particularly. I just need to pick up my son, George, from school at quarter-past three." Then cold fear crept over her as she glanced at her watch. "Oh my God, is that the time?"

It was a quarter to three. With everything going on, and chatting to Anya, she'd totally forgotten she needed to collect George. Sometimes the school day just wasn't long enough to enable her to concentrate on her work uninterrupted. Rummaging desperately, she fetched her phone out of her handbag.

"How old is he?" Joe asked. She could tell what he was thinking; she looked too young to have a son at school.

"He turned six in September — at the start of term." With a huff, she found her phone and dialled her brother's number. "Oh, Jason! Thank God."

"Hey, Beth, what's up?"

"Pingu has a flat tyre." Beth walked away from her car to talk to Jason in private.

Jason laughed. "Why do you insist on calling your car Pingu?"

"You know that's what George calls it," she said, "and I think it's cute."

Her brother laughed again. "I'll grab my tools and come out, where are you?"

"No, no, can you please collect George from school? I'm not sure I'll get there in time."

"What about your tyre?"

Beth looked over at Joe confidently fixing her wheel. He looked like he knew what he was doing. "Don't worry. It's being sorted."

"Beth, please don't wait for the AA. I can come out," Jason said. She could hear the exasperation in his voice. Jason was a self-employed mechanic. "It'll still be quicker collecting George, then coming to you."

"The AA aren't that slow." She rolled her eyes. "But it's okay, don't worry, someone's helping me now. Just take George back to your garage, and I'll collect him from there."

"Okay. If you're sure."

"I'm sure. Thank you, love."

Ending her call with her brother, Beth then made a quick call to the school to inform them that George's uncle, Jason, would be collecting him. She relaxed slightly now, although she was still anxious to be back on the road. As she tucked her phone into her handbag, she heard a rumble coming towards them and a small tractor pulled up behind Joe's Range Rover. Her eyes narrowed. The driver turned off the ignition and jumped down.

"Joe!"

"Tristan!"

"Need a hand?" Tristan gestured to the car.

Beth watched the exchange, trying to hide her scowl. She was able to get a better look at the man now. He was annoyingly attractive. Dark hair and eyes, good looks, somewhere in his late twenties, she presumed. Younger than Joe. They were similar in looks. Could they be brothers?

"Nearly there," Joe said. "Just hand me that wrench."

The younger man did as he was asked, then wiping his hands down his jeans, turned towards Beth. "Hi."

Joe looked up as he manoeuvred the spare wheel into position. "Oh yeah, Beth, this is my cousin, Tristan. Have you two met?"

"No, I don't believe we have," Tristan said. He stepped forward, ready to hold out his hand for Beth to shake it, but Beth scowled at him.

"Yes, we have! You nearly ran me over earlier!"

"That was you?" Tristan's expression darkened. "Well, you should have been looking where you were going!"

"I was following Google Maps. I thought I was lost." Beth folded her arms. "You were driving like a bloody maniac!"

"I was in a rush."

"Yeah, to kill me!"

Joe stood up, dusting his knees down. "Beth, the spare wheel's on." Then more dryly he said, "Tristan, you were a lot of help." He eyed his cousin knowingly. His silent message, Beth hoped, was *don't be such a prick*. Joe put the tools back in his vehicle. Tristan grudgingly picked up the flat tyre and laid it in the boot of Beth's car.

"Thank you so much." Beth instinctively hugged Joe, then nodded curtly at Tristan as she opened her car door. "I truly am grateful."

"Not a problem. But you best get another tyre organised," Joe said.

"It's okay, Jason will sort it," she said, waving at Joe, while studiously ignoring Tristan.

She started the car, but in her haste to get away, released the clutch too quickly and accelerated too fast. Her front wheels spun as she pulled away, sending loose gravel flying.

Well, now she knew who the arrogant prick on the tractor was. Unfortunately, it looked as if he worked at Trenouth Manor. Hopefully, he would have little do to at The Stables, because the less she saw of him, the better.

CHAPTER 2: TRISTAN

Tristan felt a nudge from his cousin as he watched Beth drive off.

"No wonder you're single," Joe said, giving him a disapproving look. "You're a real charm a minute! She couldn't wait to get away."

Joe was probably right. He should have apologised to her, not made out it was her fault. He would never have forgiven himself if he had run her over. He *had* been driving too fast. October was usually a quiet month, but with half-term looming, which was his last lucrative week in the glamping field, some bright spark had decided to block a toilet with a disposable nappy.

"Who's Jason?" Tristan asked, tucking his hands into his jeans pockets.

"I don't know! I wasn't listening. Her boyfriend or husband, I presume. She needed to collect her son from school, so she was a bit stressed out."

Tristan hadn't noticed a wedding ring, just a gold necklace that she'd been chewing anxiously. "And anyway, the reason I'm single is that I'm too sodding busy running this estate." Tristan caught up with Joe's first jibe and scowled. He'd be grey before Joe at the rate he was going. "Besides, I'm perfectly happy." He had dates from time to time. They didn't lead anywhere, though. Life was too busy. Women wanted time he couldn't give. "And you're one to talk. How many years were you single?"

"I'm a changed man these days."

"Good." Tristan smiled. The past couple of months, he'd seen the difference in Joe since he'd admitted his feelings for Rhianna, the owner of a local bistro. And now they were engaged. The man was clearly happy, and back to his relaxed, surfer dude self. If only some of it could rub off onto him.

It was totally like Joe to help a woman in distress, he thought, as he watched him wipe his hands on an old cloth he'd retrieved from the back of his Range Rover.

"And that's why I came to see you." Joe put his arm around Tristan's shoulders.

"Oh yes?" Tristan tried to focus on his cousin, and not think of the pretty red head, with her freckles and scowling green eyes — and how badly he'd handled the encounter with her. He doubted he'd see her again, so maybe he should just forget the whole thing. Today had been a bad day. And it wasn't over yet.

"Rhianna and I are planning a small party, to celebrate our engagement."

"That's great. Tell me when, I'll be there."

"We might have it at Rhianna's bistro." Joe opened the driver's door and leaned against it casually.

"Or you could have it at Trenouth Manor," Tristan said.

"It gets rather busy this time of year, doesn't it?"

"I have a bit of a lull, before the Christmas craziness starts."

"I'll ask Rhianna."

"She might appreciate the break. If you hold the party at the bistro, she's bound to get involved and not actually relax and enjoy the evening."

"You have a good point there," Joe said with a nod.

The two men shook hands. It was Tristan's way. He had a habit of ending a conversation with a business-like handshake, even with his cousin. He mounted the tractor as Joe drove off.

Back at Trenouth Manor, he called in at the office to check for any messages.

"Someone's interested in the vacant unit," Anya said, catching him up on the day's events.

"Great."

"And I think they're keen to move in quickly. They're letting me know tomorrow." Anya flicked the switch on the kettle. "Coffee?"

"I would love one."

"Sort the toilets out?"

"Yeah, I've got a plumber over there now," Tristan said, pushing his hand through his hair in an attempt to relax. "One nappy and a few disposable wet wipes, and the whole bloody facilities get blocked."

"At least it didn't happen during half-term."

"That is true." Tristan squatted down and stroked his Border Collie, Flash, who gave a whine of approval. He'd want another walk later, but he knew now wasn't the time.

The rest of the afternoon was spent running through business and bookings with Anya. He told her his suggestion to hold Joe and Rhianna's engagement party at the manor and wanted to check availability.

"It's busy leading up to Christmas; we have the fayre at the beginning of December, and a couple of weddings and Christmas parties including your charity event." Anya flicked through the pages of the Trenouth Manor diary. "When was Joe thinking of?"

"I didn't ask. Let me know some dates we can do, and I'll get back to him."

Around four o'clock, the office phone rang, breaking the silence. Anya answered with a cordial, "Trenouth Manor, can I help you?"

Tristan paid little attention to the telephone call until she put her hand over the receiver and spoke to him. "It's for you. You're not going to like it. It's Dennis Bower." Her expression had hardened. Anya transferred the call.

"Hi, Den," Tristan said, picking up his phone once it began to ring.

"Hey, mate, I'm sorry to have to do this to you, but I've realised I've doubled booked the casino for your charity do." Dennis didn't sound very sorry, though.

"And? Can't you tell the other customer you're sorry?"

"They were in the diary first, it seems. Just a mix up in the office."

"Dennis, it's only six weeks away, if that! I've sold tickets! What the hell am I going to do for entertainment now?"

"Get a band?"

"I've already got a band! For the dance afterwards. I wanted something to make people part with more money for the charity." Tristan couldn't disguise his anger. He'd never used Dennis Bower's business before, and he wouldn't be using him again. He'd booked the casino months ago. He did not need this stress this close to Christmas. And he didn't want to let his mother down. This was as much her charity function as it was his.

"I'm sorry, mate." Dennis was not Tristan's mate, but he bit his tongue.

He took a couple of breaths to calm himself and to keep the tone professional. "Thank you for informing me. Goodbye."

He slammed the phone down back on its base. Combing his hands through his hair, he stood up and paced the small, carpeted area behind his desk. Flash's gaze followed him. But even the dog knew to keep quiet.

"I think you need another coffee." Anya stood up from her desk.

"Not coffee, tea. I won't sleep otherwise. Actually, is there a bottle of brandy in the cupboard?" That would help him sleep later.

Anya gave him a reproving look.

"Somewhere in the world it's nine in the evening," Tristan said wryly. "But okay, tea will do." Admittedly, he would need to drive back to the glamping site later. A long walk with Flash after that might ease his stress.

CHAPTER 3: SEBASTIAN

Beth's Fiat 500c was not exactly the most practical vehicle for running a pop-up boutique, considering the amount of clothes she sometimes had to transport, so Jason sometimes lent her his van. They were both insured on each other's vehicles, so meanwhile he could nip around in Pingu. He tended to wear a baseball cap and sit low in the seat when he did, which both Beth and George found hilarious.

She was shoving boxes of clothing and dismantled clothes rails into the back of his camper van. She was learning to handle it down narrow country lanes.

The sporty version of the VW California camper van had been a decision with George in mind. Remembering the fun times they'd had as kids, it was ideal for the three of them to take a trip to the beach or have a weekend camping. It doubled as Jason's work van, and although a VW Transporter possibly would have been a better option, Jason wouldn't have it any other way. Besides, he also had a Ford Ranger pickup, which he shared with his business partner Archie for work purposes.

When she had returned from viewing the business unit at The Stables, Jason had encouraged Beth, with no hesitation, to take the lease on. Now, she was moving into her new premises. It was exciting but daunting, but if her big brother said she could do it, she would. He was her safety net. He had been since she was eighteen. If she fell, he'd always catch her. She didn't know what she would do without him in her life. As an uncle, he was a great father figure to little George, too.

She wasn't sure how she would have survived without his support when George was a baby, and she'd struggled with the crying, not sure whether George needed his nappy changed, feeding or sleep, and her patience had run thin. And then she'd had to juggle childcare when she'd started her pop-up boutique. Jason was quite simply her hero.

"That's the room cleared." Jason pushed the last box into the van, slamming the sliding door shut.

It was a Sunday. George was on a play date and Jason didn't work on Sundays unless it was an emergency, so they'd picked this day to move her stock. Half-term had just started, so she'd have to have George with her while she set about putting the boutique together next week. She'd found a second-hand corner sofa on Facebook Marketplace, and Jason had a mate with a flatbed truck who was going to collect it for her. He was off to do that now, while she drove to The Stables. He kissed her on the forehead and left, and Beth drove slowly, in trepidation and excitement, down the narrow lanes to Trenouth Manor.

Beth had collected the keys from Anya earlier in the week. As soon as she'd phoned to say she'd take the unit, Anya had arranged for the workshop to be decorated and cleared, agreeing that it would be ready to move into this weekend.

The VW California rumbled slowly over the cobbled courtyard of The Stables, making the boxes in the back jiggle, and the clothes rails rattle, until she came to a halt outside her unit. Eagerly, she went to unlock the door of her new business premises, taking photos of the moment on her phone so that she could update her social media. Inserting the key, she took a deep breath. This was it. Her new start, the expansion of her business.

As she opened the door, she was relieved to find Anya had been true to her word. The two desks and the filing cabinet had been removed and the place smelled of fresh paint. The walls were bright with no more scuff marks or grubby fingerprints around the light switches. The creamy magnolia colour was perfect as Beth found neutral colours were the best backdrop for her collection of clothes. A business card had been left by the decorators on the windowsill: Rosdew Painting, Decorating & Carpentry — with a mobile number and a handwritten note: *Any problems, I can come back and touch up. Regards, Noah.*

Now empty, the unit looked much larger, especially with plenty of light flooding in through the windows. But it was time to fill it. It being Sunday, Beth thought she'd have The Stables to herself, but it looked like some people were working. As she started unloading the van, she waved a cheery hello to Poppy, the florist, who was arranging a couple of bouquets inside her shop.

As Beth struggled with a heavy box, an older man, probably in his late fifties, with greying hair and a stocky build, hurried out of his workshop opposite and across the cobbled courtyard to take the box off her.

"You look like you need a hand," he said, the creases beside his friendly eyes deepening as he smiled. "Where do you want this?" He was tall and his checked shirt and corduroy trousers gave him a fatherly air. She'd met him on the day she'd come to visit the unit but couldn't remember his name. He reminded her of her own dad — not that she'd seen him in a few years.

"I'm actually taking it upstairs, as I need the rails and furniture to go in first."

The man nodded and carried the box up the stairs for her, Beth following with a lighter box. "I'm Sebastian, by the way. But everyone calls me Seb."

"I'm Beth."

"Nice to meet you, Beth. What's your business?"

29

"I own a boutique — a pop-up boutique, actually. I want this space to be my permanent shop where I run my business from. And hopefully, it'll encourage my customers to visit me here."

"Oh, this will add something to The Stables," Seb said approvingly. "We'll be glad you've decided to *pop-up* here."

Once they'd unloaded the van, Seb invited Beth over to his workshop for a cup of tea, as she didn't have a kettle yet. The older man was friendly, having chatted about his family as they'd unloaded the van. He had two daughters, one apparently around Beth's age. With a pang, she wondered if Seb would have kicked her out of home for getting pregnant, as her own father had.

As she entered his workshop, Beth's eyes widened with amazement and appreciation. It was full of wood carvings, ranging from small creations to much larger magnificent sculptures.

"Wow," she said, admiring the detail on one of the pieces. She touched a carved owl, feeling the intricate feathers with her fingertips.

"The wife got fed up with me having everything lying around the house and taking up the garage. Plus, the garage got cold in the winter, as I needed the door open for natural light, so I decided to rent a workshop, hoping some sales would make it pay." He gestured towards his workspace. "I got made redundant a few years back and decided to take early retirement."

"I don't blame you. This must be truly satisfying."

"It is my absolute passion — apart from my wife and daughters, of course — but sometimes people don't realise the amount of time I put into some of these pieces, and they think they're too expensive." Seb handed Beth a hot mug of tea. "That's why I tend to stick to smaller, more affordable pieces now and take commissions for bigger work." Amongst the smaller carved objects, there were wooden keyrings, trinkets, and plaques. These hung from the branches of a tree made of twisted willow. A couple of the larger sculptures looked like showpieces to display what Seb could really do.

"Do you always work on Sundays?"

"No, but my wife, Marie, is out with our daughters. They're having a girly day, so I thought I'd escape here for a couple of hours." He had a twinkle of mischief in his eye.

"Hey, who does this van belong to?" a voice shouted from the courtyard.

"Sorry, it's mine," Beth said, coming out of the workshop.

"You can't park there!" Beth's heart sank when she saw it was the tractor man from the other day. Tristan — was that his name? "Oh, it's you!" he scowled. The sun was low and he'd placed his hand over his eyes to shield them.

Beth returned the scowl. "I was unloading my stock."

"Well, now it's unloaded, the van should be moved. I like this courtyard kept clear," Tristan said, placing his hands on his hips. "Parking is provided... Oh, hi, Seb." His expression softened as Seb emerged.

"My fault, Tristan, I encouraged Beth in for a cuppa."

"Oh, right, okay," Tristan said, shoving his hands in his pockets. He gave a whistle and a Border Collie appeared out of nowhere. The same dog Beth had seen sleeping in the dog bed when she'd come to look at the unit. "Come on, Flash!"

Beth watched Tristan walk off, the dog loyally following. God, that man rubbed her up the wrong way.

"Is he always like that?" Beth returned to Seb, hugging her tea. "Not even a please or thank you." She knew her cheeks would be flushed red with anger. Red hair and freckles meant she blushed far too easily.

31

"Ah, I think that young man is just a little stressed lately."

"Doesn't mean he has to take it out on the rest of us. And what does he do, for heaven's sake, to get that stressed?"

Seb laughed. "You don't know who he is, do you?"

"No. Only he tried to run me off the road the other day in a tractor."

"He manages the Trenouth Estate. His old man owned it. He passed away some years ago, I believe, leaving it in a bad state. If it wasn't for Tristan's hard work, having these stables converted and the house renovated and hired out for functions, the family would have had to sell up a few years ago."

Beth hoped he wasn't going to be a royal pain in the arse. "Please tell me he's not around too often." She didn't think she could cope with him constantly popping up in her life, rocking her confidence and her mood.

"Who's to say? He's a busy man. Fingers in lots of pies."

Tristan had done it again. He'd made a complete tit of himself. He'd thought the walk might help him shake off the foul mood he'd woken up in, but apparently not. Seeing the modern camper van parked in the courtyard, his hackles had risen as he'd assumed that it was some tourists parking for free to look around the listed house.

On Sundays, he usually walked Flash through the large grounds. Today, knowing Anya had said the new business owner was moving into one of the units, he'd cut through The Stables on the way to his cottage at the edge of the estate. A former gatehouse, it was small with two bedrooms, but perfect for his needs. And Flash's.

He hadn't realised *Beth* was the new business owner. It all made sense now. She must have been walking to Trenouth Manor to view the empty unit the day he'd nearly ran her over.

He wondered if he should return and offer her a hand with moving into the unit. On Sundays he tried to keep his workload to a minimum, to give himself a day off. So he had the time. But considering he kept making a complete fool of himself in front of her, maybe it was best to get on with some chores that needed doing at home. Housework he didn't get around to because he was too busy managing the estate. With two smallholdings, a glamping and a camping field, plus the house being hired out, Tristan had his work cut out. Luckily, Anya was a godsend. The most organised woman on the planet.

The cleaning company that maintained the house also visited his cottage. But they couldn't fix a leaking tap or put a lick of paint on the walls. And he didn't expect them to do his washing, although he did pay someone to iron his shirts. Admittedly, he got Noah to do the decorating.

He should try to relax today and catch up on life at home. He was visiting his mother later for a Sunday roast. The conversation was bound to revolve around the estate and his mum's charity work.

After her cuppa, Beth moved her van, not so much to appease Tristan, but because she knew Jason would be here soon. Then she set about frantically cleaning the downstairs of the unit ready for her new furniture to arrive. She'd brought with her the vacuum cleaner from home, plus a mop, dusters and cloths.

She'd finished cleaning by the time Jason turned up in the flatbed truck, with the cream leather corner sofa strapped securely on the back. Between him and his mate Scott, they managed to get it unloaded and in position up against the back wall of the unit. It only just fitted.

Beth had never met Scott before. He was a new friend of Jason's. Someone in a trade by the looks of him, as he was wearing khaki work trousers with extra padding at the knee for protection.

While Beth cleaned the cream sofa with some leather furniture polish, the two men set to work assembling the flat pack storage units she had ordered. They spent the afternoon hanging mirrors, pictures, and blinds, assembling the shelves and the rails so that by the time the light was fading, the downstairs area of her boutique was almost ready. It just needed the clothes unpacked. Beth couldn't help wondering if Scott was Jason's new boyfriend. Perhaps not, as they acted more like mates than lovers. Seb kept them provided with teas and coffees as Beth still didn't have a kettle.

Once they'd finished, Jason swept her into his arms for a hug. "All ready for the next stage, little sis?" he asked, as he bent down and kissed the top of her head.

"Thank you, both of you," she said. She hid the nervous wobble she felt inside. This was such a big step, moving out of the house and into her own unit. It meant extra overheads for her business, but Jason was confident she could make a success of it. With George in school, she did have more time on her hands. Only the school holidays would be a problem, but Jason had promised that he would help her look after George. Plus, there were holiday clubs, playdates… She was worrying for the sake of worrying.

Now, at last, George would have his own room at Jason's house. She might even be able to help Jason with the bills if the business really took off. This could lead to financial independence.

All that was left to do was to put the changing screen in place — which Jason said he'd bring along the next day — and get the clothes out of the boxes. That would be tomorrow's job. She needed to fetch George from his playdate — he'd been there long enough — and have some quality time with her son before she put him to bed. At least she didn't need to worry about his dinner, as he'd have eaten at his friend's house.

Tomorrow, George would be with her while she did the remainder of the unpacking. He'd have to play games on her phone and do puzzles. Half-term was only a week. She would manage.

CHAPTER 4: FLASH

Up and out early on Monday morning — much to George's disgust, as he'd had to eat his cereal so quickly — Beth set to work steaming and hanging her winter range on the clothes rails. A top-up delivery had come in, so she had some new items to display, and hoped these would encourage her customers to visit her new premises.

"But it's not a school day," George had grumbled. He'd been up earlier than if he'd been going to school, but had hoped he'd get to sit in front of the television and watch his favourite programmes, which he didn't get time for during the school week.

Seb popped over upon his own arrival at The Stables to say hello and check if Beth wanted a drink. "Can't start the day without tea," he said.

"Thank you, but I'm more of a coffee person in the morning," she replied.

"Hello, little fella." Seb spotted George on the floor doing a puzzle and crouched down to beside him.

"George, this is Sebastian. He has a workshop across the courtyard."

"Hello ... Seb-as-ian," George stammered.

"It is a mouthful. Don't worry, all my friends call me Seb," he said to George, who eyed him warily. "You can come see my workshop later, if you like, once I've got some work done." Seb gave him a smile and George grinned back, a gap visible where he'd lost his first baby tooth the other day. "It'll give your mum some time to work."

"Did you want a cuppa? I've brought provisions today." On her way to The Stables, Beth had picked up a kettle and the essentials for making teas and coffees. She'd stolen a couple of mugs from home, but would purchase something more in keeping with the style of her boutique later. And she wanted to buy some champagne flutes, for those special occasions when she would offer prosecco to her customers. Once George was back at school, a shopping trip to Truro was very much needed. The poor boy didn't want to spend half-term being dragged around shops. Plus, he'd go straight to the toy departments, which would cost her more, either in money or tears. Gone were the days when he used to fall asleep in his pushchair.

"Maybe later. I can see you're busy. I'll let you get on." Seb gave Beth a wink and smiled at George.

Later that morning, Jason arrived with the folding screen she'd purchased from a second-hand shop to create a changing area. The tall screen was made up of four narrow wooden panels, whitewashed in emulsion to give it a rustic look, with brass hinges between each panel.

"Jay-Jay!" George got off the floor and hugged his uncle around the leg.

Jason always mussed George's hair. "Hello, little man. Helping your mum?"

George pointed to the jigsaw puzzle he was in the middle of. "I'm being a good boy." He sat back down as if to prove this.

He certainly was being good. Beth smiled fondly at her son, sitting cross-legged on the laminate flooring, his tongue poking out with concentration as he found the next piece and placed it in the puzzle.

The screen fitted concertina-style under the stairs, which was the perfect place for a changing area. Behind it stood a full-length mirror and hooks for hanging clothes, so customers could try clothes on in comfort.

"Right, better go, or Archie will be cursing me," said Jason. "We've got a few MOTs booked in for today."

Beth walked out with Jason to his camper van. They'd had to put the seats down to fit the screen in. Together, they put the inside of the van back together.

"All settled in?" A voice behind Beth made her jump.

She turned to see Tristan standing there, his dog beside him. "Yes, thank you," she replied coolly.

Jason gave Beth a kiss on her forehead, then with a nod to Tristan got in the driver's seat of his van. Starting the engine, he lowered the window and poked his head out. "See you tonight. I'll get home early and cook supper."

"Thanks, you're amazing." Beth smiled fondly at her brother and waved as he drove off.

"Anything you need?" Tristan asked once Jason was out of sight.

"I think I'm all good, thank you." Beth tried to keep her tone friendly, but she knew it carried some sharpness. "I need to organise a telephone line so that I can have broadband, but I can use my mobile for now."

"There are lines connected to each unit, so it's all quite simple once you find a provider."

"Doggy!"

Before Beth realised what was happening, George was running from her unit, his arms stretched out towards Tristan's Border Collie. Beth grabbed him in time and pulled him back.

"George, what have I told you? You don't approach dogs like that. They might bite," she scolded. George looked ready to burst into tears.

"He doesn't bite," Tristan said defensively, ruffling the fur at the back of the dog's head. The Border Collie gave a whine as if in agreement.

Beth looked at him sternly. "You know that, but George doesn't. He needs to learn to ask first before petting an animal. Some dogs don't like other people, even kids." And he was the perfect height to be bitten in the face. Which didn't bear thinking about.

Tristan nodded. "Good point."

Wow, the man was actually agreeing with her. "So, George, what do we say?" Beth knelt down to her son's height, her expression softening so that he knew she wasn't cross with him any longer.

"Is he okay?" George asked, looking at Tristan and eager to stroke the dog. "What's his name?"

"Yeah, he's a softie, unless you're a rabbit. His name's Flash."

"Like the superhero." George reached out his hand. Flash sniffed his fingers but waited patiently.

"Yes, I suppose so," Tristan said, shoving his hands into his pockets. "And the white on his nose zigzags slightly like a lightning bolt."

"Oh, yeah." George was eagerly stroking Flash now, and the dog was even licking his hands.

Beth and Tristan watched in silence as the dog and child bonded.

"George, we need to get on now, come on. I'm sure Tristan is a very busy man."

Flash gave a couple of friendly barks, wagging his tail.

"Bye, Flash." George gave him one more stroke, nuzzling his face into the dog's long fur.

Tristan turned to Beth. "Remember, if you need anything, and I'm not about, leave a message with Anya."

Beth nodded tersely. "Will do."

Back inside the safety of her unit, she took George into the toilet and washed his hands. "Why do I have to?" he asked, as water splashed his jumper.

"Because after petting an animal, you should always wash your hands," she said, sternly.

"Like when we go to the farm?"

"Yes."

Just as George was about to sit back down to his puzzle on the floor, she noticed dog hair all down his clothes — something she really didn't need on the clothing in the boutique. So she found herself back outside, spending several minutes brushing down her struggling son to remove the dog hair before allowing him back in her shop.

George was not happy and complained the whole time, his eyes welling with tears. Beth had learnt over the years that being a tough mum didn't mean George would love her less. She mentally cursed Tristan, though. Why did he have to show up with his dog?

Okay, she couldn't really blame him, but she could have done without this inconvenience when she had so much to do.

Tristan walked off towards the office, calling Flash as he went. The dog adored small children. Maybe he thought they were sheep, and he could round them up and play with them.

It looked like his attractive new tenant did have a partner, not to mention a small child in tow. He just needed to make sure that the first thing that came out of his mouth when speaking to her didn't sound defensive. Of course she needed to teach her son not to approach dogs without asking the owner first. He had been taught the same as a child, too.

What was the matter with him lately? Was it stress? He was always stressed. But maybe seeing Joe settling down was making him a little envious? It wasn't that he didn't want a relationship, he just didn't have time for one. Did he?

Without needing to be told, Flash took his place in his dog bed next to Tristan's desk. Anya glanced across at him and waved and smiled, the phone pressed to her ear as she concentrated. As soon as the call ended, she turned to him.

"Coffee?"

"Yes, go on. Any news you need to fill me in on?"

"We've got a couple coming to look at the house for a wedding next summer. And Isabella Le Bon has demanded to come see the house again today, for final arrangements for her wedding in December. That was her just now." Tristan listened and opened post on his desk. "If that woman thinks I'll believe she's a relation of Simon Le Bon, she can think again!" Anya was red-faced as she poured hot water into each mug. "I had to google him anyway. How was I supposed to know he was in an eighties band called Duran Duran?" She shrugged. "I think I remember my mum playing their music occasionally. But I wasn't even born then!"

Tristan chuckled as Anya handed him a steaming mug of coffee. "Where's Cathy?" She usually opened his post.

"She's got the week off — half-term, remember?"

"Maybe we should have got a temp in."

"I can manage for a week," Anya said confidently.

"Yes, but can I?" They'd agreed to split Cathy's work between them when she was off.

Anya laughed. "After this week, it'll all go quiet with the campsites."

"I suppose so." Although then he would have to make a start on the long process of getting them shipshape again, ready for next season.

"Boss?" He realised that Anya was still standing by his desk. "Is it okay if I slope off an hour earlier today?"

He frowned. "Why, what you got planned?" It was only Monday.

"Theo's taking me out. For our anniversary."

"Have you really been with him a year already?" Tristan couldn't believe it if she had. The man treated her like a doormat at times. But he didn't dare say anything. He wasn't exactly an expert on relationships, but his mother had brought him up to believe that men should treat women with respect. But the times he'd caught Anya crying into her coffee mug...

"No, silly. Six months."

"Oh right." Was that the thing now? A six-month anniversary? "Well, yes, of course you can go early. You work so hard. Just make sure he spoils you."

"I will."

"Order champagne!"

"He's taking me to The Beach Front Bistro. I'll order cocktails."

"Even better!"

CHAPTER 5: POPPY

"Hello!"

As she was sorting out her office space and her excess stock upstairs, Beth heard a knock at the door and someone entering the boutique. Realising George was downstairs on his own, she immediately stopped what she was doing and dashed down the stairs.

"Mummy, someone's here to see you."

Beth was relieved to find George on the floor, crayon poised over his colouring book, as if unsure what to do as the stranger stood in the doorway.

"Hi, I'm Poppy, the florist. I spoke to Seb this morning, and thought I'd come to say hello this afternoon, now things have gone quiet for me." The older woman held out her hand. Her other arm cradled a bouquet of flowers wrapped in pink paper. With her long floaty skirt and baggy blouse, she looked a little like a hippy. Beth recalled a dress that had come in that might suit Poppy's boho taste. "I think we met briefly when you were viewing the workshop."

"Yes, we did." Beth shook her hand. "I'm Beth. This is my son, George. It's half-term, so he's my helper."

"I'm being good," he said with his toothy grin.

"Anyway, these are for you." Poppy handed the bouquet of pretty flowers to Beth, a mix of roses, gerberas, and other flowers, in different shades of pink. "A welcome gift, and I thought they might brighten up your boutique."

"Oh, thank you, they're beautiful." Beth inhaled their sweet fragrance. They would add a beautiful touch to the boutique. She might put an order in with Poppy regularly.

"I didn't include lilies, as their pollen tends to stain."

Just then Sebastian appeared through the open door. "Hi, Poppy, nice to see you two have met," he said. "Beth, I was wondering if this little fellow wanted to have a go at wood carving?"

"Can I?" George jumped up. "Please, Mummy."

"Are you sure? Is it safe?" Beth frowned, trying to dispel visions of George cutting himself and having to be rushed to A&E.

"Don't worry, I'll do most of it," Seb said with a wink and held out his hand for George to take. As she watched them go, Beth felt a momentary pang of sadness, and she feared tears were welling in her eyes. Her father was missing out on George growing up. He could be doing things with his grandson, just as Seb was prepared to do.

"Don't worry about Seb. He's so good with kids," Poppy said, misreading Beth's expression. "He entertained my two from time to time, when they were younger."

Beth shook herself from her sad reverie. "Oh, no, I'm sure George will be fine," she said brightly. "I'm more worried about Seb! Would you like a tea or a coffee?"

"Yes, please. A tea would be lovely. I've come to discuss the Christmas fayre with you. Anya suggested I see you."

"Great, I'll go and put the kettle on."

"Do you mind if I browse?"

"Please do. I'd be interested to know what you think of the collection."

Beth nipped up the stairs two at a time, taking the bouquet with her, and flicked the switch on the kettle. She had been relieved to find the kitchenette had a small fridge under the worktop and a couple of cupboards above the sink. She'd be able to serve drinks and nibbles at special customer event evenings. Ideas kept forming in her head. Having the boutique separate from her house would make things so much easier to run, and evenings wouldn't be a problem because Jason would be there to babysit George if she needed to stay on. She could offer late appointments to customers who worked during the day.

She left the flowers in water in the sink, making a mental note to buy a vase. Once the teas were ready, Beth returned downstairs and handed Poppy her mug, noticing that she had pulled a couple of items off the rail, including the long, dark floral dress she'd had in mind. Poppy had laid them out over the back of the sofa, the rich colours and autumnal patterns of the clothes standing out against the cream.

"Could I try these on? And do you have this in a size 12?" Poppy held up a top.

"If I don't, I can order it in for you to try."

While Poppy tried on the clothes, she told Beth about the Christmas fayre that was held at The Stables at the beginning of December every year. "If we hold it in November, some feel it's too early to buy Christmas presents, but holding it too late doesn't work either. They've usually bought all their gifts or are too busy with parties etcetera. So, we've found the first Saturday in December usually works best. It's been very successful the past couple of years. If it falls a little late, say the 6th or 7th, then we sometimes hold it on the last Saturday in November. You'll probably do really well with people buying Christmas party outfits or a gift for a girlfriend or a wife."

By the time Poppy left, Beth felt she'd made a new friend. Not only had they come to an arrangement for Poppy's florist to supply flowers for the boutique, but she had left carrying one of Beth's smart paper carrier bags containing a new outfit delicately folded in tissue paper. Beth's first sale in her new boutique! She hadn't officially told anyone she was open yet, wanting to ensure the shop was ready before going public with the news. She intended spending the rest of this afternoon on Facebook and Instagram, advertising her business and setting up her appointments page. With George occupied with Seb, she would be able to do this easily if uninterrupted.

"Mummy!" Beth's peace was obliterated, and she jumped as her concentration broke. Because she didn't have a desk upstairs yet, she'd been sitting on the corner sofa with her laptop, engrossed in updating her social media channels. George came running in, followed by Seb at a much more sedate pace. She didn't have time to get off the sofa. She put her laptop aside as George clambered excitedly onto her lap. "Look what I made!" He was holding a wooden car, the size of a dinky toy.

"Wow! Aren't you a clever boy?"

"Seb helped with the really tricky bits." He cuddled into her as she admired the car. It had clearly been teamwork. Not quite as perfect as if Seb had made it on his own, but still pretty good.

She looked at Seb and he shrugged his shoulders as if to imply George did all the hard work. "What do you say to Seb?"

George turned around and grinned. "Thank you."

Seb waved. "Not a problem, young man. Maybe I'll see you tomorrow."

"Can I, Mummy? Can I? Please?"

"We'll see." She smiled at her son, ruffling his hair.

"I'd best head home, or Marie will wonder what's happened to me."

"Thanks so much for having George this afternoon. I got so much done without having to worry about him."

"You're welcome. He was fun to have around. Catch you tomorrow."

Beth glanced at her watch and realised she needed to head home, too. George got grumpy if he didn't have his tea on time. He needed his routine. As did she.

Unlocking the front door, they were greeted by a sweet tomato-and-garlic aroma. As promised, Jason was already home and had the dinner on.

"What are you cooking?" Beth asked, slinging her bag down in the hallway and helping George take his shoes off.

"Spag bol."

"My favourite!" George beamed. It wasn't Beth's, though, because of the state he got in trying to eat spaghetti. He usually had more sauce round his mouth than in it, not to mention down his clothes.

"Go put the TV on, young man," Jason said. George didn't argue. He was straight in the lounge, grabbing the remote control and making himself comfy on the sofa. Once he was out of earshot and glued to the television screen, Jason said to Beth. "Neither of you are allowed upstairs. Especially George."

"Right, okay." Beth wondered what her brother was up to. "Good job we've got a downstairs toilet." She chatted to Jason as he cooked, excitedly filling him in on her day at the boutique, about Poppy and Sebastian. Then apprehension laced her thoughts. "I hope I can do this. What if it fails?"

"Of course it won't, Beth. I'm so proud of what you've achieved already; you can do this! Come on, even being heavily pregnant didn't stop you from getting fantastic grades in your A-levels," Jason said.

"But I never made it to university." Sitting her A-level exams, clearly pregnant, seemed a trauma of the past now. An ordeal she could forget.

"You've plenty of time to follow that dream." He elbowed her encouragingly as he stirred the Bolognese sauce. "This is a great opportunity to grow your business."

She would only be twenty-five this December. The irony was, considering how heavily pregnant she had been, she'd still managed to get the A-level grades to go to her chosen university. But with her parents' lack of support, forcing her to leave when they'd learnt of her pregnancy, Beth had decided she'd made her bed, and would lie in it.

"No regrets," she said.

"No regrets," Jason concurred. Their motto. She had a beautiful son she was proud of and a close relationship with her brother she'd never quite had when they'd lived under their parents' roof. Exciting things were coming together.

As predicted, and even with her strict table manners, George ended up with Bolognese sauce all over his face. But he ate the lot. Jason and Beth both snuck vegetables into his meals without him knowing, and it was easy to do with this dish.

"I've got a surprise for you, little man," Jason said after dinner, as Beth was doing the washing up. "Come upstairs with me. And you, Beth."

She turned off the hot tap, dried her hands and followed her brother. Jason carried George up the stairs and kept his hand over the boy's eyes.

The door to the small third bedroom which had been Beth's Boutique was closed.

Jason placed George on his feet. "Go on. Open the door."

"Wow!" George entered the room, dumbfounded.

Inside was a cabin bed, and the room was Spiderman-themed, from the duvet cover to the curtains and even the lampshade. It had already been a pale blue, so it hadn't needed decorating, but with the change of curtains and the new bed the room was now perfect for a six-year-old boy.

Beth felt herself welling up at seeing her boy so happy. She swallowed to push down the lump that had formed in her throat.

"When did you do all this?" she asked, blinking back her tears. "And where did you get the bed?"

"I had the day off today."

"But you said you had loads of MOTs."

"So, I lied." Jason shrugged with a coy smile. "Don't worry, Archie was fine about it. We're allowed to take time off." Jason rested his arm on Beth's shoulder. "The bed was on Buy, Sell, Swap, too. Don't worry, it didn't cost a fortune."

"You can't have done all this by yourself." Whatever he said, she was worried about the cost. Jason owned the garage with Archie but it didn't make him rich. And this had been a lot of work for one man to do. There was even a blue wardrobe in the room.

"Scott helped."

"Is there something you need to tell me about Scott?" Beth eyed him suspiciously. George was oblivious to them, discovering his toys under the cabin bed.

"He's just a friend," Jason said coolly.

"Uh-huh. You should invite your friend over for dinner one evening." She smirked, and Jason gave a sheepish smile back.

"I worry about George."

"George will be fine. He's too young to fully understand, but as he grows up it will help him to learn that homophobia is not okay."

"It's early days yet. Maybe when it gets more serious."

Beth nodded her understanding. Then, feeling a sob rising in her throat, she hugged her brother tightly. "Thank you," she said. "I don't know where I'd be without you."

"Ditto, Beth. Ditto." He squeezed her before releasing himself from the hold.

"Let's have a glass of wine to celebrate. I had my first sale today, too, at the new boutique!"

"Great! There's red wine left over from making the Bolognese. But let's get George in the bath first."

CHAPTER 6: NANCY

Tristan, fresh out of the shower, heard a knock at his door. Flash gave a sharp bark, as if to make sure his master had heard the sound. It was close to seven o'clock in the evening. Who could it be?

Shit, it's Monday, thought Tristan. *Nancy.*

"Stay," he commanded Flash as he came down the wooden stairs that led into the open-plan lounge. Flash was still curled up in his bed. He lifted one ear, angled towards the front door, and then closed his eyes again. Exhausted from his long walk earlier, he was not fussed about a visitor. Tristan answered the door wearing nothing but a towel wrapped around his waist. A blast of cold air spread goosebumps over his damp skin.

Nearly as tall as him in her heels, Nancy looked him up and down, frowning. "I thought we were going out. Aren't you ready?" She entered the cottage and kissed him on the cheek. He shut the door quickly on the cold night, trapping in the heat from the wood burner. She dropped her small holdall by the bottom of the stairs. Tristan didn't have time for a lot of things, but he made sure he worked out regularly, and even though things between him and Nancy were very different now, he could see the lustful approval in her gaze.

"Sorry, I got held up at the office." A lie. He'd totally forgotten she was visiting.

"Well, hurry up. I'm starving. I've been at work all day. And then travelling here." She made her way over to the fire, holding out her hands to the heat.

"Okay, let me get dressed. Where do you fancy eating?" Tristan asked, heading for the stairs and picking up Nancy's bag. He'd stow it away in the spare bedroom.

"I'd like to go to the bistro in Kittiwake Cove, please." Nancy sat down on his leather couch.

"The Beach Front Bistro? It's half-term. It might be fully booked."

"But aren't you family? They're engaged now. Surely they'd find you a table?"

"Rhianna owns it, not Joe. And anyway, how did you know about them being engaged?"

"When a player like Joe Trescott gets engaged, the whole of Cornwall hears about it, darling." Nancy chuckled at her own little joke. She'd never really confirmed it, but he wondered if Joe and Nancy had once had a thing, many years ago.

Nancy was older than Tristan by around eight years, and when they'd first met, she'd teased him about being her toy boy. They had met a few years ago when her family had hired Trenouth Manor for a party and, newly divorced at the time, she'd wanted some fun. Or, as she'd put it, someone to play with. Oh, and they had played, until the very early hours of the next morning.

But now their relationship was totally platonic. They were just friends, especially as Nancy had a thing for a guy at her office. Besides, they were complete opposites; Nancy preferred city life, whereas Tristan liked to walk his land and feel the sea air on his skin.

Nancy's parents had retired to Cornwall, not far from Kittiwake Cove, so she visited occasionally and tied it in with seeing Tristan. She preferred staying at his rather than under the scrutinising gaze of her parents, who felt that her life would only be complete once she had a baby. Tristan appreciated

Nancy's head for business, so they usually had a lot to talk about.

"Give me five minutes," Tristan said as he climbed the stairs to his bedroom.

As he dressed, he reflected that when they'd first met, Nancy had pointed out that he wasn't much different to Joe. The old player Joe.

It hadn't been planned that way. He didn't fear commitment or being hurt like Joe had, even though before meeting Nancy his trust had been yanked from right under his feet. No, he just didn't have time for a serious relationship. Or was that what he told himself after his ex, Kimmie? Like Joe, he'd had a series of holiday romances, short flings. Since Kimmie, no one had caught his attention enough to make him slow down and make time for them. Tristan lacked Joe's natural charm, though. People liked Joe instantly. Tristan had to work at it.

Maybe because he spoke before he thought... He had the old *open mouth, insert foot* syndrome.

Beth came to mind instantly. The attractive red head with the fierce green eyes.

He really needed to try harder at putting things right there. With her boutique in one of his units at The Stables, he was going to see her regularly. Plus, Flash liked the little boy, and his dog was always a good judge of character.

While Tristan picked out a clean Ted Baker shirt and pulled on some trousers, he made a call to The Beach Front Bistro. Fortunately, they could fit them in, but they might have to have a cocktail until the table was available. Nancy wouldn't mind that. He knew why she liked the bistro; it was trendy, and the cocktails and the quality of the food gave it a city ambiance. But Tristan liked it because it was by the ocean.

Leaving Flash asleep in his bed, Tristan made his way out of the house with Nancy. With the press of a button, Tristan's double garage door opened, revealing two vehicles — a sports car (his red Audi R8) and his more practical Range Rover Sport — a much newer model than Joe's vintage Range Rover. He beeped open the Audi, knowing Nancy would prefer to be chauffeured around in that. Her Mercedes convertible was parked in front of his cottage.

At The Beach Front Bistro, Nancy and Tristan were greeted by Yasmin — Rhianna's right-hand woman, who had great experience in preparing the perfect cocktail. After removing their jackets, she hung them on the coat stand.

"No Rhianna?" Tristan asked, glancing around.

"Night off," Yasmin said. "Your table will be another ten minutes. Did you want to go upstairs to Shakers for a cocktail first?"

"Sounds like a marvellous idea," Nancy said, beaming her terrific, red-glossed smile. She tucked her arm through Tristan's and he led her up to Shakers.

Later, over dinner and a bottle of wine, which Nancy mainly drank due to Tristan driving, they caught up on each other's news.

"Have you found an alternative attraction for your charity ball yet?" Nancy asked. Tristan had filled her in about what had happened over the phone the other day.

He shook his head. "It's hard trying to find another casino or something similar this time of year — they're already booked up for Christmas parties."

Nancy sipped her wine thoughtfully. "Something will come up. I'll have a think about it, too." Nancy usually helped with the charity ball. She liked to donate a prize and get other larger organisations to part with their cash, as well as generating some publicity for the event.

"But the good news is that we have filled the empty workshop unit. A boutique is in there now."

Nancy's interest sparked at the mention of clothes. "Oh, I might have to take a look before I leave tomorrow."

"Yeah, I'll introduce you to the owner, Beth."

"That would be lovely."

As always, his evening with Nancy was pleasant. They'd caught up over delicious food, a couple of cocktails (mocktails for Tristan) and had shared a few laughs too. Tristan paid the bill and walked Nancy back to the car park that overlooked the cove.

The sun had set long ago over the ocean. All that could be heard were the waves crashing on the beach in the distance. The night sky was clear, and the moonlight glistened off the sea. In other circumstances stargazing together would be romantic, but he knew Nancy felt as he did. She didn't hold his hand; she only had her arm hooked through his. She didn't want children or commitment, and neither did he. Not with her, anyway.

He did care about Nancy as a friend. They helped each other, supported each other. The great thing about her was that she didn't complicate matters.

She gave a shiver. "Shall we go? It's a bit cold," she said, giving his arm a tug.

Tristan gently rubbed her hand that was resting on his arm. "Yes, let's."

CHAPTER 7: ELOWEN

After a light breakfast, Tristan walked Flash across the grounds towards The Stables. Nancy had decided to drive over, complaining that in her heels she'd never make it.

She was stepping out of her car as Tristan arrived with Flash.

"It's this way," he said. "Be careful on the cobbles." Why Nancy insisted on wearing four-inch heels, he'd never know. How did she even drive in them?

He made Flash sit and stay by the old water fountain before walking Nancy over to Beth's Boutique, taking her arm to steady her as she teetered over the stones. He knocked on the door, then pushed it open.

"Hello," he called.

"Oh, hi." Beth was dressed in smarter clothing than he had previously seen her in, perhaps from the range she sold in the boutique. She looked surprised to see him.

"Hi, this is Nancy," Tristan said, but Nancy didn't let him finish. Unaware of the friction between Tristan and Beth, and her feet now on a smooth floor, she let go of him and moved eagerly towards Beth.

"Hi, lovely to meet you," she said, holding out her hand. A startled Beth shook it. "Tristan told me you run a boutique, so before I left for Bristol, I thought I'd come take a look. A woman can never have too many clothes."

"No, indeed. You're more than welcome to browse." Beth gestured to the rails. Nancy gave Tristan a peck on the cheek. "Catch you later, darling."

Heat rose in Tristan's face. But he wasn't sure why. Nancy always kissed him on the cheek and called him 'darling'. She did it with all her friends.

George came bumbling out of the toilet with wet hands. "I used the soap, Mummy." But Beth was busy with Nancy, who was already asking her all sorts of questions about the clothes.

"Hey, I tell you what, George, would you like to walk Flash with me?" Tristan said, squatting down to the little fellow's height. He knew Nancy was allergic to children. One of the reasons for her divorce, apparently. And why he'd known Nancy would never be his future, but only a friend. He'd love to have kids one day. It was something he kept to himself.

"Can I walk Flash, Mummy?" The boy's eyes lit up and a grin spread across his face. He had the same green eyes as his mother, Tristan noticed.

Beth frowned. "Oh, I don't know." She looked at Tristan as if to check he was sincere.

"I don't mind. Then you can concentrate on Nancy."

"Thank you. That would be very kind. I do have a busy morning ahead of me," Beth said as she handed Nancy another garment.

"Grab your coat, George. It's a bit nippy out there," Tristan said.

The little boy tried to reach his jacket that was hanging on a hook by the door. Tristan grabbed it and handed it to the lad. Then, realising that the child was still having difficulty, he helped him into the coat and zipped him up. George ran from the building and out towards Flash, burying his face in his fur. The dog reciprocated with a wag of his tail and an affectionate lick.

Tristan liked to walk around the grounds every morning, to make sure all was in order. If he spotted anything the groundsmen needed to attend to, he could get them on to it. As he strolled, Tristan soon doubted if his offer had been a good idea. After all, he hardly knew the lad and wondered what the hell to talk to him about. Luckily, he didn't need to worry too much. Flash seemed to be enough entertainment for George, as he followed the dog happily.

They approached the Victorian walled garden, which always made Tristan think of his mother reading *The Secret Garden* to him as a child. Flash wasn't allowed in as it was a working kitchen garden, and the produce was sold locally to businesses: shops, cafes, and restaurants within Kittiwake Cove. After telling the dog to sit and stay outside the gate, he led George into the garden.

With autumn setting in, the beds were not looking as vibrant as they had in the summer, and much of the summer planting was fading and dying back, especially the tall dahlias, carnations, cosmos and lilies used for cut flowers. One section was bare, fully dug over, ready for further planting. Another had recently been planted with spring bulbs, and in a few months would be filled with an abundance of tulips and daffodils. Espaliered apple and pear trees grew along the red brick walls, most of the fruit now harvested. At the centre of the four symmetrical sectors was a pond with a fountain, which George made a beeline for. Tristan hurried after him and took his hand. He didn't want him falling in. That certainly wouldn't go down well with Beth.

"Come on, there's more to see." Tristan gave the boy's hand a gentle tug, and he followed him back out of the garden to where Flash was waiting patiently. Another time he would show George the tunnel for the raspberries and strawberries, and the old Victorian greenhouses used for growing grapevines and tomatoes. Maybe he should ask George if he'd heard of

The Secret Garden. But with Flash trotting beside them again, George had let go of his hand and resumed following the dog.

"What's that?" George said. He'd run on ahead with Flash. Deeper within the grounds, past the Victorian garden, they'd followed a path that led to an old elm tree. This area of the grounds remained wooded and natural, in contrast to the gardens nearer the house, which were formal and beautifully landscaped. These paths were as old as the house, and would once have been used by the Victorian household to take a turn or exercise in the garden. A brook ran alongside, the trickle of water a constant sound.

George was pointing at a large stone near the old elm. Fresh cut flowers lay beside it, probably the last from the walled garden. There was a bench where his mother used to come to sit. She still visited, but not as often these days.

"It's a memorial stone," Tristan replied as he approached.

"It looks like a gravestone," George said, rubbing his hand along the slate.

The words read, *Elowen. Sleep tight, little one*, with the date she was born and died.

"Yes, that's what it is." Tristan's sister was buried here. She'd only been a baby, so it was a small grave. This spot had been chosen because his mother had often come to read in the shade of the elm tree in the summer months when she'd been heavily pregnant with her. She'd found the sound of the brook calming. This was when Tristan and his parents still lived in Trenouth Manor.

"Whose grave is it?"

Flash sniffed the tree, then ambled down to the brook for a drink.

"It belongs to my sister, Elowen." Tristan stood by George, looking at the stone. He needed to give it a clean, otherwise his mother would be upset. "She was stillborn."

"What does that mean?"

"She wasn't breathing when she was born. And the doctors couldn't save her."

His sister would have been three years younger than him — twenty-five now, if she'd lived. A similar age to Beth, he assumed, who looked in her early twenties. Too young to have a six-year-old, if he was honest. Though he'd nearly became a father at twenty-three...

Tristan could barely remember any of his mother's pregnancy. Just brief snippets of memories, like him laying his hand or head on her growing tummy. After the devastating loss of Elowen and nearing her forties, she had decided she didn't want to try again. Tristan was her son; she'd been blessed with one child. One would be enough. He'd often heard her say this to friends, when they'd tried to encourage her to try again. But he'd only learnt of her depression when he was old enough to understand.

What would his life have been like if Elowen had lived? If she were here, would she be bearing some of the stress and hard work of running the estate? Would she have helped rescue it from the brink of being sold off to cover the debts? Or would his father have taken better care of his inheritance and his own health?

"Would you like a sister?" Tristan found himself asking George out of nowhere. He was just intrigued really, to make conversation with a six-year-old. His own child would have been around four or five now.

George pulled a face. "A brother, maybe. To play Lego with."

"Hopefully you'll get a brother someday." Tristan ruffled the boy's hair.

"I'll ask Santa this Christmas."

"Well, um, it's not something Santa has a say in. I'm sure your mummy and daddy will work on it." Tristan started walking again. How had he managed to put his size tens in it again?

"I don't have a daddy." George kicked up the gold and yellow leaves starting to cover the path as he walked beside Tristan. The small boy had taken his hand instinctively. Flash followed them, darting off occasionally when he found a scent.

Tristan frowned. "What do you mean? Who was the man with your mummy? Is he your stepdad?"

George shook his head. "No, he's my Uncle Jay-Jay, silly." He laughed. Letting go of Tristan's hand, he started picking up leaves.

"Oh."

"We live with him. I have a Spiderman bedroom now Mum's moved the boo-tick."

"What happened to your daddy?" As soon as he asked, Tristan realised it was none of his business. And maybe something not to ask a six-year-old.

George shrugged his shoulders and carried on collecting the colourful leaves. Some still green, some orange, gold and even red. "Mummy says my daddy doesn't know about me."

What? Tristan kept the thought to himself. What kind of woman kept a son from his father? His hands tensed into fists as anger filled him, so he shoved them in his jacket pockets. Kimmie returned fresh to his mind. "We'd best get back, George." He whistled for Flash to follow and they trudged back up the gravel path into the gardens and across to The Stables.

George presented his mother with the gift of collected leaves. Crouching down, Beth took the leaves gratefully, as if they were freshly picked flowers, and ushered her son inside. Tristan couldn't look her in the eye.

"Thank you for taking him off for a walk," she said with a smile. "Nancy bought some clothes."

"Good." He nodded. He knew Nancy couldn't resist some retail therapy, especially if the clothes couldn't be found on the high street.

"She said she'd call you later. She told me to tell you she had to head off."

"That's fine."

Anxious to get away from Beth before he said something he'd regret, Tristan quickly made his way along the path to the office beside the house, Flash obediently following. His thoughts in turmoil, he tried to not think about his past, the child kept secret from him. But George's innocent remark had stirred up some deep-seated hurt and resentment.

He was close to the office when he heard someone running on the gravel behind him. He turned.

"Tristan!" Beth came sprinting after him, red-faced and incandescent with rage. "Please don't tell my son he'll get a brother. What were you thinking?"

"I didn't mean it that way. Geez, he's six, he's misinterpreted me," Tristan replied, his hackles rising. "And don't you think the boy deserves to know who his father is? It takes two to conceive a child, you know!" As soon as the words escaped his mouth, he wished he could take them back. But it was as if Kimmie had come back to haunt him, and he was remembering all the things he wanted to shout at her.

"What?" Beth stepped back, taken by surprise at his question. "It's nothing to do with you! What have you said to my son?" Her cheeks were blotching red and her eyes looked shiny, as if filling with tears.

"Nothing, nothing. But I do believe George's father should be told he exists!"

"I've worked so hard to do right by George. This is none of your business. He doesn't need a father. Jason and I look after him just fine." Beth's jaw was clenched. She glared at him, lips pursed, her chin jutting out.

"The man deserves to know he has a son." Tristan towered over her, meeting anger with anger.

Beth blinked and a tear escaped, trickling down her cheek. But her green eyes were ferocious. Her voice lowered to a hiss. "I don't know who he is."

"But surely...? You must...?" Tristan was dumbstruck. Beth had turned, wiping her nose, and was running back to The Stables. Now Tristan felt sick. He'd clearly upset her. How could she not know who the father was? Was George the product of something more sinister?

CHAPTER 8: GEORGE

What was it with that man? Beth stormed back into her shop and slammed the door, startling George, who was sitting on the sofa arranging his leaves.

It had felt like they were making progress. Tristan had been really sweet to suggest George go for a walk with him. The boy hadn't stopped talking about Flash. And it had allowed her to concentrate on Nancy, who she assumed must be his girlfriend, judging by the way she spoke about Tristan. She was older than him, probably somewhere in her mid-thirties, and came across as pretty intense, asking constant questions and pulling clothes from the rail with exclamations of, "Oh, I like this. And this." Beth had lost track of the outfits she'd wanted to try on. Nancy was clearly high maintenance and not used to seaside life and the relaxed approach to everything. She came across as a driven career woman; business-focused and certainly no kids. Beth couldn't help admiring her no-nonsense, assertive approach. She'd had a meeting to attend in Bristol later that morning, so she'd constantly checked the expensive watch wrapped around her slim wrist. Before dashing off, she'd purchased two new outfits from Beth's evening range that she'd said would be useful additions to her work wardrobe.

With less care than she should, anger bubbling in her chest, Beth shoved the discarded clothes back onto the hangers. George's father, or lack thereof, was nothing to do with Tristan. *How dare he!* she thought.

"Mummy, have I been naughty?" George looked up at her, doe-eyed. With his bottom lip protruding, he looked on the verge of tears. She'd snapped at him when he'd repeated what

Tristan had said about having a brother one day. Then she'd dashed out after Tristan, shouting at George to stay where he was.

Beth took a deep breath. This was not George's fault. It was not his fault that on the evening of her eighteenth birthday she'd had a one-night stand. A drunken, what she thought was protected, one-night stand. What a way to start her adult life.

"No, sweetheart, Tristan just said something that made me cross."

"What did he say?"

"Nothing you need worry about." She scooped George into her arms and gave him a cuddle. Instant stress reliever. "Now, what shall we do with all those pretty leaves?" She ruffled his hair, combing her fingers through it. It was blond, like his father's. Although Beth couldn't remember much about George's father's features, she could remember the colour of his hair. She did wonder if the blond would change to her red as he grew older. "Did you want to stick them down on some paper and make a collage?"

"Yes!"

"You might need to do it upstairs, so that you don't get glue everywhere."

"I'll be careful."

Once George had been settled upstairs with paper and glue, Beth finished hanging up the clothes Nancy had tried on with a renewed sense of calm. She had a couple of personal styling appointments today. She had convinced both customers to come to her, rather than take her stock to them. She was determined that the boutique would mean less travelling for her and a better shopping experience for her customers. Nancy turning up and buying two outfits had been an unexpected bonus this morning, so she could not complain. Unfortunately, it meant thanking Tristan for the introduction.

"You know you were telling me you were struggling to find something to replace the casino at your charity ball? Well, I've had an idea." Nancy was calling Tristan from her car, on her way to Bristol. He could hear the rumble of her engine in the background.

"I'm listening," he said.

"You should get Beth to run a fashion show."

"How would it work?" Nancy had no idea of their recent argument, so he'd hear her out, but he doubted Beth would want to help him. Not now.

"Well, you charge to get bums on seats."

"Which I've already done."

"Then, with the sales from the clothes, a percentage of the profits could go to the charity. And it would give Beth some great media coverage in the area, too. Think of the publicity for her boutique! Her clothes are beautiful, by the way."

Tristan wondered how much Nancy had spent on clothes at Beth's Boutique. Nancy was quite a private woman, so he hoped she hadn't revealed too much about their relationship. Not that it was any of Beth's business … just as George's father was none of his.

"But I don't have the slightest idea how to run a fashion show," he said, rubbing his temple.

"It'll be fine. I'll help. I've got some girlfriends who could help model the clothes."

"Has Beth ever done something like this before?"

"I'm not sure. You'll have to ask her." After this morning, Tristan wondered if Beth would be interested, but what Nancy said made sense. "I'll have a think on it some more and see what I can do this end. But ask Beth. She might be able to donate a couple of pieces from her range for the silent auction, too."

"Okay, good idea, I will. Thanks, Nancy. Drive safely."

He might give it a day or two first. Or see if something else came up.

Don't be such a coward, he rebuked himself. *This would be a good opportunity for Beth. And something different for the charity ball.*

And it might be a way to redeem himself, too. Show her that he wasn't a complete tosser — or at least not all of the time.

Tristan always ran an auction at the ball, and this year he'd decided to run a silent one, so it took up less time during the evening. This way, guests could come and go as they pleased during the first part of the evening, to place silent bids. The casino had been planned to generate some more charitable cash before his guests sat down for dinner. After that, he had a band booked to end the evening with dancing. Because everyone loved a good boogie at this time of year.

But Nancy could be on to something with her fashion show idea. It would be something different and could be quite fun. And there was already going to be a marquee in place ready for a wedding the following week. He decided to run the idea past his mother. After all, it was her charity the event raised money for.

December got awfully busy at Trenouth Manor. There was the Christmas fayre at the beginning of December, the charity ball was the weekend before Christmas, and this year they had a Christmas wedding — fortunately not on Christmas Day itself. He'd talked Isabella Le Bon, the Bridezilla from hell, out of that. Instead, he'd convinced her to have her wedding on Christmas Eve.

The more he thought about it, the more he could see that it wouldn't make very good business sense for Beth to refuse this opportunity to promote her boutique.

With this in mind, Tristan resolved to use this business proposition as a chance to make amends with Beth. He just hoped she'd agree to speak to him.

CHAPTER 9: A PROPOSITION

Fortunately, Beth had organised a last-minute playdate on Wednesday for George. One of her regular customers had asked to see the new top-up additions to her winter collection, which had arrived recently. Beth had convinced her to visit the boutique and bring a couple of friends. She'd brought in a bottle of prosecco — already chilling in the fridge — because this was her first ever group personal styling event at the boutique, so she wanted to celebrate in style.

As she bustled around, getting ready for her customers, she thought back to the day which had started her on her fashion journey. With George only a baby, she'd attended a clothing party run by a mother she'd met through her post-natal classes and baby weigh-ins. Her name was Eva, and although she was a good ten years older than Beth, her daughter was only two weeks older than George. Beth had gone along for some adult company, as her health visitor had recommended she should socialise more. She liked the idea of supporting a new mum trying to make some money as a stay-at-home mother. She'd bought an item in the sale, as that was all she could afford, and had stayed on to help Eva pack away the clothes while both their babies slept soundly. Over a cup of coffee, Beth had shared her pre-baby dream of becoming a fashion designer, and Eva had given Beth the initial spark of an idea to set up her own fashion business. They'd become good friends, Eva being her initial business mentor. From then on, Beth had built her venture around George, and as he'd grown, so had her business.

The French label she was signed to designed beautiful pieces which could be mixed and matched, and Beth had an eye for creating striking outfits. Her most loyal customers were those she'd been honest with. She'd refuse to sell an item to someone if they loved it but wouldn't feel confident enough to wear it. And she made sure she always told customers when an item of clothing didn't flatter them. They trusted Beth's opinions. The result was happy customers who loved wearing her clothes and referred their friends to her.

Eva and her family had emigrated to Australia a couple of years ago, but they stayed in touch via email and social media. Beth did miss her friend, and made sure to take some photos of the boutique to send to her. Eva would have been cheering her on.

As she was making sure the boutique was spotless and arranging the clothes, she noticed Seb wasn't in his workshop yet. She supposed, as a retiree, he wasn't so tied to his studio as she was to her business. She aimed to be here nine to five, fitting around George where possible.

She would have to remember to lock the door if customers started stripping off in the middle of her shop. She might need Seb to make her a sign that read, 'Please Knock, an Appointment is in Progress'. Her plan was to the run the shop through appointment slots. That way, her customers would get a personalised shopping experience, rather than the high street free-for-all. She was limited on space, after all. She wanted to be able to give each customer her full attention and that personal touch. It was her unique selling point.

With a spare half an hour before her customers' appointment, she checked her emails and her online shop. It was the way forward — she could reach a wider customer base, and if a shopper had seen an item they'd liked at a pop-up party but couldn't afford it at the time, they could order it when they wanted.

The three ladies arrived punctually. Megan, who entered first, Beth already knew. She introduced her friends as April and Briony. Beth guessed all three women were in their early thirties.

"Lovely to meet you, ladies. Now, did you bring your accessories? Boots, shoes?" Beth said.

"Yes!" All three women gestured to their cloth tote bags slung over their shoulders.

"Right, well, let's get started."

The three friends made themselves comfortable on her corner sofa as Beth gave her spiel about the fashion label she represented, where the clothing came from and how long she'd owned her boutique. This was more for April and Briony's benefit rather than Megan's, who was a regular customer.

"You won't find any designs in this boutique on the high street."

"Oh, I like that idea," said April.

"Yes, no showing up to a party and finding someone wearing the same dress as you!" Megan said.

"Well, ladies, have a look through the rails and I'll go make some drinks. Is it too early for a glass of prosecco? This is my first week of opening Beth's Boutique. I want to celebrate."

"Yes, why not… It's wine o'clock somewhere on the planet," April said with a mischievous smile.

"Just a small one for me, as I'm driving." Megan pouted disappointedly.

"Yes, we can't go mad either. Need to look after the kids later." Briony was already browsing through the clothes rail.

"Oh, who's looking after your children?" Beth asked, remembering it was half-term.

"I've left mine with my mum for a couple of hours," Megan said.

"Yes, my mum's looking after mine too," April chipped in whilst Briony nodded. "What would we do without our mums, hey?"

"Yes, yes…" Beth wished she had a mother who was interested in her grandchild. But hey ho. Her mother's loss. Today was a day to celebrate.

Upstairs, Beth popped the cork on the prosecco and carried the three glasses filled with bubbles down on a tray. Already she could see the ladies were busily holding tops and dresses up against themselves. Some items that they'd picked out as favourites hung on the hooks around the walls.

"Feel free to try on as many items as you like," Beth said, handing each lady a glass. "Even the ones you're not sure about. You might surprise yourself. There's room behind the screen, but you must come out and show us."

Before long, each woman was happily trying on different outfits. Beth was on hand with styling tips, such as a faux leather jacket to put over a top or a dress. She showed them how to mix and match the items for the perfect capsule wardrobe. The women swapped clothes left, right and centre, laughing and joking as they did, while Beth, with their permission, snapped photos of the frolics so that she could share the event on her social media sites.

"Oh, this is so much fun." April came out from behind the screen in a dark blue jumper dress.

"Oh, April, that looks gorgeous on you," Megan said, standing in front of a mirror, clearly undecided about a yellow top with a flowery print.

An hour later, the clothing range had been exhausted by all three women, and they'd all decided what to buy.

Briony hesitated about a blouse she liked, holding it up to herself in front of the mirror by the hanger. "Oh, I love this so much, but I can't afford this as well."

"Why don't you hold a pop-up party at your house? As the host, you'll get a discount. You could buy it then." Beth smiled, trying to concentrate on all three women at once. She handed a receipt over to Megan, who'd already paid for her items, then turned her attention back to Briony.

"So you're still doing pop-ups, then?" Megan asked.

"Oh, yes. This shop space is to free up the third bedroom at home. And this just adds to the shopping experience, doesn't it?" With the light-coloured walls, laminate flooring, mirrors and carefully selected ornaments, Beth was impressed with the chic look she'd achieved. And in only a matter of days, too. "I'm keeping it as appointments only here too. It wouldn't have been half as much fun if you'd had other shoppers getting in the way. I want to offer a personal service as well as selling a fantastic clothing range."

"I don't really have the room at home," said Briony, frowning.

An idea popped into Beth's head. It could be a way forward. "Well, you could hold it here, then." This would be a good way to get people into the shop, it would save her hauling the clothes to someone's house, and she could offer the same reward scheme to the person who booked the party.

"Oh, now that's an idea." Briony beamed. Beth grabbed the shop's appointment diary, and between them they booked a date.

"It has been so much fun, and so relaxed. I usually hate clothes shopping," said April as the group said their goodbyes. Encouraged by Beth, they were going to browse the other shops before they went home. Beth was slowly getting to know all the other business owners at The Stables. Maisie, the jewellery maker, had asked to display some of her jewellery in the boutique in return for business cards and leaflets from Beth's to put in hers. The two shops did cross over rather nicely. Customers could buy bespoke jewellery to go with their not-on-the-high-street clothing.

With a pop-up boutique for Briony booked in a month's time, and over three hundred pounds in sales this morning, Beth was feeling positive about her business. With the new shop, she had the opportunity to make it grow. Clearing away the glasses and making sure the prosecco bottle's top was secure, she prepared the boutique for the next appointment that had come in via Facebook. She had confirmed it after Megan, April and Briony had left.

"Hello … Beth, are you there?" She heard a male voice downstairs. Assuming it to be Sebastian, she ran eagerly down the stairs to greet him and then stopped short. Her smile faded.

Not Seb. *Tristan*.

She eyed him suspiciously. "Can I help you?" she said in her most supercilious voice, hoping it would annoy the shit out of him.

"Actually, it's maybe how I can help you."

"Oh?" Her heart betrayed her with a skip of excitement. Why did he have that effect on her? When he smiled, he was quite handsome.

"Are you busy?" He stepped towards her hesitantly, aware that he was walking on eggshells with her.

She checked her watch. "My next appointment is in half an hour." She tried to keep the tone professional, and not snappy.

"Right, I'll make it quick, then. I've got a business proposition for you."

Beth nodded, still hesitant and unable to forget their earlier animosity.

"Well, I run a charity ball every year in December to raise money for various children's charities. The charities are my mother's choice, really. She rotates them each year. I just organise the event and hold it at Trenouth Manor for her," Tristan said, keeping his focus on Beth. She felt herself softening under the intense gaze of his dark brown eyes. "We're running a silent auction this year, so it doesn't eat too much into the night's events, and there's dinner and dancing later. Anyway, sorry, I'm digressing... The company I'd booked to lay on some entertainment and generate more money for the event has pulled out."

"Oh, that's short notice! What was it?"

"A casino." Tristan shoved his hands into his trouser pockets. "Anyway, Nancy came up with the idea of holding a fashion show — with your clothing range."

Beth realised she was holding her breath. "Oh, right."

"So, I'm wondering if you'd like to do it? We'd have everything set up for you and Nancy said she could get you some models, so perhaps we could come to an agreement about a percentage of your profits being donated to the charity."

"Did you want a cup of tea?" Beth didn't know what to say, and realised Tristan had come to her with an amazing offer. Okay, it had been his girlfriend's idea, not his, but even so. After the row they'd had yesterday — more like Beth biting his head off — she now felt the need to eat humble pie.

"Thanks, but I'm all tea'd out." Tristan shook his head. "Look, I can see I've caught you off guard with this. Have a think about it. But you would be doing me a huge favour, and it would be great publicity for your boutique."

"Yes. Yes, it would. Okay, I'll have a think." There was nothing to think about really but again, it was probably good to sleep on it, run it by Jason. "Come and see me tomorrow morning. Oh, you'd best let me know the date too."

"It's the Saturday before Christmas."

"Okay, I'll check the diary. Might have to make sure Jason can look after George."

Tristan nodded, making his way to the door. "I'll come and see you tomorrow morning, and we can discuss the finer details if you're okay with it."

"I look forward to it."

Tristan closed the door behind him and Beth exhaled heavily.

I look forward to it.

But would she look forward to spending time with this man, who rubbed her up the wrong way whenever she saw him?

If she agreed to this fashion show, she would be seeing a whole lot more of Tristan than she desired. However, she would be mad to turn down this offer. The publicity her boutique would receive — and potentially the sales. She'd need to work out what she could afford to donate to the charity, but she would be silly to turn this offer down just because she and Tristan didn't see eye to eye.

Sleep on it first. You have a habit of making rash decisions.

CHAPTER 10: THE WRONG CAR

"When you see him this morning, are you going to tell Tristan that you are doing this?" Jason stood in the kitchen, making packed lunches for the three of them.

"I can do this, can't I?" Beth hovered beside him. She knew she sounded hesitant.

"Yes. You. Can." Jason looked at her fiercely. "Putting your differences aside, this fashion show will be a brilliant opportunity for your business. Think of the exposure. Everyone at that charity event will be ready to spend money for a good cause too."

Last night, Beth had discussed Tristan's proposal with Jason and number crunched to see what percentage of sales she could afford to donate. They circled the date on the calendar in the kitchen. Jason would babysit George that evening. He hinted at a cosy night in, just the boys. He said he might even invite Scott over, having confessed to them being a little more than just friends.

"There you go." Jason handed Beth two sets of sandwiches in boxes. She grabbed a carton of juice for George, plus a bag of crisps and an apple for each of them. She'd also put a mix of red and green grapes in another tub, which she knew were George's favourite.

On her way to The Stables in Pingu, Beth detoured past her old family home. She occasionally stopped by this house but would never admit it to Jason. It didn't matter, as her mother and father no longer lived there. She'd seen the 'For Sale' sign go up a few years ago, when George was not even one. And now she no longer knew where they lived. They were permanently estranged. While her parents had lived at the house, Beth had hoped that one day reconciliation would be possible.

Jason had also been eighteen when he'd washed his hands of their parents. She'd only been thirteen at the time and hadn't understood why, until she'd turned eighteen herself and he'd given her refuge in his small, pokey flat. Her parents, embarrassed by Jason's sexuality, had hidden their real reason for kicking him out from Beth.

Usually, she didn't like to drive by the old house with George in the car, but she hoped he would be too preoccupied to notice.

"This isn't the way, Mummy."

Damn the boy for being so observant. Your own fault for encouraging him to look out the window. "I just wanted to take a look at something."

That first Christmas, when George was only a newborn, Beth had sent her mum and dad a Christmas card and enclosed a photo of George. Neither of her parents had got in touch. Beth was gutted.

And now, having relocated, it felt as if her parents had moved on without their two children. Beth couldn't understand it. She simply couldn't imagine life without George. She would always be there for him.

She gave herself a mental shake and drove on, trying to suppress any negative thoughts. She always started feeling low and regretful at this time of year, in the lead-up to Christmas. George should be seeing his grandparents. It was so sad that he had no contact with them. That's why she was so grateful to Sebastian. She'd barely known him a week, yet the man was already the closest thing to a grandparent for George.

Trying to think more positively, she concentrated on the boutique. She had several appointments booked today. Seb, bless his heart, had agreed to look after George in his workshop during those times. Those two were becoming real buddies. Next week would be easier, as George would be back at school.

Beth let herself into the shop, and placed a heavy lump of wood Sebastian had given her in front of the door to hold it open. The late October morning was sunny and mild, so it would be nice to let some fresh air into the building. She busied herself cleaning, checking emails for orders, and setting up the coffee machine, so she had filter coffee on tap for her customers, as well as for herself. A delivery driver arrived early with a box of goodies: more clothes to replenish items she'd sold from the autumn/winter collection.

She always loved unpacking deliveries. Today, she even allowed George to help her open the box. With a marvellous grin on his face and his eyes lit up, he watched as she pulled different items of clothing from the box. He understood not to touch them — well, almost. He was as intrigued as she was by the feel of the fabrics and the different array of colours. Yellow and red appeared to be the in colours this season. More brochures and stationery were included in the delivery and she filed them away appropriately. She used one of the lower box shelves to store the paper carrier bags, and took the rest of the stationery upstairs.

There were bins located at the back of the stables for the businesses to use. She was relieved to see a large bin provided for recycling, so she placed the flattened cardboard box in it. As she walked back towards her shop, she caught sight of Tristan coming towards her with Flash obediently to heel.

"Hey, I thought I'd call in on my way past. Any thoughts on the fashion show?"

"It's a yes. I'll do it." She checked her watch. "Could you call in later so we can arrange the finer details? I've got customers due any minute, and I need to take George over to Sebastian. And he'll want to chat."

"Did you want George to come for a walk with me and Flash?"

Beth could see Tristan was hesitant about making this offer, after their recent altercation. "It's okay, Sebastian said he'd look after him. I think the pair of them are up to something, if truth be told."

Tristan nodded as he threw Flash's lead over his shoulder. "What time are you free later?"

"Midday."

"Okay, let's have lunch and talk it over then. I'll come and get you."

"That's great. See you at twelve."

Jason's sandwiches could wait until tomorrow. They would survive in her fridge.

At ten o'clock, with George safely in the care of Sebastian — he'd even brought hot chocolate in to make for George when he stopped for tea — Beth had a group of six women in her shop trying on clothes. Louisa was another of her regular customers and wanted a styling session in Beth's new boutique now that she'd got her figure back after having two children. Beth had thought she was only bringing a couple of friends, but when five women trooped in after her she realised this would be a great test for the shop.

She decided it would be easier if the women took it in turns to try outfits on. With their choice of beverages on the coffee table — tea, coffee or Buck's Fizz — three of them sat on the sofa while the other three changed and showed off their chosen outfits. Beth realised that six customers was probably the maximum she could have in the shop to keep the experience comfortable and enjoyable. They were tag-teaming the changing area; as one came out, the other went in. Then one would sit on the sofa in the outfit she was wearing, while another tried on clothes. It was perfect. The atmosphere was fun and light-hearted, just as Beth hoped it would always be. The friends encouraged each other to try on different items, but Beth gave each woman her honest opinion. She would never sell a garment to someone if it looked awful on them. Some colours flattered, while some washed a person out. A design that did nothing for one woman's figure, suited another perfectly.

With their chosen items purchased and carefully folded in her Beth's Boutique carrier bags, six very happy customers left her shop. It gave Beth such a buzz seeing them chatting enthusiastically about what they'd bought, planning a night out when they could all wear their new outfits. And they all promised to return with more friends.

"See you in the spring, if not before," said Louisa, kissing Beth on each cheek as she left.

After clearing up the shop, Beth went to collect George from Sebastian, conscious he had been in the workshop for over an hour. "No rush, we're having fun, aren't we, little man?" Seb reassured her, and ruffled George's hair. It needed a cut before he went back to school.

Midday approached, and Beth's nerves gave a flutter. Lunch with Tristan.

Why should she be nervous? It was hardly a date. She had to take George with her. *It's a business lunch. Get over it.*

Beth brushed her hair, applied some light make-up, including lipstick, and gave her outfit the once over. She always wore her label in the shop as her work uniform. She'd given George strict instructions to behave at the meal table and explained that Mummy was having a business lunch and needed him to be good.

Beth heard the rumble of the engine before she saw the car.

An Audi R8 — red to make it stand out more than it already did — slowly drove into the courtyard. It had to drive slowly, because a low sports car and cobblestones were not a good combination.

It pulled to a halt, and Tristan jumped out. "Ready?"

Holding George's hand, Beth locked up her shop and then walked towards the car, frowning. She knew a bit about cars thanks to her brother being a petrol head. Therefore, she knew there was no way George would fit in a two-seater sports car. Annoyance bubbled inside her but she plastered on a smile. In Tristan's defence, she hadn't said she'd need to bring George with her.

Tristan looked at George, who'd let go of Beth's hand and was approaching the car eagerly. "Are we going to lunch in this car? Red's my favourite colour."

"Don't be silly, George, we can't all possibly fit in this car." Beth looked at Tristan questioningly, aware that she sounded rather like Mary Poppins scolding one of the children.

Tristan, realising his blunder, pushed his hands through his hair and approached Beth. "I'm so sorry, it should have occurred to me that of course you'd need to bring George. I'm such a twat."

"Language," Beth scolded. Fortunately, George was too busy looking around the car. Beth feared he was too close and didn't want him scratching the pristine paintwork.

"Twit," Tristan said quickly. "Look, wait here, I'll get my other car."

George's face dropped. "But I want a ride in this car."

Before checking with Beth, Tristan opened the passenger door. "Tell you what, buddy, come with me."

"But he hasn't got his car seat!"

Tristan was already placing the seatbelt over George. "Don't worry. I'm only going as far as my house, within the grounds, and I won't take it out of second gear. Promise."

She could hardly say no. George's face was a picture inside the sports car. "Okay, I'll fetch his car seat from my car, then."

"I'll meet you there in five minutes."

"No speeding!"

"Ten minutes, then." Tristan gave a grin from the driver's seat and started the engine. It purred to life. A little press of the throttle and there was the growl of the lion beneath the bonnet.

The gleaming Audi R8 glided out of the courtyard with George eagerly waving at Beth and Seb, who'd stepped out of his workshop to admire the car. Beth wondered if Tristan's slow driving was due more to the cobbles than her stressing that George wasn't properly secure in the car. Seb waved back to George.

"What a happy little boy," Seb said whimsically.

Beth smiled fondly. "With his uncle a mechanic and mad about cars, it's clearly rubbed off on George."

CHAPTER 11: LUNCH DATE

Tristan could have kicked himself for being so stupid. Of course Beth still had George with her. It was half-term.

Concentrating on keeping the car at a slow pace, he drove it back to his cottage, glancing at the very eager little boy sitting next to him. Because George wasn't in a child's car seat, he was sitting very low, and straining to look out the window.

"Can you go fast?" George asked, glowing with excitement.

"I promised your mother I wouldn't. Besides, the drive is all gravel, and not really designed for a sportscar to speed along it." It would guarantee chips in the paintwork.

"I won't tell her, if you won't."

Tristan laughed. "I'm already in trouble with your mum for a number of things. I don't want to add this to the list. Another time, when you're in your car seat, I'll take you out."

At the cottage, Tristan pressed the button to the garage and with a beep the large door lifted open. He pulled up the Audi alongside the Range Rover.

"Wait," he said firmly to George. He knew the doors would be too heavy for a six-year-old and didn't want trapped fingers or the door swinging into the garage wall.

He helped George out, then lifted him into the back of the Range Rover. George was now equally excited to be up much higher and in something just as impressive. Tristan put the seatbelt over George's shoulder and lap, then reversed the vehicle out. He let George, who was loving every minute, press the button to the electric garage door to hide the Audi away.

Again, Tristan took it slowly and made his way to where Beth's Fiat 500c was parked in The Stable's designated car park. Next to the Range Rover, Beth's car looked minuscule.

Because Tristan had no clue how to fit a child's car seat, he let Beth make the adjustments required. He helped by removing the headrest, so that the car seat was secure. At times, as they adjusted the seats, he was close enough to catch the scent of Beth's perfume. While she fastened George's belt, he couldn't help watching her appreciatively. He had to admit, when she wasn't red with anger at him, she was very attractive.

Tristan glanced at his watch. Good job he hadn't reserved somewhere swanky for lunch, now they had a small child in tow. He decided to drive to Kittiwake Cove to eat at The Cormorant, Joe's pub. This way, he could kill two birds with one stone and catch up with his cousin. Also, some of Joe's charm might rub off on him, and he might not put his size ten feet in it with Beth — again. He needed her assistance. But so far so good. She seemed to have forgotten his Audi R8 blunder.

The pub was quieter than it would be in the summer months, and Tristan was relieved that they were serving food. The aroma of Cornish ale and steak and chips made his stomach rumble.

"What would you like to drink?" Tristan asked as they approached the bar. "Wine? I'm driving, remember."

"And I've got to drive home tonight. Remember."

"Yes, sorry…"

"And I have another appointment booked this afternoon, so I can't be too long."

Tristan noticed Beth glance at the clock behind the bar, then Joe appeared.

"Hi, Tristan." He leaned over the bar and shook Tristan's hand warmly. Joe looked at Beth, then the penny dropped. "Oh, it's Beth, isn't it? Did you get your puncture fixed?"

"Yes, I did. And thanks again for helping me out."

"And you've moved into The Stables, Tristan tells me. I'll have to take Rhianna along for the shopping experience."

"Yes, it would be lovely to meet her."

Tristan watched as Beth blushed shyly. Joe's charm was at full wattage.

"So, what can I get you?" Joe beamed his million-dollar smile. The one Tristan needed to master.

"Can I have an apple juice, Mummy?" George piped up, tugging at Beth's sleeve.

Joe leaned over the bar. "Hey, I didn't see you down there, little fella."

"And the magic word, George?" Beth said.

"Please."

Tristan ordered the drinks and paid. All soft drinks. He didn't want to risk a pint or even a shandy with George in the car. They found a table near the window. The Cormorant sat up the hill, so the large bay window at the front of the pub looked over the town and the beach. With the sun shining, and hardly a wisp of clouds in the sky, it could have been a summer's day outside.

"Some days, I forget this is on our doorstep," Beth said, after fetching a colouring book and crayons out of her large handbag and handing them to George. Tristan found himself wanting to ask where she lived, whether she visited the beach often, but he remained quiet, watching mother and son.

"Can't I play games on your phone?" George asked. The boy looked at his mother innocently. Tristan's admiration for her increased as Beth ignored the 'don't say no to me' look.

"No, darling. Maybe later, do some colouring first." She pushed the book closer and George picked up the crayons, turning the pages to find something he wanted to colour in.

Tristan handed Beth a menu. Once they'd chosen, including a kids' meal for George, Beth went to hand Tristan some money. He gently pushed her hand away and felt a fizz of electricity as the heat of her fingers tingled inside his palm.

"My idea, my treat. Besides, you're going to be doing me a huge favour." He gave her a smile — not quite Joe's megawatt one, but he hoped he looked sincere.

At the bar, while ordering the food from Joe, Tristan hoped to discuss his engagement party. But Joe had other ideas.

"Kissed and made up, did we?" Joe said with a twinkle of mischief in his expression.

Tristan rolled his eyes. "She's a tenant of mine, renting a workshop at The Stables. I have to play nice." Tristan quickly looked over his shoulder, to check that Beth couldn't overhear what he was saying. "What I mean is, I'm trying to make amends for being an arse."

Joe nodded. "Better."

"I still managed to be an arse, though." Tristan explained about his poor choice of transport this morning, which Joe laughed at, and how he had questioned her about George's father. "I thought she wasn't letting the man see his son, so I just saw red."

Joe shook his head. "Maybe find out the facts before you leap to conclusions, huh?"

"I don't know what it is about that woman, but I keep putting my foot in it with her."

Joe smirked.

"What?" Tristan frowned.

"Nothing." Joe shook his head, then silently gestured towards Beth, who was sipping her drink and gazing out the window. "Go sit down. Number one rule, Tristan. Don't keep a lady waiting."

Tristan nodded. "But I do need to talk to you about your party."

Joe waved him off impatiently; perhaps he would be better off speaking with Rhianna about the arrangements.

Back at the table, with George engrossed in his colouring, Tristan and Beth got down to talking business. Tristan couldn't help studying Beth's pretty face; the freckles on her nose, her fierce green eyes that had softened now she'd relaxed and wasn't so wary of him — finally. He observed how her red hair shone in the light, and how she'd tuck a strand behind her ear nervously as she talked about her clothing line and the boutique.

Beth had pulled out a notebook. "I can donate a percentage of the sales profits to the charity, and I have an outfit to donate for the silent auction, too." She sucked her bottom lip, looking at her notepad, then up at Tristan, who couldn't stop watching her. "Fifty per cent okay?"

"If that's what you can afford. I don't want you losing money; you do have a new business to run, with start-up costs etcetera. It's extremely generous of you."

"Well, I'm envisaging huge sales, so fingers crossed, hey?" Her green eyes widened with excitement.

Tristan returned the smile. "Yes, fingers crossed."

Their food arrived quickly, and they continued their discussion while eating.

"Did you say you could get me some models?" Beth speared a chip with her fork.

"Yes, Nancy said she'd rope in some of her friends. Or do you have people in mind who wouldn't mind volunteering?"

"Not really, this is a first for me. And if Nancy's friends look anything like her, it'll look like we've dragged in professional models. But we need some older women as models too, to showcase that the clothing range suits all ages."

"Good idea, because the guests will be a mixed bunch." Tristan nodded. "I might be able to convince my mum to model. In fact, she'd probably love it. What about yours?"

Tristan watched as Beth's gaze dropped and the colour rose in her cheeks. She looked out the window, avoiding meeting his eyes. "No. No, I can't ask my mother," she said faintly, the mood suddenly chilling.

Tristan was on the verge of asking why, but stopped himself just in time. "I'll ask my mother, and my Aunt Rose might like to do it, too. How many models do you think we'll need?"

"Depends on how much space we have for them to change. I'll need their sizes, so that I can get the right outfits for each of them. We need enough so that while some are changing, others are on the catwalk."

"I'll check with Nancy and get the dress sizes." Tristan finished his food, pushing his knife and fork together.

"Great. Thanks for lunch and for asking me to do this. As you say, it might give my business the boost it needs, while supporting a fantastic local cause."

"Might? It definitely will!" Tristan was starting to pick up hints of Beth's lack of confidence. "Anyway, as I said before, it was Nancy's proposal really. She came up with the idea of a fashion show."

Why did he have a way of pouring cold water onto something that was just warming up? Why mention Nancy?

"Oh, yes." Beth's gaze dropped. They'd become quite intense in their conversation, relaxing in each other's company, and Tristan had blown it — once again. "I must remember to thank her, then."

"Well, if she ends up modelling for you, you'll have an opportunity." Tristan really wanted to get things back on an even keel with Beth. "I'm a bloke. I never would have thought of a fashion show. You know what us men are like." He tapped his head to indicate he was a dunce, and George laughed, which made Beth smile. "Hey, if it goes well, it could be a regular thing. The fashion show, I mean…" God, now he was stumbling over his words.

"Yes, yes… Gosh, is that the time?" Beth glanced at her watch. "I need to be getting back." In a panic, she started packing her notebook away.

"Yes, sure, and I have things I need to be doing. Can't leave it all to Anya."

They sat in companionable silence on the drive back to Trenouth Manor. Tristan dropped Beth and George off at The Stables, then parked the Range Rover outside the office. His heart felt lighter. One, he'd secured a fashion show for the charity ball, and two, he might have made some progress with Beth.

CHAPTER 12: TRICK OR TREAT

Beth was relieved that Halloween had fallen during half-term this year, which meant the inevitable late night wasn't on a school night. She had finished early in the boutique to be home with George, so that they could spend the afternoon hollowing out a pumpkin and carving a spooky face. Once darkness had fallen, they had placed it on the doorstep with a lit tealight inside, giving its toothy grin an orange glow. For tea they had spicy pumpkin soup with fresh, crusty, wholemeal bread and lashings of butter, followed by homemade Halloween-themed biscuits that they had made the day before. They had baked enough to be handed out to trick-or-treaters, too.

Beth usually went all out for Halloween, from the pumpkin carving to biscuit baking, because, as kids, she and Jason had never been allowed to participate in the trick-or-treating at Halloween. So, they both agreed that George should have the pleasure of dressing up. And so many more kids did it nowadays, they didn't want him missing out on all the fun. They remembered their own misery, listening to their friends at school talking about their Halloween plans. By walking George around the houses, it also meant she and Jason got to share in the fun too, making up for what they had missed out on as children. Jason, as chaperone, usually got dressed up as well. Beth couldn't work out which of the two was the bigger kid! Sometimes, Beth stayed at home to answer the door to other trick-or-treaters. The younger ones were usually out early, just as it got dark. Beth always made sure she wore a witch's hat as she answered the door and gave a good cackle for dramatic effect.

Her mother had insisted the tradition was nothing more than begging and would not permit it. Conscious of this, Beth ensured that George only knocked on doors of houses with decorations or pumpkins outside to avoid troubling those who didn't participate in the festivities.

Although the shops were full of costumes these days, Beth always enjoyed making George's outfit. She liked sitting and sewing in front of the television, usually upcycling some old clothes or pieces of fabric. For her twenty-first birthday, Jason had found her a sewing machine in a charity shop, and she tried to use it whenever she could.

Fortunately, the evening was dry but cold; perfect for George and Jason to roam the streets. Beth insisted they stick to the houses in their close. They usually received enough sweets and chocolate on their doorstep, without the need to go much further afield.

This year, she'd transformed an old tablecloth into a cape and waistcoat, dying it black, for her own cute Dracula. With George's hair spiked up and his face painted white, with dark circles around his eyes and red lipstick on his lips, he made a great little vampire. Jason was happy to dress as a ghost in an old white sheet with eyes cut out, and holes for his arms. Beth waved her ghouls off while answering the door to other mini monsters.

When they returned, George emptied his little pumpkin bucket on to the table to review his treats, and shared the things he wasn't so keen on with Jason. Jason, a sweet-o-holic, gladly took what George did not want as his reward for accompanying him.

After George's bath, his white make-up removed, Beth made him a hot chocolate before bed, allowing him a couple of Halloween treats while he watched some television. CBeebies had finished, so she'd stuck a DVD on. A quick story in bed and George was soon fast asleep. He looked angelic. Beth gave a sigh as she kissed his warm cheek. A wave of sadness swept over her after the fun they had shared today. Her mother really was missing out on seeing her grandson grow up. But what could she do?

November had started chilly, and the trees were losing their leaves fast in flurries of golds, reds and yellows. George loved going to the park and running through them, kicking them up with his welly boots. And the odd Saturday when Beth brought him with her over to The Stables, he found great enjoyment in the grounds. Today, thankfully, he was in school.

Beth's Boutique was taking off and it was such a relief not to run it from home anymore. George loved his new bedroom, and when he was naughty, Beth loved it even more, because she now had somewhere to banish him to. Then, she'd catch him happily playing with his toys, the television long forgotten. This always made her smile, her heart melting a little more with love for her son. It also meant she could go home and switch off, treating her business like a proper job. She would still organise pop-up boutiques in homes, workplaces, salons and gyms, as they were a great way to advertise what she did. But she hoped over time she would need to do this less and less, as she was finding her clients were enjoying coming to her. It took away the stress of them having to entertain guests. Plus, the feedback she was getting from customers was that they liked having the retail experience, but in a more exclusive, intimate way — exactly what Beth was aiming for.

She had just finished another session and was hanging clothes on the rails, when there was a knock at the door. Seb had crafted her a reversible plaque which read 'Appointment in progress, please knock,' or 'Open, please come in.' It hung outside the door. Maybe she'd forgotten to turn the plaque over.

"It's open, come in."

"Hey." It was Tristan. He closed the door behind him and rubbed his hands. "Nice and warm in here." The scent of his aftershave wafted pleasantly around the boutique.

Lately, she hadn't seen much of him, having been dealing with Anya with regards to the charity ball and the Christmas fayre. When she didn't have any customers in the shop, she was busy ordering clothes to replenish her stock. In truth, she was more than happy to avoid him. Less chance to rub each other up the wrong way. Or more importantly, for him to piss her off.

So why did her face feel like it was bursting into flames?

"I have to keep it warm in here with customers changing," she said. She worried it could be too warm sometimes. It was about finding that perfect temperature. It felt too warm now in Tristan's presence. "How can I help you?"

"Are you free Monday evening?"

"I think so. Why?"

"It's Joe and Rhianna's engagement party, here at the house, and I wondered if you'd like to come along?"

"Oh, I'm not sure. I'll feel like I'm imposing; I won't know anyone." Beth and Jason lived closer to Wadebridge. She didn't belong to the Kittiwake Cove clique. And with her brother being gay, and she a single mother, would they ever fit in? Twenty-first century or not, some people's mindset was still judgemental and belonged in the dark ages. Like her mother and father's.

"Nonsense, and it's the best way to get to know people. I thought you might enjoy the networking opportunity." Tristan must have picked up on her apprehension because he added, "Seb's coming with his wife."

"I'd need a babysitter." She fiddled with the coat hanger in her hands.

"Couldn't your brother do it?" Tristan said hastily, then more gently, "I mean, could you ask him?"

Beth blushed. He knew she was just making excuses. She was a little disconcerted by this new, concerned Tristan. "I'll ask him. He does enough for me already, though. I don't like to impose."

"Okay, let me know." Tristan gave a nod. "I'll come and collect you." With that, he gave a small wave and let himself out, shutting the door behind him. The temperature in the room dropped a few degrees.

Why would Tristan want her to go to an engagement party with him?

Networking opportunity ... not a date!

"Er, hello? Of course you should go!" Jason waved his fork at Beth before tucking into a roast potato. He'd made toad-in-the-hole. "I'll look after George."

"I didn't like to ask."

"Is it a date with this Tristan? I thought you thought he was an arsehole?"

"No! It's not a date," Beth said coolly. But was it?

"But you said he'd pick you up?"

Beth shrugged. "I don't think he meant it that way. Maybe he's offered so I don't have to walk in on my own. He said it would be a great networking opportunity."

"It is, so you will tell him you'll go. You need a life, little sis."

"But what about George...?"

95

"George will be fine with his Uncle Jay-Jay, won't you, matey?" Jason winked at his nephew. "And he won't love you any less for having a night out and enjoying yourself. We all need some time off occasionally."

The next morning, Beth made her way down to the office to find Anya was the only one in the room.

"Oh, hi, Anya. Is Tristan about?" Beth hovered in the doorway. Mild relief that Tristan wasn't there washed over her. For some reason, the man made her feel flustered.

"He's running a team-building event today. Can I give him a message?"

"Oh, he asked me about Joe and Rhianna's party, and I just wanted to say, yes I'd love to come."

"Oh, great, the more the merrier!" Anya's face lit up. "I'll leave him a note."

Although relieved not to face him, Beth would have liked to confirm whether it was a date or not. However, Beth reasoned, Anya's reaction to her attending meant that she must have known Tristan was going to ask her. So maybe it was just a networking opportunity and she was overthinking things. As usual.

CHAPTER 13: THE ENGAGEMENT PARTY

Monday evening arrived. Over the weekend, Tristan had been in touch with Beth to confirm that he would collect her. As she fussed about in her bedroom, getting ready for the evening, she was still confused about why Tristan had invited her, but decided to try to treat the event as a networking opportunity.

Still, she was wearing the best dress she owned — one from her Vivienne Rémy collection — as it was a party, after all. She had straightened her hair properly and applied make-up more heavily than usual. It was a rarity to get dressed up for an evening out. She couldn't remember the last time she'd spent this long getting ready, undisturbed by her son.

Since having George, she had rarely gone out, let alone dated. If she did go out, it was with Jason and George. After her disastrous one-night stand, even if George was the product of it, she hadn't trusted herself. She didn't want to make the same mistake twice. And besides, who wanted to date a young, single mum? Guys her age weren't interested in kids. They were at the start of their lives, their careers, having just left university … just as she should have been. And the ones that were interested in children already had their own — some by several different mothers. She didn't want that in her life either.

It was a strange thing, having a child. Beth thought she would have gained confidence, but instead it had made her less sure of herself. The stretchmarks on her body didn't help.

But the young woman gazing back at her in the mirror, in the floaty, olive green tunic dress, which rested just above the knee, looked confident, classy, and even, dare she think it, sassy. Could that really be her in the mirror?

Jason was putting George to bed, reading him a bedtime story. She tapped on the door.

"Will I do?" she asked nervously from the doorway. Then she did a twirl, more for George than Jason. She hadn't been sure what the exact dress code for the party was, so she'd gone for a smart casual look.

"You look great. Enjoy yourself," Jason said.

"You look lovely, Mummy." George was under his duvet, hugging his favourite teddy.

"Ah, thank you, George." She kissed him on the forehead, then gave it a rub, having left a red lipstick mark. She turned to Jason. "Thank you for babysitting."

"It's not a problem. Scott's coming over later once this boy is asleep."

"Oh good." Beth had still only met Scott briefly. She hoped Jason would introduce him properly soon, but maybe their relationship was in the early stages.

"I want to meet Scott," George piped up.

"Another time, little man." Jason ruffled his hair, spiking it up.

The doorbell rang and Beth froze. Jason probably glimpsed the flicker of panic that flashed across her face.

"You'll be fine. Go enjoy yourself."

"Go, Mummy, go!"

Beth grabbed her small handbag, which contained keys, phone, lipstick and cash. Oh, and a small packet of tissues — the mother in her always wanted to be prepared.

She opened the front door to find Tristan standing on her doorstep, hands behind his back. His smile dropped as his eyes widened.

"Wow, you look lovely. Is that one of your dresses?"

"Well, clearly it's *mine*." Beth couldn't help the sarcastic reply. That was her defence mechanism. Then, remembering her manners, she added more softly, "But yes, it's from this year's winter collection."

"That is what I meant."

"It's okay, isn't it? Your face dropped. Am I underdressed?" *Or overdressed?*

"No, no, you look ... great. Perfect, in fact." He stumbled over the words and Beth wondered if he was trying to think before he spoke, as they both tended to say the wrong things to one another.

"Are you sure you're okay giving me a lift? I mean, you live on the estate."

"I can't drink anyway. I'll be keeping an eye on things, to make sure the party runs smoothly." Tristan led her to his Range Rover. Secretly she'd hoped for the Audi R8, but now she saw why he wasn't driving the sports car.

Nancy was sitting in the front passenger seat.

"Allow me." He opened the back passenger door, behind Nancy, and Beth stepped in. Tristan held his hand out, which she took, for fear of making a fool of herself. Luckily the dress wasn't tight around her thighs, or she would have struggled to get up into the seat gracefully. Once she was in, and putting her seatbelt on, he closed the door.

"I didn't realise Nancy was coming down. And she insisted on coming along for the ride," Tristan said. Was Beth imagining it or was there an edge of annoyance in his voice?

"I wanted to talk about the fashion show, and tell Beth how much I love my clothes. I have a couple of friends interested in coming to see the new range." Nancy twisted round and beamed at Beth. She had an amazing smile with beautifully straight teeth.

"Are they the friends who have agreed to be models for the charity ball?" Beth asked, glad to be discussing something they had in common — a passion for clothes.

"Yes! They'd like to see the collection."

Beth smiled back. She couldn't dislike Nancy. She'd been the one, after all, to convince Tristan to hold a fashion show for his charity event. And she had bought clothes from her, too. She was supporting her. However, it was a clear reminder that this was never going to be a 'date' with Tristan. He had a girlfriend.

Besides, would she have wanted it to be a date?

Tristan rattled her in so many ways. Probably best to remain friends. Or perhaps they were more like business associates? She wasn't sure that 'friends' was the right word to describe their relationship. It was fairly rocky at the best of times.

Beth would have to put aside that he scrubbed up well in a suit. *Really* well. Even without the tie. Seeing him on her doorstep had made her breath hitch and her heart quicken. And for a brief moment she'd panicked she had forgotten to apply deodorant, as a flash of heat had spread across her skin.

"It does seem weird to have a party on a Monday evening," Nancy said. As usual, she looked immaculate. Beth had thought the same.

"Rhianna shuts the restaurant on Mondays during low season, so this was the best night for her. Plus, it allows her staff to attend the party, too."

"Oh, I see." Nancy nodded.

"And Trenouth Manor was definitely not going to be booked on a Monday evening."

When they stepped out of the car, Beth noticed Nancy's dress. It clung to her body like a second skin. It was long, a deep midnight blue, and its tiny sequins and beads shimmered in the light. Nancy looked impossibly elegant, wearing heels that made her tower over Beth even more than she already did. Beth, next to Nancy, now felt underdressed for the party. But at least she felt reassured that Nancy would be the perfect model for the fashion show. With a figure like that, she could wear a black bin-liner down the catwalk and still look amazing. Beth could see why Tristan was attracted to her. They were certainly a striking couple.

Tristan escorted both women towards the imposing front door of Trenouth Manor, Nancy tucking her arm through his. Beth, he could tell, felt awkward on the other side of him. With a reassuring smile, he gestured for her to loop her arm through his, which she hesitantly did.

Although it was great to have Nancy here to talk to Beth, he had hoped to have the evening with her to himself.

But Nancy had called him in the afternoon, uncharacteristically upset — not all teary and blubbering, just frustrated about something she hadn't wanted to discuss. She wanted some company, some space to get away from her home and her office, and so here she was. Why she couldn't have stayed at a girlfriend's... He had really hoped to concentrate on looking after Beth. He wanted to build a better friendship between them and learn not to keep putting his foot in it with her. There was something about her that intrigued him.

When he had knocked at the door, and Beth had answered, for a moment she'd been unrecognisable with the heavier make-up and an olive green dress that suited her complexion perfectly. The dress, cut above the knee, revealing fantastic legs that had always been hidden away, had taken his breath away and made his mind go momentarily blank. He couldn't deny the spark of attraction he felt for her.

As he led Beth through the front door, he placed his hand on her lower back, trying to reassure her. At first, he feared he'd made a mistake, and she would glare at him, but the gesture appeared to go unnoticed. Or at least not discouraged, which pleased him. A waitress was standing in the hallway, holding a silver tray with tall glass flutes. A welcome glass of champagne for each guest. He handed a glass to Beth and Nancy in turn. The two women tapped glasses before taking a sip. He took the non-alcoholic option: orange and elderflower spritzer. With Rhianna involved, there were bound to be cocktails available, but Tristan would be surviving on coffee during the evening.

Music could be heard throughout the house. The morning room at the front of the house was set up with a dancefloor and the DJ was up on a stage. Lights flashed in time to the dance tunes he was playing. The stage was also set for a band to come on later, littered with mic stands, guitars and a drum kit. The drawing room, which led off the morning room, was set with several small, circular tables and chairs. In the grand dining room, the large table was pushed to one side and laid with a buffet of delicious finger foods and canapés, all chosen by Rhianna. Tristan had caterers manning the kitchen and the bar, who were busy toing and froing with silver trays. He didn't want Rhianna or Joe worrying about a thing. The sitting room had a couple of comfortable sofas, for those wanting a quieter moment away from the party.

"Excuse me for a minute, ladies, I need to find Joe." Tristan left Beth and Nancy in the drawing room, swaying to the music.

He found Joe and Rhianna in the kitchen. Tristan always discouraged guests from entering the kitchen to enable the catering staff to work efficiently. The former working kitchen of the old house, which was around the corner, was where the bar was set up. Rhianna had a selection of ready prepared cocktails for guests to help themselves to.

"You two, out of here! It's your engagement party. I don't want you both stressing. You need to be enjoying yourselves."

Rhianna popped a canapé into her mouth and saluted him. Joe, who also had a mouthful of food, mumbled, "Yes, boss."

Tristan led them towards Nancy and Beth, who were now in the dining room. The music wasn't so loud here, so they could talk easily. "Rhianna, this is Beth. She's going to be running the fashion show at the charity ball," Tristan said.

"Oh, yes, Joe and I have already bought our tickets!" Rhianna said. "Lovely to finally meet you, Beth."

"Nancy here is going to model for us," Tristan said.

"And I've roped in three friends." Nancy lifted her champagne glass in celebration.

"And I've asked Mum and Aunt Rose to be our older models," Tristan said. Rose was Joe's mother, the sister of Tristan's father.

"Mum agreed? And Aunt Janine?" Joe's mouth fell open. "This I have to see!"

"It'll be great," Beth said.

Tristan was relieved to see her more confident. Maybe the champagne was kicking in. He needed to find his mother and Rose to introduce them to Beth. He politely excused himself from the group and returned a few minutes later, with two older ladies in tow. "Mum, this is Beth. She runs the boutique I was telling you about, and is organising the fashion show for us," Tristan said, over the music. "Beth, this is my mother, Janine."

"Lovely to meet you." Janine shook Beth's hand. "I can't wait to model for you."

"I have to admit I'm a little nervous about it all." Beth chewed her lip.

"So am I, if truth be told," Rose said. "Not sure what my favourite nephew has signed me up for." She nudged Tristan.

"Nothing to be nervous about. It will be perfectly fine, my dear," Janine said cheerily.

"Do you need any more models, Beth?" Nancy asked.

"No, six should be perfect," Beth replied. "And I'll be the compère."

"I'll happily help the models change backstage," Rhianna said.

"Thank you, that would be amazing. I will need a couple of helpers behind the scenes for it to run smoothly."

The women started talking, Nancy leading the conversation, telling Rhianna, Rose and Janine about the amazing clothing line Beth's Boutique stocked. Joe rolled his eyes at Tristan, amused.

"Is this okay?" Tristan said. He was never usually nervous about events being held at the house, but when it was his own flesh and blood, he wanted it to run smoothly. Joe felt more like a brother than a cousin.

Joe, laid-back as ever, replied, "Of course, it's great. But I'm moving on to beer soon." He gestured towards his empty champagne flute, which he placed on a passing waiter's empty tray.

More people arrived, taking up Rhianna and Joe's attention. Tristan flitted between guests, as most of them were locals from Kittiwake Cove who he knew. He worried he was neglecting Beth and Nancy. Fortunately, Nancy really liked Beth, so stuck to her like glue. In between making sure the party was running smoothly, as he'd given Anya the evening off so she could attend as a guest, he tried to introduce Beth to as many people as possible.

Tristan warmly greeted Tilly, who owned a gallery in Kittiwake Cove, and her surf instructor and gardener husband, Liam. He found a beer for Liam and an orange and elderflower spritzer for Tilly, who was expecting their first child.

"I don't think you'll have clothes for me this size," Tilly said to Beth after introductions. "But I'll pop in once I've lost my baby weight."

"When are you due?" Beth asked eagerly, gesturing to Tilly's bump. Nancy looked bored.

"The fifteenth of December. Four weeks and one day to go — not that I'm counting!" Tilly laughed as she rubbed her stomach. "But I'm hoping it comes early."

"You don't know what sex it is?" Beth asked.

"No, it was a surprise in the first place —" Tilly nudged Liam — "so it'll be nice to have a surprise at the end too."

Next to arrive were Noah and his brother Olly. Olly's wife, Rachel, had only just given birth a month or so ago and had decided to give the party a miss, much to Tilly's disappointment. She'd wanted to coo over the new baby. "Tell Rachel I'll call in soon," Tilly said to Olly.

Noah introduced himself to Beth, telling her he was the painter and decorator for her boutique.

"Ah, great, nice to get a face to a name," Beth said, shaking his hand.

Anya arrived alone, joining them in the drawing room. She looked upset, as if she'd been crying but had covered it up with make-up. Her eyes showed signs of puffiness.

"You okay? Where's Theo?" Tristan asked tenderly, taking her aside. He'd only met Theo a couple of times. He wasn't really sure he approved. He didn't think the guy appreciated Anya enough.

"Oh, it's not really his thing," Anya replied miserably. "I nearly didn't come."

"No, it's important that you're here."

"That's what I told him. Besides, I've not been to a party in ages."

Tristan grabbed a glass of champagne and placed it into her hand.

"Oh, I'm driving." She tried handing the glass back, but Tristan shook his head.

"You can leave the car here. I'll take you home. Let your hair down. It was the whole point of you having the evening off."

"And how am I to get into work tomorrow?"

Tristan scratched his head. "I'll come and get you, or your loving boyfriend can drop you in." He winked. "I won't mind if you're a little late. You deserve to enjoy this party, you helped organise it."

"I should be the one taking on the stress."

Tristan shrugged. "It's my family, so tonight it can be my stress. Enjoy yourself."

Anya gave him a grateful smile. "Thank you, boss."

"Here, Noah and Olly will look after you tonight." Tristan welcomed Anya into the group of friends forming and made introductions where needed. She'd met most of them before, but Anya looked as lost as Beth tonight, so maybe the two women could enjoy the party together. He didn't want to push Anya on whether she'd had a row with Theo, but it was the stupid man's loss if he didn't want to join his girlfriend on a night out. Anya had only been seeing him six months; the relationship was still new. Tristan had to keep his opinion of Theo to himself. Anya would have to discover for herself if he was truly right for her or not. But he hoped she'd find out sooner rather than later. What kind of a relationship was it if your partner didn't want to accompany you on a night out?

The Range Rover came to a stop outside Beth's house. Nancy had been dropped off at his cottage first, so she was sitting in the front, alone with Tristan.

He was supposed to drop Anya home as well, but she'd already been picked up by Theo. That had been interesting. Anya's phone had three missed calls and a zillion text messages from Theo. They had discovered them when they had both nipped off to the loo, giggling and light-headed from the cocktails. Anya hadn't been ignoring them during the night, but she'd been too busy on the dancefloor, and her phone had been tucked in her bag, left in a pile with everyone else's. But Theo wanted her home — even though they didn't live together. Apparently, she was staying at his tonight, so he'd collected her early. Too early.

Beth felt sorry for Anya, being pulled away from the party. At first, she'd been pleased to see Theo, thinking he'd changed his mind about coming, but he didn't stay longer than ten minutes. Maybe he hadn't been pleased to see Anya happily dancing with Noah and Olly. Not that Beth had much experience to go on where men were involved, but Theo came across as the jealous, controlling type. He didn't like what Anya was wearing, that she was drinking... Beth hadn't warmed to him at all in the brief time he was at the party. Judging by the look on Tristan's face, he didn't think much of Theo either. Beth found it quite endearing that he had a protective streak.

"Thanks for inviting me to such a fun evening." She hadn't danced so much in all her life and had drunk quite a lot of champagne. She was worried her words sounded slurred to a very sober Tristan. "The house is beautiful."

"You want to see it when we put the Christmas trees up. You'll have to bring George along. He can help decorate them."

"Oh, he would love that." Beth hiccupped. "Oops, excuse me."

Tristan gave a chuckle. "That's okay, I'm glad you enjoyed the evening."

"Yes, I really did." Tristan, although busy making sure the party ran smoothly, had constantly checked in with her. Luckily, Nancy had been so nice to her, as well as Olly and Noah. And she'd had a real giggle with Anya — until Theo had turned up.

Before she realised what she was doing, Beth leant across and gave Tristan a kiss on the cheek. Her face reddened. Luckily, the dull glow of the interior light wouldn't show her awkwardness. Then she hiccupped again.

Cringing with embarrassment, she quickly jumped out of the vehicle. Carrying her shoes, she hurriedly walked barefoot up the garden path to her house, feeling a little like Cinderella. She had no idea what time it was, probably easily past midnight. Jason had left the outside light on and, with the moon shining from behind the clouds, her pathway was well lit. A dull light also came through the front door's two frosted panes of glass. But could she find her keys?

Tristan didn't drive off, and after watching her fumbling to find her keys for a couple of minutes, he jumped out of the vehicle and went to her rescue.

"Here, let me help you." He took her bag, his warm hands briefly touching hers.

"I don't want to knock in case Jason's gone to sleep," Beth whispered, her whole body aware of their close proximity. His aftershave intoxicated her further. "And once George is awake, it's hard to get him to go back to sleep."

She watched, holding her breath and trying not to hiccup, as Tristan found the key. He put it into the lock and opened the front door. An orange glow from a lamp left on in the hallway leaked out, highlighting his handsome features.

"Goodnight, Beth."

He hovered. She hovered. Her lips parted as she placed a hand on his chest. His dark eyes focused on hers. She'd already kissed him on the cheek. She shouldn't do it again. But what would his mouth feel like on her lips? To be kissed... She hadn't been kissed in such a long time. She missed that more than sex. He dipped his head closer to hers...

The sound of a car passing brought her back to her senses, and before she could think twice, she'd darted into the safety of her house.

From behind the front door, heart racing, she heard Tristan's Range Rover pull away. She touched her lips lightly with her fingertips. Tristan Trenouth was not right for her.

Besides, he had a rather stunning girlfriend — who Beth liked — waiting for him back at his cottage.

CHAPTER 14: ALL LIT UP

Late November

Beth noticed the arrival of the Christmas trees before Tristan mentioned anything. They had come yesterday on a lorry, wrapped in netting. Today, a large one was already erected outside the front of Trenouth Manor. Earlier in the week, the groundsmen had started putting lights on the bushes and evergreens around the grounds and gardens, making it look magical at five o'clock in the evening, now the sun was setting earlier and earlier. The gardens sparkled as if they had been covered in stars.

Since Joe and Rhianna's engagement party, Beth had been so busy with Christmas orders and organising enough stock for the Christmas fayre, which was next weekend, and then worrying about making sure she had the outfits for the fashion show — which was two weeks after — she hadn't seen much of Tristan. The party had only been a week ago, yet it felt like longer.

Ever since that night, Beth hadn't been able to stop thinking about him. She'd seen how relaxed he was around other people, his friends. They all liked him. So why had he ever been such an arse to her? But he hadn't been that night. He'd been a gentleman. She couldn't stop thinking of that buzz of electricity she'd felt stood on her doorstep as he'd unlocked her front door. His heat, his scent, the millisecond they'd paused, as she'd been immersed in his dark eyes. Every time she thought of that moment, a tingle of pleasure flowed through her body.

Her birthday was next week too, on the first of December. George thought she was incredibly lucky to have her birthday on the Advent calendar. This year it fell mid-week, meaning she would have to work. Especially at such a busy time for retail. She didn't want to miss opportunities with bookings at the boutique.

Jason usually got a takeaway in and they would share a bottle of wine. Once George was in bed, they'd watch a film. Since having George, Beth's birthdays hadn't felt significant. She had made such a big deal of her eighteenth, and it had only landed her in trouble — pregnant and chucked out by her parents. The memory made her maudlin at this time of year. Her throat tightened, and she could feel the tears stinging her eyes.

She missed her mum. But clearly her mother did not miss her, otherwise she'd try to find her.

Beth sniffed, pulling out a tissue. She dabbed her eyes and blew her nose. Luckily, her mascara was waterproof. Maybe it was the time of the month, too. Her emotions usually went haywire then. She tried to focus on the bouquet of flowers Poppy had brought over to brighten the boutique. They were in autumnal shades of orange, red and yellow in a glass vase by the tissue box. Flowers usually brightened her heart.

"Hey, are you alright?" She hadn't noticed that Tristan had entered the boutique. He came towards Beth with a concerned expression.

She shook her head and laughed it off, pulling another tissue from the box. What a moment to get caught having a little cry. "It's okay, I was just thinking about something, and it upset me. I get a little emotional this time of year." Her tears halted at the appearance of Tristan. To pretend she really was okay, she started hanging clothes on hangers from an order box she'd received, giving the occasional sniff. It meant she could avoid eye contact with him.

"Christmas is hard." He stood beside her and to her surprise, started helping with the clothes.

"No, it's not Christmas, it's my birthday next week. It's an annual reminder of a mistake I made … what will be seven years ago this year."

Tristan looked at her questioningly, holding out a coat hanger.

Beth shook her head, not wishing to divulge her past to Tristan. What would he think of her? "It doesn't matter. It's not really a mistake now. Can't go back and change it, and well, I wouldn't go back if I could anyway." Her throat tightened again; she swallowed to ease the tension and stop the tears forming. She didn't want to become a complete soggy mess in front of Tristan. "So, what brings you to my boutique?" she said, plastering on a smile.

"Oh, yes, the Christmas trees. Did you want to bring George over this evening to help decorate them?"

"It can't be too late; he has school in the morning."

"Of course, bring him straight after school. We're starting to put the Christmas trees up in the house. Anya reminded me we have a Christmas office party booked this weekend, so they have to be ready for that." He rubbed his chin. He hadn't shaved today, and dark stubble was forming. Beth thought it made him look tired.

"Christmas party in November?"

"The end of November. The house gets so booked up in December. Plus, with the charity ball … and a wedding…" Tristan huffed as he scratched the back of his neck.

"Are you sure you want a six-year-old decorating your Christmas trees?" Beth raised her eyebrows. "I usually have to go around after he's finished — and in bed — and move some of the baubles."

Tristan laughed and suddenly looked less tense. "I'm sure with you supervising him, it will be fine."

"Okay, shall I meet you in the house around three-forty-five? George finishes school at three-fifteen."

"Sounds like a plan."

Later, standing outside George's classroom, wrapped up in her coat and scarf, Beth waited for the school bell to ring. The chilly air bit at her cheeks. But the cold couldn't dampen her mood. Tristan's visit had lifted Beth's spirits this afternoon. She'd shed no more tears and squashed any thoughts of missing her parents. What would be, would be. Funnily enough, her mother had used to say that to her as a little girl.

Usually, Jason and Beth didn't get their tree in until the week before Christmas, so decorating the Trenouth trees was going to be a real treat for George. He hadn't seen the grounds all lit up with the fairy lights yet either, so tonight would feel very magical for him.

The school bell rang, and minutes later George came running out with a big smile. He wrapped his arms around Beth's thigh, as he wasn't quite tall enough to reach her waist.

"Have you been a good boy today?"

"Yes, Mummy."

"Good. Because I've got a surprise for you."

Beth parked in The Stables car park, and, holding George's hand, walked along the gravel path that led through to Trenouth Manor. It was lined with evergreen trees already decorated with fairy lights. She couldn't wait for the grounds to be lit up later. She laughed to herself, imagining George's awestruck face. On the lawn, at the front of the house, the large Christmas tree that had been put in place the day before now had two men wrapping lights and decorations around it. One stood on a small cherry picker to reach the higher branches.

Beth and George entered the house via the kitchen.

"Hello!" Beth called out.

"In here!" she heard a female voice reply, coming from down the hall. She walked into the sitting room to find a bare tree in a stand, still with netting wrapped around it. The room smelled of pine. They walked through, into the dining room, where another tree, even larger than the one in the sitting room, had the netting removed and Anya was fanning the branches out.

"Hey," Anya said with a smile. She stood back to admire the tree. "Tristan's helping to put up the other trees. Do you want to help me decorate this one?" Her last question was directed at George more than Beth.

"We'd love to," Beth replied, because her son was dumbstruck by the size and beauty of the Christmas tree, even if it was still bare.

"Do you mind helping me with the boxes?"

"Not at all. George, stay here a minute." Beth pointed to a chair and George jumped up onto it. "Don't touch anything." Then she followed Anya out into the hallway to find Tristan and another man carrying a large Christmas tree between them. Beth and Anya stepped aside, backs against the wall, breathing in, as the two men passed. Tristan was almost unrecognisable in casual, old, dirty clothes covered in pine needles and bits of tree. The sweat around his hairline and his ruddy cheeks proved he wasn't afraid of some hard work.

"Hey, I'll come see you once this tree's in place," Tristan said over his shoulder. "And don't lift anything heavy. I'll be with you guys in a minute."

They watched the two men struggle up the stairs. Tristan could be heard huffing and puffing, and saying something about how it was a shame the tree couldn't fit in the dumbwaiter.

In the ground floor bedroom, there were piles of cardboard boxes. Anya chose the boxes marked 'Dining Room' and handed a large one to Beth, who carried it back the way she had come. George was still sitting patiently but had been joined by Flash, who was happily pushing his nose into George's lap to be stroked. The little boy giggled at the dog's eagerness.

Between the two of them, with the aid of a stepladder, Beth and Anya wrapped the lights around the tree. To involve George, they asked if it looked even from where he was sitting. He nodded eagerly.

The lights were white LEDs. "We don't have colour, to keep the look more Victorian, like candlelight," Anya had informed them.

Once they were happy with the lights, George was allowed to help with the decorations. The dining room had a red and gold theme. Flash remained by the boy's side, giving him the odd lick on his hand.

"Flash!" Tristan entered the room, his stern tone making George jump. He almost dropped the glass bauble in his hand. The dog obediently went to his master's side.

"Oh, he's okay," Beth said, feeling sorry for Flash.

"Yeah, he's helping me." George beamed as he placed the bauble on a low branch. Anya was now on the stepladder, decorating the higher branches, with Beth handing her the glass baubles and ribbons in alternating colours and sizes.

Tristan waved the dog away to re-join George. "Sorry, I don't like him pestering people."

He came to stand beside Beth, wiping his forehead with the sleeve of his jumper. His scent, strengthened by the heat radiating off him, enveloped Beth. She could feel the warmth spreading through her and up to her face.

Don't blush. Don't blush.

"Is that all the trees in?" she asked.

"One more. The morning room. Don't worry, I don't expect them all decorated tonight." He nudged her with his elbow, which took Beth by surprise. "We have a couple more days before the party." Tristan stood with his hands on his hips, admiring the work so far, still torturously close to Beth.

"Hello!" A female voice trilled from the kitchen. "Thought you might want a hand."

"We're in the dining room, Mum," Tristan replied. He poked his head out of the door and into the hallway to beckon her in. Flash greeted the woman, wagging his tail and giving a welcoming whine. Beth recognised her from the engagement party — Tristan's mother, Janine.

"Hello, Flash, no I don't have any treats." She stroked the dog under the chin, then gave Tristan a kiss on the cheek. She was tall, though shorter than her son, with a slim figure and dark shoulder-length hair. She was somewhere in her early sixties, Beth guessed, but it was hard to tell. Her face was lightly made up, and unlike Tristan, she radiated a natural charm. Beth felt at ease in her company.

"Hello, Mrs Trenouth," Anya said, stepping off the ladder.

"Oh, please, Anya, I must insist you call me Janine." She kissed Anya on the cheek. "Hello, again," Janine said to Beth, planting a kiss on her cheek too. Chanel No. 5 replaced the smell of fresh pine and the spicy undertones of Tristan's aftershave. In a smart trouser suit, Janine looked overdressed for Christmas tree decorating. "Is this your son?" Janine

116

gestured towards George. "Hello, young man." She crouched to greet him, and George managed a timid smile.

"He's called George and has gone very shy suddenly."

Janine laughed. "Tristan was exactly the same at that age."

Tristan rolled his eyes. "Please do not subject Beth or Anya to my childhood horror stories, Mum."

"I've already heard them," Anya laughed.

Janine gave her a teasing shush and a wink. "Right!" She clapped her hands together. "I think I should put the kettle on. You lot look parched. Once I've made tea, point me in the direction of the tree you want dressing."

Janine soon returned, her designer clothes protected by an apron, carrying a tray with six steaming mugs. "Look who I found loitering."

Another woman walked in with Janine. She was in her early thirties, and Beth recognised her as Cathy, who worked in the office in the mornings, supporting Tristan and Anya. Cathy removed her jacket, hanging it over a dining room chair while saying hello to everyone.

"I've made five teas and one hot chocolate." Janine put the tray down on the dining room table. She left, then returned with a jar of biscuits and offered it to George first. He looked at Beth for permission, and when she gave the nod, his little hand delved in.

"Thank you," he said sweetly.

"I bet you get spoilt rotten by your nanny and grandad," Janine said, ruffling George's hair.

"I don't have a nanny and grandad," George said meekly.

"Oh." Janine looked up at Beth in surprise, then realising it wasn't a subject to be discussed in front of the boy, she said, "Well, I might have to adopt you." Her voice lowered.

"Because waiting for my son to give me grandchildren is like waiting for snow to fall in summer."

"Mum!" Tristan frowned. Then, placing his tea back on the tray, he gave a huff and left the room. Anya and Cathy looked at each other, sharing an expression between concern and amusement. Beth carried on rummaging through the boxes for more decorations, feeling it was best to stay out of it.

Wondering what had possessed him to think it was a good idea for Beth to meet his mother for a second time, Tristan returned with two boxes marked 'Sitting Room'. He placed them by the tree and cut the netting. Of course, the two women needed to meet with the fashion show on the horizon, but he now wished he'd told his mother not to embarrass him.

But he hadn't wanted Beth to feel awkward about her family, either. Why did George have no grandparents? That time they'd had lunch, Beth had said her mother couldn't help with the fashion show. He hadn't pushed it, not wanting to rub Beth up the wrong way. But were her parents dead? He could empathise there; he'd lost his father at twenty…

"Here you go, Mum," he called. Maybe if he got her away from Beth, she wouldn't embarrass him so much in front of her. Although, why he was worried Beth might be put off him, he had no idea. He watched from the sitting room doorway as his mother gathered up her mug of tea.

"Would you like to come help me?" Janine asked George.

"You can, if you want to," Beth said gently, as her son looked up at her for approval. Tristan thought he would have been the same at George's age with his own mother. It made him sentimental.

Flash and George obediently followed Janine into the sitting room. What was it with his mother when it came to small

118

children and animals? She was like Mary Poppins — firm but fun. He had plenty of fond childhood memories of his mother. Not so many of his father, who'd always been busy, supposedly working on the estate. Only he'd failed to manage it efficiently, and the combination of stress and not looking after his health had led to his death at the early age of sixty-five. At just twenty, Tristan had been left to take over the management of the estate.

He watched as Janine picked up the jar of biscuits. "Don't give them to Flash," he said. "And I'm sure Beth wants George to have room for his dinner."

"I was going to return them to the kitchen." Janine winked at George. "Take one more, George." Once the boy had taken a biscuit, Janine dutifully took the jar away.

Tristan stayed to help with the Christmas tree lights, fanning the branches, then left his mother to it. He had another tree to bring in yet. Tristan also knew she wanted to dote on the boy, not to mention Flash — the dog was the closest thing she had to a grandchild.

If only he could confess to her that she might have been a grandmother once. At the time he couldn't bear to tell her, and as the years had passed, he'd decided it was best left as a secret between him and Kimmie.

Banishing these thoughts, he found the gardener who had been helping with the trees, leaning against a flatbed truck with a mug of tea.

"Ready?" Tristan asked him.

The man nodded. The pair of them hauled the last Christmas tree off the truck and had the fun of negotiating it through the house and into the morning room.

Christmas songs were playing in the dining room now, and Tristan could hear the women singing along to 'Last Christmas' by Wham! Any minute now Flash would start howling. But it reminded him of fun times as a child at Christmas. Rose and Janine always made it a grand affair for the kids. Three cousins who had treated him like a baby brother meant he hadn't grown up too much as an only child. Even though he was much younger than Sam, Joe and Heather, they'd always included him and played with him. Joe especially had always looked out for him.

Family meant the world to Tristan, and Christmas highlighted that. If only he could admit to his mother how much he wanted a family of his own one day.

CHAPTER 15: A GIFT

Beth's stomach rumbled, and a glance out of the window showed her why. It was dark. Checking her watch, she saw it was five o'clock. The nights drew in so quickly.

"I'd best get George home," she said, hanging the last of the decorations on the tree in the sitting room. Anya and Beth had finished the tree in the dining room and had come to help Janine. Tristan hadn't been about much, liaising with the groundsmen about various things, she assumed. Or was he avoiding her? Or even his mother? She'd seen how he'd told Janine off. Not that Janine had taken a blind bit of notice, having had Cathy, Anya and Beth in fits of giggles with her stories. The types of stories Beth wished she could tell her own mother about George; the antics he got up to as a small boy. And would get up to in the future, she was sure, after listening to Janine tell tales of Tristan's childhood. Beth had warmed to her instantly, and so had George.

Janine had George on her knee now, and she'd been lifting him to put baubles on higher branches. Beth had feared she might put her back out. But Janine had assured the three women that at sixty-two she was still in her prime. She swam most days, walked a lot with friends, and visited the gym twice a week to keep her bingo wings at bay. Beth admired her and had already thought of the outfits that would suit Janine best for the fashion show.

"I think Cathy and I will put the lights on the tree in the morning room, then call it a night too," Anya said.

Beth gathered her things and kissed each woman on the cheek. Janine had helped George don his coat, zipping him in. As Beth walked out of the kitchen, holding George's hand, Tristan came striding in.

"Oh, you're still here. Good. I was worried I'd missed you," he said. He still had pine needles stuck to his scruffy jumper and a couple in his hair.

"Yes, but I must go. George needs his dinner." The little boy was rubbing his eyes now.

"I'll walk you to your car. Where did you park?"

"In The Stables' car park. I thought George could see all the lights that way."

"Oh, yes." As if Flash could sense Tristan's presence, he joined the party and trotted alongside his master as they walked down the gravel pathway and through the courtyard. Now it was dark, fairy lights glowed around the windows and doorways of each workshop. There was also a tree in place that hadn't been there earlier, which needed decorating.

"Tomorrow's job," Tristan said, gesturing towards it.

"Shame I'm at school, or I'd help," George said.

"You can always come after school."

"We'll see." Beth ruffled George's hair. "It's been a long day for him."

"I was going to ask you, have you bought your Christmas tree yet? Do you have a real one?"

"Oh, yes, we usually get a real one, but we haven't bought it yet."

"Don't bother buying one. I've got a spare one here you can have."

"Oh, right … well, thank you," Beth said, nervously fetching her car keys out of her bag as they reached her car, surprised by Tristan's generous offer. "Do you want something for it?"

"No, honestly, it's a gift."

"Okay, I'll bring Jason's VW California. The tree should fit in there."

"Or I can drop it off. That might be easier."

Beth pressed the button to unlock her car. Before she could reach for the handle, Tristan had opened the passenger door so that George could climb into his car seat in the back, helping the lad in. Beth needed to pass Tristan but stood awkwardly, the proximity of him befuddling her brain. "I need to strap George in," she said hesitantly.

"Yes, you'd better do that. Not my forte." Tristan stepped aside.

Once George's seatbelt was on, Beth got in her side, and Tristan leant against the open car door.

"Thank you for helping today," he said.

"No problem. George enjoyed it. So did I. It was good to get to know your mum."

"I forgot what a chatterbox she can be." Tristan chuckled.

"She's lovely, and I've got the ideal outfits in mind for her for the fashion show."

"I'll have to bring her over so she can try on the clothes."

"No need, we've already made arrangements." They'd discussed it during the tree decorating. Anya was miffed she couldn't model, but knew she would need to be available as the events co-ordinator to make sure things ran smoothly. Cathy had politely declined, saying she'd rather buy a ticket and participate that way. Anya had roped her into helping out backstage with the models.

Tristan wore a worried expression. Beth laughed. "Don't worry, we'll keep the conversation strictly about clothes."

Tristan nodded. "Right." He sounded unconvinced. He was still holding the car door. Flash sat by his feet, staring up at him. "Beth…"

"Yes?"

"You'll need to let me thank you properly for helping with the Christmas trees."

"No need. It was fun. Wasn't it, George?" The boy nodded.

"Yes, but Anya was getting paid, and Cathy will get time off in lieu."

"Oh, that's okay. You're treating us to a Christmas tree."

"No, no … maybe you'd let me buy you dinner?"

"And me! I helped too!" George had been sitting quietly in the back of the car, but now woke up.

"Oh, er, and yes, you too, George." Tristan leaned in to acknowledge the boy.

"It's okay, you don't have to," Beth said.

"We could go for Mummy's birthday," George blurted out.

Beth blushed.

"When's your birthday?" Tristan asked.

Before Beth could shrug it off, George said, "It's the first day on the Advent calendar!" For a child that had been tired, dawdling to the car, he was now wide awake. "She gets chocolate on her birthday."

"I'll take you out. Tuesday."

"You don't have to." Before Tristan could argue, Beth continued, "Look, I'd best be off. This boy needs his dinner."

"Of course. Thank you." Tristan shut the car door, waving as he watched Beth drive off.

"Can I come to dinner with you and Tristan?" George asked.

"I'm not sure that's what he meant."

"He did."

Beth shook her head and smiled. "No falling asleep, little man."

"I won't."

When they arrived home, George could not stop telling Jason about the size of the Christmas trees, the decorations and the fairy lights. Janine's name came up frequently, too. "Janine let me put the star on the top," he said, eagerly eating his dinner, which Jason had dished up from the slow cooker. Beth had had the good sense to put a casserole on in the morning.

"Who's Janine?" Jason asked.

"She's Tristan's mum," Beth answered. "And before you judge, she's extremely lovely. She took a shine to George immediately."

Jason must have caught the slight sombre tone to Beth's words, well aware she wished their mother could be a part of George's life. He had no grandparents. It had been awful when he had admitted that to Janine. He did not know why he had no grandparents, and Beth never wanted him to feel he was to blame. Her issues with her parents were not his fault. Fortunately, Janine, with more tact than her son, had known not to push the matter.

Jason touched her hand. "That's nice for George."

"Yes, it was."

"Tristan asked us to dinner," George said after he'd wiped his mouth with the back of his hand.

"Did he now?" Jason turned to Beth, his eyes wide with intrigue.

"It's not like that. It's a thank you for helping today." Beth's gaze dropped to her dinner plate.

"He's taking us out on her birthday!"

125

"George, stop speaking with your mouth full!" Beth said, hoping to change the subject.

"Do you think Tristan wants to just take your mummy out?" Jason asked George.

George frowned. "No, he said me, too."

Jason and Beth giggled. Beth was quite sure Tristan had meant just her. It had certainly felt like he'd been asking her out on a date.

But how could it be a date when he was seeing Nancy?

CHAPTER 16: A BIRTHDAY CONFESSION

1st December

The best thing about owning a boutique was that Beth had a great many clothes at her disposal. With all these stunning outfits, surely she could find something to wear?

Apparently not, judging by the piles covering her bed.

The effort of trying on different outfits was now making her feel hot and bothered. Her armpits were damp and she'd already applied deodorant three times. Staring at her reflection in the full-length mirror, she pulled off another top and threw it onto the bed.

Tristan was collecting her in thirty minutes. Jason had appeased George by convincing him that it was too late for him to go out on a school night.

Should she go dressy or casual? It *was* her birthday. But Tristan hadn't told her where he was taking her. Plus, it was winter, and therefore cold. So, she had narrowed her outfit choices down to smart, black, skinny trousers, so she could wear her boots. She was also concerned that a dress may give all the wrong signals. But now she couldn't decide on a top. She didn't want it to be too revealing — again, wrong signals. Tristan was only taking her out to dinner to thank her for her help. And Nancy was his girlfriend, wasn't she?

However much she and Tristan didn't always see eye to eye, she didn't see him as a cheat. Although lately they had been getting on very well. He no longer got on her nerves … in fact, quite the opposite…

She huffed and picked up another blouse.

With minutes to spare, Beth decided to go for a floaty black top with a floral print. She checked her make-up, brushed her hair, then waited nervously in the lounge, studying her hands and wondering why she hadn't painted her nails.

What does it matter? she asked herself sternly. *Nancy could be coming along too, for all I know!*

She had opened her presents from Jason and George earlier. Her brother always spoilt her. He'd bought a massive chocolate cake and George had helped blow out the candles. In fact, he'd helped with unwrapping most of her presents, too. But that was okay. It was all part and parcel of being a mother. Jason had bought her favourite perfume. He'd obviously noticed she'd been running low. It meant she could wear it more liberally now. She'd been saving the last drops in the bottle for special occasions — not that she had many. New earrings, bath bombs, and her favourite chocolates had also been amongst her gifts from her son and brother. Jason's colleague Archie had kindly sent over a bottle of prosecco.

Earlier in the day, Beth had been surprised by all the business owners at The Stables, each spoiling her with a gift. Poppy had dropped over a bouquet of flowers, Seb a hand-crafted heart-shaped plaque that George had helped with, and Lisa, with her pottery, had given her a small rabbit ornament. Beth had decided to keep him at the boutique. Chrissie the sugar crafter had delivered six cupcakes, each delicately iced with sugar-crafted pink flowers. Maisie the jewellery maker had given her a pair of silver earrings shaped like oak leaves, which she was wearing now. Dan, the glassblower, gave her a paperweight, with intricate swirls of colour inside it. Again, she'd decided to keep it at the boutique.

Cards from some friends had arrived, including one from Eva, but nothing from her parents. She faced the same disappointment every year. But what could she do? Was her mother thinking about her today? Giving birth was a very memorable moment. She couldn't imagine ever forgetting George entering the world and changing her life — for the better — forever. The pain had been instantly taken over by all the joy of having a child.

God, she needed to improve her mood before Tristan arrived. He had no idea why she didn't really like celebrating her birthday these days.

Tristan pulled up outside Beth's house. He really hoped George didn't expect to come for the evening because he'd turned up in the sports car, and not the Range Rover. When he'd made the arrangements with Beth the other day, she had assured him that she would set George straight. He had booked Rhianna's bistro in Kittiwake Cove, because it was the best for food locally. And as Rhianna was almost family, he liked to support her.

He nervously fiddled with his cufflinks, straightened his jacket, then rang the doorbell.

Beth answered immediately. She looked amazing with her smoky eyeshadow and long black eyelashes, accentuating her pretty green eyes.

"Bye," she called behind her, shutting the door. "Sorry, I didn't want to make a fuss, just in case George plays up for Jason," she explained as she popped her door key into her small handbag.

"I understand." Tristan nodded. "You look lovely, by the way."

"Oh, thank you. I couldn't decide what to wear."

"Really?"

"Ironic, I know." She gave a nervous laugh. "I wasn't sure where we were going either. And the weather isn't great."

"It is important to be comfortable and warm," Tristan replied, realising he felt nervous. Upon reaching the car, he opened the passenger door for Beth to get in.

It didn't take long to drive into Kittiwake Cove. Tristan parked in front of Tilly's gallery, White Horses, then ran around as quickly as he could to hold the door for Beth to get out.

"Thanks," she said, as she stepped out of the car, coming tantalisingly close to him. She paused for a moment, looking out to sea. The moon was peeping out from the clouds, reflecting on the ocean and lighting up the beach. "I forget how lucky I am to have this on my doorstep sometimes," she said.

"Me too. Being up in the valley, busy with the estate."

"I must try to bring George here more, even in the winter."

"Joe could take him out surfing." Tristan felt a strong urge to put his arm around her but stuffed his hand in his pocket instead.

"There's a thought."

"I think he and Liam run a surf school during the school holidays."

"I'll wait for the warmer weather. Or I'll be stood on a freezing cold beach, watching him."

They both stood for a moment in silence, listening to the sea. Then, Beth gave a shiver, and Tristan, shaken out of his own reverie, touched her arm to lead her towards The Beach Front

Bistro. He ensured he reached the door first, opening it for her. He was ardently trying to get everything right tonight.

They were greeted by Rhianna, who showed them to their table.

"Shall we get a bottle of wine?" Tristan asked, once seated.

Beth shook her head. "Oh, just a glass will do me. I don't think it would be wise for me to drink too much on a school night."

"But it's your birthday."

"I think I'd rather try a cocktail or two after." Beth had picked up the drinks menu.

"Now there's a good plan." Rhianna's cocktails were her speciality.

They ordered a glass of wine each then perused the menu. Beth couldn't decide what to have, so Tristan, who ate there regularly, was able to provide some recommendations. Rhianna gave the two of them plenty of time to order the food. Tristan wondered if it was deliberate. What had Joe told her?

Once the food was ordered, Tristan leaned forward, resting his elbows on the table, and said, "While we're here, I thought this would be a good opportunity to talk through the fashion show."

"Oh, yes," Beth said. She looked a little taken aback by his suggestion.

"Do we have enough models?"

"Yes, I think so. Nancy and her three friends, and there's your mum and your aunt."

"Have you enough outfits?"

"Yes, the great thing about Vivienne Rémy is that items are made to mix and match. So, for example, I might pair the same blouse with a different pair of trousers or a skirt. I'll be able to showcase the capsule wardrobe."

Tristan nodded. They both fell silent as their starters arrived.

Beth continued the conversation as she buttered her crusty bread roll that accompanied the soup. "I'm sure Nancy told you she's coming down with her friends on Friday to try on the clothes."

Tristan frowned. "No, she didn't." Would he have to put Nancy and her three friends up? "Nancy does her own thing." He shrugged.

"Oh, well ... they wanted to do it on Saturday, but I said it would be too much with the Christmas fayre, so they're coming on Friday — I've blocked out the whole afternoon. Nancy said they will pop in to support the fayre."

"Nancy is good like that." So she was staying over on Friday night. But where?

"I've tied it in with Rose and Janine too. I'll have all six models in, so we can work out the fashion show's running order. It'll run for twenty minutes. Half an hour at the most."

"That sounds perfect."

Trying not to think about his mother being in the same room as Nancy, Tristan concentrated on running Beth through the programme he had planned for the evening of the charity ball — or at least, what Anya had planned. He'd never been completely honest with his mother about his relationship with Nancy. But he was sure Nancy would be discreet. She wasn't the sort to gossip, certainly not to his mother. And they were just friends now.

It did make sense for Janine to be a part of the fashion show. It was in aid of her charity, after all: The Elowen Trust. Each year, her trust chose where the money would go. It usually went towards a children's charity, after the loss of Elowen all those years ago.

Beth pushed her dessert plate away, content that she could not eat another thing. After a delicious starter of a hearty vegetable soup and a main course of pan-fried chicken breast in a red wine sauce, Beth had fully relaxed in Tristan's company. They'd talked mainly about business — his estate, her boutique and the fashion show, which had suited her, even if initially it had felt like a business meeting and not a birthday treat. She'd touched on George and Jason slightly, but had kept the topics of conversation safe. To her surprise, she'd been able to sit with Tristan the whole evening and he hadn't upset her once. He must have been improving. In fact, the more time she spent with him, the more he grew on her. But she needed to push her attraction to him aside.

"That was delightful," she said, wondering if she'd scraped up all of the crème brûlée.

"It's a little early to go home yet. Would you like that cocktail?" Tristan leaned back in his chair, throwing his serviette onto the table.

"Yes, why not? If you don't mind?"

"Not at all," he replied eagerly. "We'll go upstairs to the lounge; there are comfortable seats up there — unless you're happy here?"

Beth shrugged. "I don't mind either way."

Rhianna came along, clearing the plates. "The wood burner is lit, and the couches are free." She raised her eyebrows at Tristan.

"Come on," he said. "We've talked enough business, let's celebrate your birthday." To Beth's surprise, Tristan took her hand, leading her up the stairs to Shakers, the cocktail lounge. As she followed, she found she was enjoying the warmth of his palm against hers but feared the heat was straying to her cheeks. At the top of the stairs, he released her hand. Beth was unsure whether she was relieved or not.

The lounge was quiet. They made their way to the brown leather couches by the wood burner, Tristan sitting down opposite Beth. Surely if it was a date, he would have sat beside her?

They made small talk over ordering the cocktails, Beth choosing the Beach Front Cosmopolitan, Tristan sticking to a mocktail, and once again they relaxed in one another's company. Beth wondered if the alcohol had made it easier for her. They were laughing a lot, Tristan jovially talking about the events coming up around Christmas, and his Bridezilla wedding. "The great thing about the wedding is that it's paying for the marquee for the charity ball," he said. "So, I'm just trying to let everything go over my head, when it comes to the bride and her demands. Luckily, Anya, who is much more patient than me, is dealing with her mostly."

Beth nearly made a sarcastic comment about never imaging him upsetting someone but thought better of it, as they were getting along so well. Just in case he didn't take it as a joke. She smiled instead, relaxing with the warmth of the fire and the effects of her second cocktail.

"Anyway, enough about the estate. Is George getting excited about Christmas?" Tristan asked. He leant closer to her, his dark eyes sincere.

Beth rolled her eyes and laughed. "Oh my God, yes." George fully believed in Father Christmas. "Jason and I have a hotline to Santa and the naughty list — or so George thinks."

"Ah, yes, the infamous way to blackmail your children to be good leading up to Christmas. My mum did it to me all the time."

"Mine too," Beth said more quietly. She thought of how her mother used to pick up the old landline phone and pretend to be dialling Santa's number. Jason and Beth used to stop fighting immediately.

"This evening has been great, you know," Tristan said. Had he noticed she'd gone quiet?

"You sound surprised," Beth teased, deciding it best to change her mood. "But yes, it has. Thank you." She raised her cocktail glass.

"I didn't mean it like that." Tristan laughed. "Bloody hell, why am I so good at being awkward? I mean, it's the least I could do, to take you out on your birthday. I've been such an arse. You and I didn't exactly start off on the right foot, and then I upset you about George's father... I didn't realise that you might not know who his dad was." His expression darkened and his tone grew serious. "But I understand it's a difficult subject ... and I admire the fact that you love George in spite of what happened to you..."

"What do you mean?" Beth interrupted, shaking her head as it dawned on her what Tristan was implying. Her back stiffened. "It wasn't that. Gosh, no... It was consensual." Heat rushed to her face. She swallowed and decided to admit the truth. Alcohol was always a good truth serum with her. "On my eighteenth birthday, I had a drunken one-night stand. I never got the guy's number, just his first name. Which I couldn't remember." Beth blushed with embarrassment and stirred the metal straw in her cocktail. What would he think of her now?

"Oh."

"So, on my eighteenth birthday, I conceived George." She took a deep breath. "I have never regretted having my son. But my parents wouldn't support my decision to keep the baby. They kicked me out."

"Oh, shit."

"We've been estranged since then, and we've completely lost touch. I don't know where they live anymore, much as I'd like to locate them to try to build bridges for George's sake." She could feel Tristan's gaze focusing on her. She couldn't look at him. She concentrated on the orange flames licking at the log inside the wood burner. "So, George has no father, and no grandparents..." Her throat tightened; she could feel tears forming.

Tristan swiftly moved off his couch to sit down beside Beth, placing his arm around her. "Hey, don't get upset, it's your birthday."

"I know, but that's why I do get upset. That's when it happened."

"So, Jason took you in?"

"Yes, he'd already been thrown out. He was the original black sheep — my parents couldn't deal with the fact that he's gay."

"God, that's awful." Tristan was still stroking her shoulder. She enjoyed the warmth, the closeness, the brush of his fingertips. It had been a long time since she'd been touched affectionately. Pretty much seven years.

"So we're both the black sheep now."

"And you've not seen your parents since?"

Beth shook her head.

Tristan frowned. "They've never met George?"

"No, like I said, we've lost touch. Jason and I moved after George was born, and my parents have sold up the family home." She took a deep breath to loosen the tightness in her chest. "Seeing your mum with him the other day really brought home what my mother is missing. And Seb, he's like a grandad to George already." Her voice faltered. She could feel the tears again. She mustn't get maudlin on Tristan's shoulder. How would that look? He was taking her out to say thank you. But it was kind of him to put his arm around her, even though she mustn't read anything into it. He was with Nancy, and she was technically a tenant of his...

"I think I'd best take you home." His fingers traced her hairline, making her look into his eyes. She held her breath, terrified he would kiss her. Wanting him to kiss her. But he gave his cheeky grin, took her hand and helped her up off the sofa. "I'm sorry I misunderstood you."

That made Beth want to cry even more. But she held it together.

Tristan pulled up outside Beth's house, feeling a little deflated that their evening had come to an end. But they both had work tomorrow morning, and Beth had the school run.

"Do you mind if I find my key first?" Beth said, fumbling in her small handbag.

Tristan pushed a button in the roof and an interior light came on. "Sure, take your time. I'm in no hurry," he said, to calm her. Should he get out of the car, escort her to the door and help her with unlocking it? Should he kiss her? Was this what she was nervous of? "Beth..." Seatbelt released, Tristan turned, resting his left arm against Beth's seat. He didn't touch her, even though he would have liked to, but he wanted to look her in the eyes. He waited until she raised her head and caught his gaze. A bolt of excitement shot right to his groin as he found himself lost in those amazing green eyes. "...I had a really lovely evening tonight. Thank you."

She smiled shyly. "I had a lovely evening too." To his surprise, she held out her right hand. "Friends?"

He took it, realising he was supposed to be shaking it, as if this were a business deal. "Friends." But he didn't let her hand go, cherishing the warmth and softness of it. Slowly, he raised the back of her hand to his lips and kissed it, relieved she didn't pull away. He then gently turned her hand over. As his lips touched her palm, he heard a gasp escape her lips.

"Tristan…" She gently pulled her hand away from his mouth, but allowed him to keep a hold of it. His thumb rubbed her skin. "Do you think we should be doing this to Nancy?"

Tristan pulled his hand away, instantly realising it made him look guilty. "Oh, me and Nancy…"

"Have you broken up?"

"No, no…"

Beth looked at him, frowning with confusion.

"Nancy and I aren't together." Tristan chuckled nervously. "We're just friends."

"Oh." Beth sat up straighter, pulling away. He lost her hand; she was back to fumbling inside her handbag.

"You have nothing to worry about. Nancy and I… We did once have a thing…" *Shit, how bad does that sound? Stop talking, Tristan.* "What I mean is, we realised we were better as friends — a long time ago." He wanted to be clear. "Look, Beth, I really like you. I know we started off on the wrong foot, but I'd like to make it up to you."

"Tristan, I don't think it would be a good idea. I've got George — do you want to date someone with kids? I'm a twenty-five-year-old with baggage." Before he could argue, she found her key and held it up. "Thanks for a fun birthday."

She kissed his cheek, just a peck, and then she was out of the car and passing through her garden gate. Not daring to follow her this time, Tristan watched to make sure she entered the house safely. She gave a brief wave and closed the front door.

Without even trying, he could always screw things up with Beth. He drove away with her words circling in his brain. It didn't bother him that she had George. He didn't see her son as baggage. In fact, he liked the idea of children. More children. He wanted his own someday. He had always envied his cousins their sibling rivalry, bickering and playing together. A family as it should be.

Probably a bit too early to fantasise about having children with Beth, though…

Driving home, his mood darkened as his thoughts turned to Kimmie. Once happy and ready to get married, they'd drifted apart after Kimmie's decision to terminate her pregnancy without telling Tristan. His friends and family hadn't understood why two people who had appeared perfect for one another had broken up, seemingly out of the blue. He'd kept what had happened secret. Instead, he had thrown himself into the family estate, and Kimmie had moved on.

For the first time in years, Tristan wondered if he'd found someone to start over with.

Confused, Beth sat at the bottom of the stairs, caressing the palm Tristan had just kissed. That instant was burned into her memory, every pleasurable moment and sensation of it. As his lips had touched her palm, heat had pooled at her core. Her whole body had tingled with excitement, ignited by his touch. Every part of her had wanted him to touch her more.

And then she'd mentioned Nancy and poured cold water all over everything. And bolted from the car as soon as she'd found her door key.

Up until that moment, the evening had been going much better than Beth had expected. She'd thought maybe this meant she and Tristan could put the blunders of their first meetings behind them. She was starting to learn he didn't necessarily mean to be tactless. Then… She shivered.

Was his past relationship with Nancy really such a big issue? But what if he got bored with her — would he just switch to Nancy as easily as turning a light on or off?

And what if Nancy didn't see her relationship with Tristan as just friends? She wouldn't put it past Tristan to be totally misreading their relationship. For all Beth knew, Nancy wanted to rekindle her romance with Tristan, hence her frequent visits to Cornwall.

With George her number-one priority, did she really want to risk getting involved in what could potentially be a heart-breaking and messy relationship?

CHAPTER 17: PROSECCO AND PREPARATIONS

As promised, Tristan dropped off the Christmas tree at Beth's house the following evening. Jason had been called out to a breakdown and was coming home late, so Beth had to face Tristan on her own.

Which was a ridiculous notion. She wasn't frightened of seeing him. She just didn't know what to think at the moment. She wasn't used to this kind of attention — especially from a man. Or maybe she was reading the signals all wrong and worrying about nothing — in true Beth style. She had discovered this tendency to worry and overthink things was one of her weaknesses after George was born. It may have even stemmed from pregnancy — worrying about eating the right foods, not overdoing it, what to do if she couldn't breastfeed...

She unlocked the back gate, and between the two of them, they carried the Christmas tree around into the back garden. Beth wasn't quite ready to install it inside. It would be too early, and she wanted it to look its best for Christmas Day.

"It'll be perfectly fine out here in the cold for a couple more weeks," Tristan assured her, looking a lot more casual in his rough work clothes, still covered in pine needles. Beth resisted the urge to brush them off his shoulders and broad back.

"Thank you again for this," she said. George was watching through the patio doors. Tristan had given him a wave, so he was aware of him too. Last night had been wonderful ... until she'd raised the topic of Nancy. Did she really want to revisit the conversation or just keep Tristan as a friend? Out of politeness, she asked, "Did you want a cup of tea?"

Tristan glanced at his watch and shook his head. "I would love to, but I still have work to do."

Relief washed over her, and she decided not to insist. Or was it disappointment? She followed Tristan back down the side pathway so she could lock the gate after him. He stopped at the gate and turned to face her. They were out of sight of George.

"Beth, you did enjoy yesterday evening, didn't you?" The darkness made it hard to read his facial expression.

"Yes, yes, it made a pleasant change from my usual birthday celebrations."

"Beth…" Tristan reached out to touch her arm.

"Mummy! I'm hungry!" George called from behind the back door at the side of the house. He was in the kitchen. She could hear him trying the handle. It was too stiff for his little hands, so it took him longer to open it. To Tristan, this was a gentle reminder of her responsibilities and who she needed to take care of before anyone else. George was her priority.

"I'd best go. I'll see you at the weekend," Beth said, holding the gate open, trying not to look too eager to get rid of him. "Thanks again for the tree."

"No problem. See you around."

Beth locked the gate, wondering if things could be any more awkward with Tristan.

Friday arrived far too quickly, and Beth was a mix of nerves and excitement as she did a last-minute clean of her shop. She couldn't wait to meet all her models and plan the outfits they would wear on the evening of the charity fashion show, but she felt some trepidation about seeing Nancy again.

Beth had never been a very good liar. With red hair and fair skin, the slightest embarrassment turned her pink. Would Tristan have mentioned anything to Nancy about taking her out for her birthday?

Beth wasn't sure if she was ready for the third degree, and what if Nancy did hold a torch for Tristan? And why did the thought of this make her green with jealousy? Nancy was stunning and did not have a six-year-old boy — who Beth loved dearly, obviously. Nancy had a lot more going for her. Tristan would be mad not to date her...

In preparation for the Christmas fayre, her shop was already decked out with elegant and sophisticated festive decorations. White fairy lights framed her wardrobes and an artificial evergreen Christmas garland, also intwined with white fairy lights, travelled up the banister of the stairs. Poppy had delivered a fresh Christmas bouquet that morning, bursting with red roses and seasonal foliage including hypericum, ilex and natural cones. (Poppy had told her the fancy names.) A large poinsettia stood on the coffee table and fresh holly with red berries and mistletoe adorned the boutique — all supplied by Poppy. She did confess that Tristan supplied the mistletoe for free, as there was plenty to find in the trees on the grounds.

The crossover support from each business in The Stables worked well. Beth had purchased a Christmassy reed diffuser, which doubled as a decoration whilst filling the boutique with the aroma of spiced plum pudding. The fridge was stocked with prosecco and polished glass flutes stood on a silver tray, beside the poinsettia. She'd also purchased some nibbles: mixed nuts, dried fruit and individually wrapped chocolates. To avoid the clothes being marked, she'd deliberately picked nothing too greasy, but there were plenty of tissues on hand, just in case.

Janine and Rose were the first to arrive, which calmed Beth's nerves a little. Apparently, Joe had dropped them off.

"Is George at school?" Janine asked.

"Yes, but Jason is bringing him along tomorrow," Beth said, a smile forming. How nice of Janine to think of George. But before Janine could jump to conclusions about who Jason was, she added, "He's George's uncle, my brother." Beth took their coats and hung them on a hook by the door.

"Will your mum not be here?" Rose asked innocently. "Have you not roped her in too?"

"No." Beth blushed. She could see Janine giving Rose a nudge. "I don't see my mum." Beth shook her head. Feeling her cheeks were about to betray her by turning a fresh pink, she turned and busied herself with the clothes on the rack.

"Oh, I'm sorry," Rose said, frowning.

Beth mentally kicked herself; she could have just said she didn't live in the area. That would have put a stop to further questions. She could tell that Rose felt sorry for her.

"Did you want to show us the clothes?" Janine beamed, tactfully changing the subject.

"Yes, I've been wondering. What will we be wearing?" Rose asked. Beth guessed she was a little older than Janine, in her late sixties probably, and although she had a good figure, she wasn't as slim as Janine. Or as tall. And unlike Janine's dark, shoulder-length hair, neat and straightened, Rose didn't dye hers, so there were wisps of grey. In fact, it was more grey than brown now, but it suited her. Janine looked dressed to impress in a trouser suit, whereas Rose looked much more casual in a long floaty skirt and a wool jumper. Tristan had said she ran a bed and breakfast in Kittiwake Cove, and she had that welcoming warmth about her.

Beth was about to answer when there was a knock at the door.

Nancy and her three friends had arrived. Nancy immediately approached Beth, giving her a kiss on each cheek, and handed her a bottle of champagne.

"Stick this in your fridge, sweetie." She gave a wink.

"You shouldn't have. And I feel embarrassed, as I only have prosecco. My budget can't quite stretch to champagne." Beth blushed.

"Oh, nonsense! But that does need chilling, so prosecco will do for now. We don't care as long as there are bubbles, do we, ladies?"

Nancy introduced Tara, Emily and Alice, and Beth was worried she'd forget the names so she wrote them down on her notepad. She would need to make notes about the clothes too.

Beth ran the bottle of champagne up to the fridge, returning with the chilled prosecco. She handed Nancy the bottle, who had the cork off and was pouring the glasses like a pro.

"There are only six glasses, where's yours?" Nancy looked at Beth. "You need to join in with the fun, too."

"Oh, okay, but just the one glass. I'm driving, remember." Beth fetched another glass from the kitchen and was soon clinking glasses with her six models-to-be.

"Ladies, you'll be modelling the Vivienne Rémy winter collection as the summer season doesn't get released until February." Sipping their prosecco, the six women stood listening to Beth before she showed them the clothes. "I was thinking the catwalk demonstration shouldn't be longer than twenty to thirty minutes."

"Yes, no more than thirty. The men might get bored, and we want them to part with their cash," Janine added.

"Right, well, the first thing is for you all to look at the clothes and try things on. I have some ideas, but I want you to be comfortable on the runway in the clothes you'll be wearing," Beth said.

"Why don't you young ladies go first? Janine and I will sit down as there's not that much room." Rose made herself comfortable on the cream leather couch. Janine joined her.

"Yes, I'll sit it out too," Nancy said, settling next to Janine. "We can tell you what we think, then it'll be your turn with us."

Beth was relieved Rose had made this suggestion. Six women looking at and trying on clothes might have been a little cosy.

"Last time I saw you, Tristan said you were going for a promotion. Did you get it?" Beth overheard Janine ask Nancy.

So Tristan does talk to his mother about Nancy, thought Beth.

"Yes, I did." Nancy smiled smugly, her prosecco glass poised before her lips.

"Oh, that's fantastic news," Janine said. "And what about your love life? Don't be coy, let Rose and I live vicariously through you young ones. Do you have a man in your life?"

"Might do," Nancy said more coyly. "We've decided to give it a proper go, but it's early days yet…"

Beth didn't get to hear the rest of the conversation because she was called to assist Tara with a zip. But did this mean Nancy considered her relationship with Tristan as more than just friends now? Had they decided to see each other more seriously? Had Tristan been about to tell her that when he'd dropped the Christmas tree off, but George had interrupted them?

If so, what was all that with Tristan on her birthday? One last fling before he had to be monogamous?

Beth pushed all thoughts of Tristan, and his gentle kiss on her palm, out of her mind and concentrated on the job in hand. Luckily, it kept her busy. But every now and then, catching Nancy and Janine laughing together, it made her wonder. But Beth could not dislike Nancy. She might have a different outlook on life, but she wasn't a bad person. She was charming, sophisticated, and beautiful, and Beth could see her appeal to Tristan.

There really is no competition.

Over a couple of hours and a couple of bottles of prosecco between the non-drivers, they'd worked out who would wear what on the evening and in what order. Nancy had been a real help, as if organising a fashion show was second nature. On her notepad, under the name of each woman, Beth had listed the garments they would be wearing and in what order. They'd even decided on the running order of the show, allowing time for each model to change. Everything from her range was going to get displayed in the fashion show.

"I might even buy this." Tara held up a black, floaty top. She gave a sigh and hung it back up.

"Save it for on the night, and then it will count towards the charity," Beth said.

"That's a nice idea. I must admit I've seen a couple of things I'd like to add to my wardrobe, too," Janine said.

With goodbyes and kisses on cheeks, Nancy departed with her three friends, leaving Rose and Janine with Beth.

While Beth cleared away the glasses, she overheard Janine say to Rose, "I do like Nancy. I always hoped she would make Tristan settle down, but she's worse than him for putting her career first, and she has no time for children. And I hope Tristan wants children. I want grandchildren — like you!"

"Oh, Janine." Rose gave a chuckle. "Maybe Tristan is who she's making a go of things with."

"Hmmm … maybe, but unfortunately Nancy isn't the maternal type."

Beth pushed the conversation aside, although it affirmed her thoughts about Nancy and Tristan.

The two older women were happy to help Beth with hanging the clothes back up and tidying the boutique.

"How are you getting home?" Beth asked as they finished up, remembering that both Janine and Rose had had more than one glass of prosecco.

"Tristan's coming over in a minute to pick us up," Janine said.

"Oh." Beth could feel her face starting to betray her with the tell-tale flush of pink. She turned away so Janine wouldn't notice.

"I'll pop to the loo first," Rose said, "if that's okay."

"Beth…" Janine waited until Rose had closed the toilet door. "Regarding what you said about your mother earlier … is it true that you don't see her?" Beth could tell she was trying to be as tactful as possible. "Does she live too far away or something?"

"Erm…"

"It's just I thought I recognised your surname. It's Sterling, isn't it?"

"Yes, it is." For some reason, Beth felt she might burst into tears. Which was ridiculous. Janine was just asking a simple question.

"Oh, sorry, darling, I'm prying. It's none of my business." Janine hung the last item of clothing on the rail.

"No, it's okay, I should try to talk about it more than I do. I just feel ashamed, and I don't want George to feel that."

"Why? What's it got to do with that adorable boy of yours?"

Beth took a deep breath. "My parents disowned me as soon as they discovered I was pregnant." Janine didn't need to know it had been a one-night stand on her eighteenth birthday.

Janine was silent for a moment, as if deciding what to say. Maybe she agreed with Beth's parents. But she threw her arms around her, hugging her tightly, and said, "Oh, you poor thing." She didn't ask about the circumstances. No judgement was made. Beth was overcome with deep affection for her.

Rose appeared, rubbing cream into her hands, and looked at the two of them quizzically. Fortunately, Janine released Beth just as Tristan entered the shop with a jolly, "Hello, everyone decent?"

Beth quickly blotted a tear at the corner of her eye with her finger and turned to smile at him. *Play it cool.* "Yes, everyone's decent. But you've missed Nancy."

Hands shoved into his pockets, Tristan shrugged. "That's fine. I'll catch up with her later. Everything okay?" He looked at his mother suspiciously. Had he caught the moment she and Janine had shared?

"Absolutely brilliant," Janine said, "but Rose and I may have had too much prosecco."

Tristan rolled his eyes at his mother. "I hope you haven't shown me up."

"Not at all, darling. Have I, Beth?"

Unable to resist a smile, Beth shook her head.

"I may have. The bubbles have gone to my head. I think I might need a lie down. I'll let Charles take over this evening." Rose giggled, then gave Beth a hug and a kiss. "Thank you, Beth. See you on the night, if I don't see you before. It's going to be fun."

"My pleasure. You're going to look fabulous."

"I know. I'll be wearing something a little different to what I'm used to."

"But you felt comfortable, didn't you? It's important you feel confident in the clothes you're wearing. And I wouldn't let you wear something that didn't suit you."

"And neither would I," Janine piped up. She gave Beth another hug, and a kiss. "I'll come and find you tomorrow, and that gorgeous boy of yours," she said with a wink.

With the boutique now empty and quiet, it felt almost eerie after the bustle of the day. Exhaustion washed over Beth. She hadn't stopped all day, helping dress and undress the six women, and she hadn't sat down once. She wanted to join Rose and have a nap, but she had her stall at the Christmas fayre to organise for tomorrow and a little boy who needed collecting from school.

After dropping off Rose and Janine, both a little giggly from the prosecco and in high spirits, Tristan called Nancy, feeling he should touch base with her as she was in Kittiwake Cove.

"We're staying at the Kittiwake Cove Hotel. The girls wanted to spoil themselves with spa treatments. Make a real weekend of it," Nancy said. "Look, I need to speak with you. Could you meet me in the foyer for a drink?"

"Of course. I'll be there in ten minutes." As long as he didn't get stuck behind a tractor.

Relieved that he wasn't being put in an awkward position, hosting four women at his cottage, Tristan drove to the hotel to meet Nancy. The hotel was renowned for its exclusiveness and brought the finer clientele to Kittiwake Cove, as only a five-star hotel could. With a prestigious spa, it was perfect for couples on romantic breaks. Or for women like Nancy and her friends.

He met Nancy in the foyer where a large Christmas tree stood, elegantly decorated with red and gold ornaments. She kissed both his cheeks, and they made their way over to the bar, where he bought them each a drink. They chose a small table in the conservatory. They had the view of the ocean in front of them, the moon glistening on the water. To anyone watching, they could have been having a romantic evening together.

Nancy clinked her wine glass against Tristan's half pint of Cornish ale. "Look, sorry, I've been a bit distant lately, but I'm back with Mark," she said, after taking a sip of her pinot grigio.

"He's the guy at your work?" Tristan knew a little about Mark. He was the guy Nancy had had flings with on and off over the years. If he remembered rightly, he was older, with children, and divorcing his wife. The man had been cheating on his wife with Nancy over the past couple of years, as far as Tristan could gather. Nancy had always openly discussed Mark with Tristan. Tristan believed the reason she'd slept with him a few years ago had been to get back at Mark. However, she'd never admitted that.

"Yes, his divorce has finally gone through, and we've realised we can't stay away from each other, so we're going to give it a go. A proper go this time."

"You're settling down?" he teased, never thinking he'd hear Nancy admit it.

"Well, one step at a time, Tristan. But he has kids who are teenagers, and he doesn't want any more. He's older than me, more mature than some of the guys I've dated." She smiled at him. "But I actually think I'm in love."

"That's great, Nancy. I'm happy for you." Tristan put his glass down. "Why are you telling me this?"

She shrugged. "I don't know. I tell you pretty much everything. Maybe I wanted a male point of view as my sounding board. And even though we're friends, I may have to stop crashing at yours. He gets really jealous about you."

Tristan chuckled. "He has nothing to worry about there."

"I've told him that."

"Why, thanks."

"You know what I mean." She nudged him playfully. "I've told him we've only ever been friends, just helping each other out on occasions when we've needed a plus one … except that one time…"

Tristan finished his drink. There was no awkwardness between them. He felt no jealousy over Mark. He truly wished for Nancy to be happy. She was his friend and always would be. "You know where I am if you need me," he said, standing up.

With Nancy happily in a relationship with Mark, and visiting him less, would this mean he could concentrate on pursuing Beth?

CHAPTER 18: THE CHRISTMAS FAYRE

It was the first Saturday of December, and only three weeks until Christmas.

All week, along with the usual running of a business, Beth had been busy with the other business owners preparing The Stables for the Christmas fayre: adding more Christmas bunting; decorating the tree Tristan had provided in the courtyard. Life would be full-on for the next few weeks with George's school running a carol concert and a Christmas play. And she still had to do her Christmas shopping for George. She wanted to give him plenty of presents, as he loved the unwrapping just as much as the gifts themselves.

However, all the tearing around took the fun out of Christmas somewhat. Beth thought her diary might explode, it was so full. In the back of her mind was the fashion show, too. After an exhausting day yesterday, Beth had made sure she went to bed early in preparation for the fayre today, as she envisaged another day flat out on her feet.

Jason had agreed to look after George, even though he had to work. Archie and Jason took it in turns to be in the garage on Saturday mornings, and today was Jason's turn. George would be safe in the office of the garage with his puzzles and colouring. There was a TV, so he could even watch CBeebies. Jason could give him jobs like sorting nuts and bolts. Archie had his own kid, so he understood their predicament.

That morning, after applying the final touches to the stalls, Beth took a moment to admire how festive The Stables looked in preparation for the Christmas fayre. Although the day was crisp and cold as only December days could be, it was at least dry, so most workshops were keeping their doors open, to entice customers in.

Poppy's had displays of Christmas wreaths, mistletoe, holly and, safely tucked inside her shop, poinsettias. Sebastian had worked busily to create a range of wood-carved Christmas decorations: hearts, stars, stockings, tiny Christmas trees, gingerbread men, even intricate snowflakes, each threaded with a red or green ribbon. He had made a large tree out of bare branches which was adorned with his creations. Plus, his large sculptures were decorated with red ribbons, tied in big bows, so they could be considered as a gift for loved ones.

The other workshops were equally rammed with beautiful artisan creations. Chrissie the sugar crafter, next door to Beth, had a selection of Christmas cakes ornately decorated. Chrissie had admitted to buying the cakes, confessing baking really wasn't her thing; her passion lay in designing and decorating. For the cakes she used a local supplier, so they were scrumptious with that home-baked taste. Her sugar-crafting was an art form; there were cakes covered in intricate flowers, as well as snowmen and reindeers.

Then there was Dan the glassblower, showcasing how he blew the glass as well as his Christmas decorations and ornaments. Maisie had sparkling jewellery on show with little gift boxes. Some samples were displayed in Beth's Boutique. And last, but not least, there was Lisa at her pottery wheel, demonstrating her techniques in the middle of her studio, with unique pieces on display. She also offered workshops, so she was selling gift vouchers as ideal Christmas presents.

To bring in the crowds, Anya had also invited small local businesses, usually women working around their children, to have a stall too. The courtyard was full of them. There was someone selling knitted items, someone who made stuffed toys, and another who sold cones of sweets and stocking fillers. Beth made a note to visit them later to look for a present for George. There was a whole array of handcrafted items for people to browse, from cards to bath bombs.

One kiosk sold mulled wine and mince pies, and another hot chocolate. These sweet, spicy aromas filled the air, adding to the festive atmosphere and the Christmas cheer. Someone was even selling roasted chestnuts.

Anya had booked a local choir to sing carols around the Christmas tree. They were raising money for charity. Wearing Victorian clothing, they looked like something out of a Charles Dickens novel. And when the choir took a break from their singing, a local brass band replaced them, playing Christmas tunes in deep baritone. Jason would be bringing George along later, after he'd finished work, and Beth couldn't wait for him to experience the excitement of the fayre.

However, she wasn't sure if she'd have much time on her hands when Jason did arrive. She'd been so busy with customers, but luckily, she'd convinced some to make appointments to come back to view the clothing the following week. Her shop was bustling with women trying on outfits. Nancy and her friends had been in to see her, as promised, but fortunately had not stayed long. Early on, due to being busier than she'd expected, Beth realised she needed to make appointment windows for people so that they received her pop-up boutique experience. She had to insist on no food or drink in the boutique too. She couldn't afford sticky fingers and marks on her garments.

To Beth's surprise, Tilly had been one of her customers, wearing dungarees over a thick, tight-fitting maternity jumper. Because Beth hadn't seen her since the engagement party, she

155

was surprised at how much larger Tilly's bump had grown. She tried not to stare.

Tilly flicked through the rails of clothes. "I know I won't fit into them yet." Chuckling, she pointed to her bump. "Oh, to be able to touch my toes!"

"You must be due soon." Beth felt an urge to reach out and touch Tilly's bump but remembered how invasive that had felt when she'd been heavily pregnant with George.

"Ten days and counting."

Later, Jason appeared, holding George by the hand. "Hey, sis, how's it going?"

Beth looked at her watch. Wow, it was three in the afternoon already. The fayre was scheduled to finish at six. She'd gathered from the other business owners that they liked to stay open until it got dark, so that the fairy lights could be seen and appreciated by the customers still browsing the stalls. It added that extra Christmassy ambience.

"It's pretty manic. I need an assistant," she joked. She looked at Jason's grease-stained hands. "But you don't need to volunteer."

"Good, because I know nothing about fashion." He laughed. "I'll let you get on, then, and I'll show George around some stalls. He's already said he wants to see Seb."

Keeping her voice low, hoping George wouldn't hear, Beth said, "Can you visit the sweet stall and pick something up for his stocking?" She gestured with her eyes to George, who was busy watching the women in the shop.

Jason winked. "Sure." He left with George, and Beth hurried over to help a woman taking a long, blue dress off a hanger. Five minutes later, Janine arrived.

"I've just seen your son, and your brother — who you can tell is your brother, by the way," Janine said, brushing Beth's cheek with hers as she hugged and air-kissed her. She smelt of Chanel No. 5 and was impeccably dressed as usual.

"Mum, there you are!" Tristan entered the shop abruptly. Beth's stomach fluttered. Then, seeing the women browsing the clothes, luckily all of them decent, he held his hand up and said, "Oh, sorry, I'll wait outside."

"I'll just be a minute, darling!" Janine called after him. She turned her attention back to Beth, who hoped the foundation she was wearing covered her blush. Heat had risen to her cheeks as soon as she'd seen Tristan, all wrapped up and looking incredibly handsome. The smell of his aftershave lingered. "Gosh, he won't give me five minutes. I just wanted to call in and see how you were doing, but I'm pleased to see you're busy."

"I am." Beth was surprised by the turnout, if truth be told. She hadn't been sure how many would attend the Christmas fayre, Trenouth Manor being a little out of the way down narrow country lanes. But it was clearly a very popular event for the residents of Kittiwake Cove.

"Do you need a hand?" Janine asked earnestly. "I can help."

Beth shook her head. "No, I'm fine, thank you. But thanks for offering."

"Not a problem. I'll let you get on then, darling." Janine kissed her again. "You look terribly busy. I'll come check on you again later."

Tristan, waiting patiently outside Beth's Boutique for his mother, had his gloved hands stuffed deep into his jacket pockets. He people-watched, pleased to see the fayre was a success yet again. Anya really did a good job of getting the event advertised. He was glad he'd walked Flash earlier and left him back at the cottage. The poor dog, however well behaved, would have been having a field day with all these children and people to make a fuss over him.

Tristan could tell his mother had a soft spot for Beth. And George. He mentally prepared himself for another onslaught of guilt for not providing her with grandchildren yet. He did remind her — constantly — he was only in his late-twenties and still had plenty of time. He knew she was teasing really, but he also knew there was an element of truth behind it. His mother yearned for a large family, like Rose had. Another pressure laid on Tristan, being an only child.

"Sorry to keep you waiting, darling. I just wanted to check on Beth." His mother appeared and kissed him. She wrapped her scarf snugly around her neck. "She's such a lovely girl. You could do worse."

"Mum!" Tristan could feel the heat rising to his face. Or was it the cold wind burning his cheeks? "Beth and I are … business associates." He shrugged.

His mother tutted disapprovingly. "I've seen the way you look at her. And the way she acts around you."

"Mum, I've managed to put my foot in my mouth so many times with Beth, I don't think she approves of me." She'd run a mile as soon as he'd tried to kiss her. His mother did not need to know about that. But he replayed the other night over and over in his head. Had he moved things too fast? What had he been thinking? Transfixed by Beth's presence, sitting so close to him in the car, he had unthinkingly taken her hand and kissed her palm. Like an animal caught in the headlights, she'd awoken from her trance and bolted before he could kiss her as he desired.

"Don't give up, Tristan. Not if you really do like her. I like Nancy, but she is not for you. There's no future with her."

"I know," Tristan said. "Besides, Nancy and I are just friends. Always have been."

"Good." Janine linked her arm with Tristan's. "Now, show me around these stalls."

They walked around the fayre, his mother ordering wreaths from Poppy, jewellery from Maisie and some pottery from Lisa. As was her custom every year, keen to support the small local businesses, she picked out Christmas gifts for friends. They were on their way over to Seb's workshop next. She usually purchased a large wood carving. Now Tristan had the estate running lucratively, as a shareholder his mother enjoyed her benefits from it too.

"Janey!" George came running out of Seb's workshop, Beth's brother following, trying to keep up. Tristan presumed George couldn't quite pronounce Janine or had forgotten her name. But his mother didn't correct George; in fact, she seemed to take it as a sign of affection.

"Hello, sweetheart, I was going to look for you." Janine crouched down to George's height. "Are you enjoying the fayre? Would you like a hot chocolate?"

Tristan and Jason shook hands. It was now dark, and the fairy lights twinkled like stars around the courtyard. The carol singers started up again, after taking a short break, with 'Silent Night'. The aroma of mulled wine wafted through the air.

"Beth had a good time the other night," Jason said. Tristan assumed this was an innocent remark, unsure how much a brother and sister would divulge to each other. "She said the food was amazing. Probably a bit posh for a mechanic like me."

"Nonsense, Rhianna accepts all sorts," Tristan joked, and hoped Jason would know he was teasing. Jason laughed, thankfully. Tristan really didn't want to upset Beth's brother now he was on an even keel with her. "But yes, yes, it was a lovely evening. I wanted to say thank you for her help with the Christmas trees. And when George let slip it was her birthday, I thought it would be a nice thing to do."

"Yeah, it was. Thank you. She deserves to be spoilt." Jason nodded. "I had to convince the lad it was too late for him to go out with you. He felt he also deserved to be thanked for helping with the trees." Jason chuckled.

Tristan laughed. "Yes, I should thank him too. Maybe a walk with Flash will appease him."

"That ought to do it. He's mad about your dog."

Tristan couldn't help wondering if George liked him too. After all, the little boy was part of the package if he dated Beth.

"Jason, do you mind if I take George for a hot chocolate?" Janine had stood up and was resting her hand affectionally on the boy's head.

"No, not at all. That's very kind of you. That was next on our agenda," Jason said, then thumbed over his shoulder as he continued, "Now it's dark, and he's seen the lights, I'll just tell Beth I'm taking him home soon."

Tristan insisted on paying for the hot chocolates. He noticed how Janine kept hold of George's hand. When Jason returned, Tristan handed him one too. "Wasn't sure if you'd want one or not. But George said you like hot chocolate."

"Thanks." Jason took the disposable paper cup and sipped. "I'd prefer something stronger, but maybe later when I get home." Jason ruffled George's hair in a fatherly fashion. Tristan felt a slight twitch of envy at the connection they had. "Need to get this one home and into bed soon."

George yawned, tired but happy.

CHAPTER 19: FESTIVE TEMPTATIONS

After seeing Jason and George off, followed by his mother, Tristan stayed behind to help dismantle the tables and pack away the stalls, the Christmas fayre over for another year. He could see the light was on in Beth's shop, so he decided to call in on her. The fayre had been a huge success by the looks of things. Every year it got bigger and better — mostly down to Anya's hard work. He'd know more after he'd talked to each business owner and found out if their takings had been high.

He knocked on the door, just in case someone was still trying on clothes, then poked his head around the door. All clear. No sign of Beth.

"Hello," he called.

"Hello?" Beth replied. She appeared suddenly, straightening her floral-printed blouse from her autumn collection. "Oh, it's you. Sorry, I nipped to the loo. Haven't had a chance all afternoon." She puffed out her cheeks.

"Yes, it's been busy. I think the dry weather helped."

Clothes were lying all over her cream corner sofa or hanging haphazardly on the various hooks on the walls. She started picking items up, straightening them on the hangers and placing them on the rails. Tristan picked up some of the garments, then handed them to Beth, as he had no idea where she would want them hung.

"You've had a very busy day," Tristan said, handing her another hanger. Beth reached for it, and their fingers touched briefly, sending a thrill of heat up his arm. He would have liked to move closer and gently brush the stray hair that wisped round her neck, but he was worried she'd think he was being too forward.

"Yes, I'm shattered now I've stopped. I don't dare sit down for fear of not being able to stand up again."

He held out another piece of clothing. "Did you want to grab some dinner once you're done?"

"Oh, um, I'd love to, but I think Jason said something about getting a takeaway."

"Oh, right, maybe another night, then?"

"Yes, sorry. I don't want to muck Jason about," Beth said. "And I think I'm ready to just crash in front of the TV."

He wanted to tell her she could do that at his. Order a takeaway, watch TV, drink wine, make love on the sofa… He stepped closer, fighting the urge to reach for her, touch her…

"Nancy was in earlier," Beth said, turning her back on him and reordering the clothes on the rail.

"Yes, she's staying at the Kittiwake Cove Hotel with her friends. They've booked a spa weekend."

"Sounds lovely." Beth rolled her shoulders. "I could do with a massage myself."

"I'm pretty good at back massages," Tristan said without thinking. To look like he was making a joke, he waved jazz hands.

Beth laughed. "Thank you for the offer, but I was thinking more along the lines of a spa treatment. It's not something I can afford."

"Oh, right, yes, it is pretty posh over there," Tristan said shoving his hands into his pockets, worried he'd do something to freak Beth out — like touching her hair. Her vibrant, red hair, that matched the freckles on her milky, smooth skin. *Stop thinking like that*. "Maybe after Christmas, with the profits from your sales, you could treat yourself?"

"Yes, maybe." Her usually defiant green eyes had softened their gaze on him now.

"Look, I meant what I said —"

"Tristan! There you are! I need you!" Anya barged in, breathless and rosy-cheeked, rubbing her gloved hands together to warm them up.

"What is it?"

"It's Nancy, she needs you."

"Nancy? I thought she'd gone back to the hotel."

"She had. You'd better come. Sorry, Beth," Anya said, as if realising she'd interrupted something.

"No, it's not a problem," Beth replied, frowning with concern. "Look, you had better go, it sounds urgent," she said to Tristan. "Thanks for your help." She smiled.

"Anytime." He touched her arm affectionately, smiling back. "I'll try to call in next week."

With a heavy heart, but with some concern for Nancy too, Tristan hurriedly followed Anya out.

"What's the matter with Nancy? Is she okay?" Tristan asked Anya. "And why didn't she call me?"

"She did." Anya waved his phone at him. "You left it in the office, and I answered it. She's at your cottage. She sounds upset. It's very unlike Nancy." Anya handed Tristan his phone, which he tucked into his back pocket.

He made his way over to the cottage, thinking how Flash must be going stir crazy, needing his second run. He was unlikely to be able to convince Nancy to go for a walk. Maybe if he gave her a couple of pairs of thick socks, she could fit into an old pair of wellies he had.

What could make her so upset? She was passionate about a lot of things, especially her work, but to leave her hotel, her friends, and come to see him... He'd never seen her upset to the point of crying. Nancy didn't shed tears. Never in front of him, anyway.

Flash barked as Tristan opened the front door of the cottage. Nancy, with her feet tucked underneath her, was curled up on the sofa, a box of tissues beside her and a bottle of red wine open and a glass poured.

"Hey, are you okay?" Tristan removed his coat, hanging it on the hook by the door, and joined her on the sofa.

"I'm sorry, I'm sorry, I shouldn't be here."

"It's okay, but your friends must be concerned. They know where you are, right?"

Nancy sniffed. "Yes, yes."

Tristan poured himself a glass of wine. "What is it?"

"It's Mark…" Nancy said, between sobs.

"What's happened? I thought things were going okay?"

"It was going great — until his ex-wife interfered," Nancy said angrily, then took a large gulp of wine. "I think she thinks I want involvement with his kids. As if!" Then she started crying again. "So he's called it all off, put it on hold — again! — and said he'll assess it in a couple of months. He doesn't want to jeopardise his relationship with his children. Who are teenagers now!"

"I'm sure it's a misunderstanding."

"Does this look like a misunderstanding?" Nancy thrust her phone at Tristan's face, having opened the text message from Mark. "No one puts me on hold!" she said indignantly, jutting her chin out. "I'm not some bloody doormat either!"

He read the message. It read ambiguously, in his opinion. "I don't think he's ending the relationship," Tristan said as calmly as he could, handing her mobile back. "Us guys can say one thing and mean another."

"His text says we need to wait."

Then another fit of sobbing overcame her, and he hugged her to his shoulder.

With the bottle of wine finished, Nancy edged even closer to Tristan. "You know, we could head upstairs." Her fingers were snaking around his neck, combing through his hair at the back; her mouth was edging closer to his. "We could rekindle that old flame..." she purred. Her tongue wet her lower lip as her lips parted. His blood pulsed faster around his body. She smelt amazing, looked amazing, even with puffy eyes from the crying, and he knew how much fun they could have in bed. Tempted, he almost dipped his head so that his mouth could meet hers, knowing the passion it would reignite between them...

Coming to his senses, he pulled back, gently pushing Nancy away, creating some space between them. "Nancy, I don't think that would be a good idea. We're just friends." Nancy would regret it in the morning. And so would Tristan. "If this is a misunderstanding, then you'll be riddled with guilt. You could jeopardise your future with Mark." He shifted further away from her. Flash whined a gentle reminder. "I need to take Flash for a quick run, so you take my bed, and I'll sleep on the sofa. Things will look different in the morning."

"You're probably right." Nancy kissed him affectionately on the cheek. "Shame, though; if I remember rightly, you're pretty good in the sack."

"And Mark can't be bad either," Tristan said, getting off the couch.

"Of course. Would I settle for anything less?"

CHAPTER 20: THE REHEARSAL

Well, that confirmed Beth's suspicions. One whiff of Nancy in trouble and Tristan had gone rushing to her side. But what was he playing at, being so solicitous and flirtatious towards herself? That wasn't right. Over the past few days, she had replayed the moment Anya had entered the shop over and over in her head, remembering the way Tristan's expression had changed when he'd been told Nancy needed him — urgently. Beth thought he'd seemed in an inordinate hurry to distance himself from her, as if guilty about being caught out.

That's what she must do too. Distance herself emotionally. Physically was going to be tougher, as she saw him every day at The Stables. She really needed to keep things strictly professional between them. She had enough on her plate, juggling the final touches to the fashion show for the charity ball, fulfilling Christmas orders and attending George's school's various events.

Jason and Beth had spent an evening wrapping the presents they'd bought for George, hiding them in the loft once he'd fallen asleep. For George, Santa's magic was real, and Beth wanted to keep it that way. They hadn't yet put up the Christmas tree Tristan had given them, fearing it was still too early for it to last until Christmas Day. That was another job to do.

During the two weeks leading up to the fashion show, Beth kept herself to herself and avoided Tristan where possible. It hadn't been hard. He was busy with the preparations for the charity ball, including the erection of a large marquee and she didn't know her arse from her elbow with Christmas on the horizon.

Somehow, sitting up late one night, she'd written all of her Christmas cards — she'd bought the ones George had designed at school and posted them off. They featured a cute stocking, hand-drawn and coloured in to the best of a six-year-old's ability.

Inside her Christmas card to Eva, she had included the latest school photo of George, smiling at the camera with his mouth closed, hiding the gap between his teeth. He was smartly dressed in his school uniform, his red V-neck jumper clashing with his blond hair.

If only she could send a card to her parents. She would include a note about her business, to prove she was doing well, and could stand on her own two feet. All she wanted was a larger family for George than just her and Jason.

It had been nearly seven years now. Beth had confessed after Christmas that she was pregnant, hiding it for as long as possible. At first, she'd thought she might lose the baby in the early stages, and her family would have been none the wiser. But as her pregnancy had become more and more apparent, she'd confessed. Surely her mother would want to see her only grandson... She thought of Janine, and how she longed for a grandchild, adopting George every time she saw him as if he were hers. And Seb, like a surrogate grandfather, unfailingly patient with George, letting him experiment with wood carving.

If only she could track down her parents ... but Jason usually discouraged it. He wasn't as prepared to forgive as she was.

She wiped a tear from her cheek. Heading downstairs, she opened the shop. She had another busy day ahead of her. She needed to bury these feelings of rejection. This time of year was always tough for her. Jason knew it, but each year she tried to make it look as if it no longer bothered her. It shouldn't anymore. Jason and George were her family, and they were enough.

The charity ball drew closer. The agenda had been set. The silent auction would be ongoing; while guests enjoyed a welcome drink, they would be able to bid for lots. The fashion show was set to open the event, followed by a three-course dinner, the closing of the silent auction and then a live band to round off the evening. There would be an opportunity for guests to place clothes orders with Beth. Cathy and Anya would assist her with that. Anya had shared the schedule with Beth, leaving her nervous and excited in equal measure.

The Thursday before the event, Beth organised the outfits for each of her models. She wanted to transport them over to the house, ready for the show. The wind had started to pick up, hinting at a storm brewing. Not unusual in Cornwall. However, apparently there was the threat of snow this weekend, which was rare. Like everyone else in Kittiwake Cove, Beth would believe it when she saw it.

This evening they were having a rehearsal: checking the music, getting the models used to quick changes, and roughly timing how long the show would last.

Trenouth Manor was the venue for the fashion show, while the marquee would be used to hold the dinner and dance part of the event. With Anya's help, Beth carried the clothes across to a room set up for changing on the night. Most of the house's antique furniture had been cleared away, put into storage in the billiard room. A catwalk had been constructed out of what looked like the portable dancefloor, with rows of chairs lined up on three sides. It stretched from the morning room, which would be where the models started from, into the drawing room. The two rooms had been opened up to make one large area, adorned with festive decorations and dominated by the imposing Christmas trees. Beth spotted where she would sit with a mic. She would be at the top of the stage, in the morning room, from where the models would enter.

Backstage, Cathy and Rhianna would help the models with their quick changes. Anya would have liked to have helped too, but she needed to be on call to sort out any unexpected problems during the event.

Once everyone had arrived and changed into their first outfit, Anya started the music and each model in turn made their way down the catwalk, doing a twirl, and then strutting back. When the first model reached the end and turned, then next model came out. Beth practised what she would say about each item of clothing, using her notecards to prompt her. She also had the name of each model.

Anya had the bright idea of printing a list of the outfits, in the order they would be shown on the catwalk, to hand to the guests. That way, they could tick what they would like to order. "Guests won't want to be hanging around too long trying to order the clothes, and we want them to place orders on the night so we can calculate how much money we've raised," she had said eagerly.

Anya was standing at the end of the catwalk, and Beth noticed Tristan join her there. He was clad in jeans and an old jumper and had a smudge of dirt on his cheek. Worried that she would lose concentration and stumble over her words, she focused intently on each woman as they walked the runway, looking fabulous in her clothing. But she couldn't help noticing Tristan giving Nancy a wink as she reached the end of the runway. Once again, she was reminded that she couldn't compete with Nancy; not only was she super intelligent, she was also stunningly beautiful with her tall, slender figure and bouncy blonde hair.

The show took no longer than thirty minutes. When all six models were called to take a bow, Anya, Beth and Tristan gave them a round of applause. Rhianna and Cathy appeared at the back to clap too.

"That was great!" Anya said. "How did it go backstage?" She turned to Cathy and Rhianna.

"No problems. Beth had all the outfits hung in order. It was easy," Rhianna said as Cathy nodded her agreement. The models had tried the clothes on in Beth's Boutique, so each knew exactly how each garment should be worn. "But you'd best come back and re-organise the outfits for on the night." Rhianna pulled an apologetic expression. "I'm not sure we've put them back in the right order."

"I wouldn't have expected you to, with such quick changes." Beth noticed Nancy and Tristan having a quiet chat together, before she kissed him on the cheek and joined the other models returning to the bedroom nearest the morning room, to change back into their own clothes. Beth went with them to assist.

"That was so much fun," Rose said.

"It was a giggle, wasn't it?" Janine said, hanging a blouse on a hanger.

"I think I'm going to be a little more nervous when the room is full of people," Tara said as she pulled on her jeans.

"Nonsense, you'll be fine. As the fashion show is first up, we can have a drink after it's all finished," Nancy said.

"Think we deserve a celebratory drink at Joe's pub now!" Rhianna said, helping Beth to hang up the dresses and blouses.

"Oh, we'll join you," Nancy said, gesturing to her three friends. They were all staying at Rose's B&B this weekend. Rose had invited them as she had the room, and since they were helping Janine's charity, it was the least she could do.

"Yes, we'll meet you at The Cormorant," Rose said. "Will you come, Beth?"

"Oh, I'd best head off home and relieve Jason. He's been doing a lot of babysitting for me lately." Much as Beth liked Nancy, she didn't think she could sit there and listen to her talk about how she and Tristan were making a go of it. And she did need to get back for George.

"Well, promise me you'll let your hair down after the show on Saturday," Janine said, giving Beth a hug. "There's a table reserved for you all, as a thank you for volunteering for this."

"I promise," Beth said, wondering if it would seem childish to have her fingers crossed behind her back.

CHAPTER 21: THE CHARITY BALL

The freezing east wind had not abated. But the white marquee stood firm, thankfully, as the wind whistled through the thick guy ropes and riggings. Beth could imagine Tristan's worry, but high winds were normal along the coastline. The snow hadn't arrived, although it was still threatened. The day had been bleak with dark grey clouds.

Wanting to be prepared for the evening, and run through any last-minute touches, Beth had arrived at Trenouth Manor early. Jason had dropped her off, wishing her good luck, with George waving in the back of the car. He'd driven her right up to the front door of Trenouth Manor so that she didn't have to walk far in her heels. She had flats on standby for later.

She'd dressed up for the occasion. The event was strictly black tie, so she was wearing a floor-length, navy blue dress, which sparkled from her halter neck to her feet. The dress had a slit at the side, revealing her legs as she walked. Her clothing line was smart casual, not quite black tie attire, so she'd found this dress in TK Maxx — her next favourite shop for clothing. Since her school leaver's prom, Beth had never had an occasion to get this dressed up and it felt good. Her nerves were mixed with excitement and anxiety. Her boutique's clothing range was going to be viewed by over a hundred people, and she hoped everything would go to plan.

Walking round the side of the house, Beth took a sneaky peak inside the marquee, wanting to see it before everyone arrived. A thicket of circular tables surrounded the stage and dancefloor and were laid ready for the dinner: white tablecloths; red cloth napkins; Christmas confetti; gleaming cutlery; polished wine glasses and tumblers sparkling under the fairy lights in nets above them, like a night sky. Red, green, and gold helium balloons rose from evergreen holly wreaths, provided by Poppy. Sprigs of mistletoe decorated the tables too. A candle flickered on each table, giving off a scent of spiced apple and cinnamon … and could she smell pine needles? A large Christmas tree stood beside the dancefloor near the stage, decorated in the same colours and white fairy lights. All the upright poles of the marquee were decorated with white lights and artificial holly and ivy. There was the traditional silver disco ball above the middle of the dancefloor, but she also spotted a couple of clumps of mistletoe hanging there too. The marquee looked magical. Everything Christmas should be. Beth found her phone and snapped a couple of photos, thinking how George would love to see it. Hopefully, she might be able to snag a balloon for him at the end of the evening.

She entered the house via the kitchen and, busy admiring the extra Christmas decorations and getting out of the way of the busy staff preparing for the evening, she bumped into Tristan. "Oh, sorry."

"Wow," he said. "You look amazing." He looked her up and down approvingly.

Her thoughts matched his. Clean-shaven and wearing a black tuxedo with a black bow tie, he looked utterly handsome. James Bond suave. A white silk handkerchief was folded neatly in the left-hand top pocket of the jacket. His aftershave, woody and smoky, which was familiar to her now, left her flummoxed. In a moment of madness, it lured her closer towards him.

"Erm, thank you, so do you…" She nervously shuffled around him, fearing her blushes would give her away, even with the amount of make-up she was wearing.

His hand briefly caught hers. "I expect a dance later."

She frowned. What about Nancy? "Um, yes, yes…" She left the kitchen as quickly as possible and made her way to the safety of the downstairs bedroom, where the models would be changing.

She was the first one in the room. All the clothes were hanging on the clothes rails, exactly as she had left them on Thursday evening. There were three rails, with two sets of outfits on each. The single bed had been shifted aside to make room. There was an ice-bucket on the sideboard, with a bottle of champagne chilling and nine glasses. Beth wasn't going to drink any alcohol until after the fashion show was over. The last thing she wanted to do was slur her words. While alone, she checked the clothes.

"Hello! Gosh, you look gorgeous! I love the dress." Nancy arrived, giving Beth an air-kiss on each cheek, for fear of smudging her red lipstick. She wore a red strapless cocktail dress, with a sweetheart neckline and a mermaid flare from the knee, accentuating her slender figure. Her red four-inch heels enhanced her natural sophistication.

"So do you," Beth said admiringly. She was no competition for Nancy. Tristan and Nancy really were made for each other. Nancy gave a twirl, revealing an open back. And the dress had a ruffle bustle. It was even more beautiful than Beth had first realised.

"I'm going to need a hand getting back into this dress after the fashion show," Nancy chuckled.

Tara, Emily and Alice entered, giggling and in high spirits. Each woman looked glamorous in their own cocktail dresses, but Nancy stood out the most. As she expertly popped the champagne cork, Janine and Rose entered. Each woman was handed a glass of bubbly, but Beth refused.

"Go on, have a little. It'll take the edge off your nerves." Nancy held a glass out to her.

"I'm worried about slurring my words."

"Not on one small glass you won't." Nancy winked. Hesitantly, Beth took the glass. "Cheers," Nancy said, raising her glass to all the women.

"Cheers!" resounded around the room as they all clinked glasses before taking a sip.

Maybe Nancy was right. One small glass might calm her nerves.

They'd all brought along black shoes, heels and flats, to wear on the catwalk. There was still plenty of time before the actual start of the event, so they chatted for a while, giggling with nerves and apprehension. Another bottle of champagne was presented by a member of the waiting staff, which Nancy happily took from them and placed in the ice bucket. Then, she and her friends had their phones out and were snapping selfies of the group and taking photos of each other.

There was a knock at the door.

"Come in," Nancy said. "We're decent."

It was Tristan.

"Oh, darling, would you mind snapping a photo of all of us before we get changed?" Nancy approached him with her phone. She brushed his shoulder proprietorially, wiping off imaginary fluff. "We're all looking beautiful and it would be great to capture it."

"Of course," Tristan said. "But come out and have a photo in front of a Christmas tree, rather than all squashed in this room."

They made their way into the dining room and could see guests starting to take their places. Beth noticed Seb and his wife, and gave them a wave. Tristan gestured to the nine women, Beth included, to stand before the tree. The Christmas tree in the dining room was the largest, so it would make the best backdrop for the photograph. Beth and Nancy had managed to be at the front, side by side.

"Oh, there you are, Tristan." Anya appeared, all dressed up and looking very pretty. "The door to the drawing room from the hallway has been closed, so no one can see the models. However, I can't lock it for fire safety purposes."

Tristan nodded, Nancy's phone still in his hand, poised to take a photo.

"What are you doing?" Anya asked curiously.

"Nancy wants a group photo."

"Oh, you get in, too." She took the phone off him. "It's only fair as the charity ball organiser."

"It's not really mine…" Tristan argued, but Nancy grabbed him, hauling him next to her. Beth shuffled to the side. "Oh, well…"

Tristan had Beth on one side of him and Nancy on the other. As Anya demanded a cheese from the group, making them squash in together to fit in the picture, Beth felt the back of Tristan's hand rest against hers. His heat against hers. A shock of electricity pulsed through her, but to move her hand away would draw attention. For a moment, she thought she felt his fingers gently take hers.

"I've taken a few, so you can choose the best," Anya was saying to Nancy. But Beth was looking at Tristan, who was gazing back at her. His hand was still touching hers. They were so close she could see the different flecks of colour that made up his dark brown eyes, how they were lighter at the pupil, and grew darker at the edge of his iris.

He leaned in and whispered in her ear, "You look gorgeous. Don't forget, I want that dance." The heat of his breath sent goosebumps from the back of her neck along her arms.

She hadn't realised she'd been holding her breath. As he walked away, giving her a subtle wink, she exhaled. Her cheeks were on fire. She watched as Tristan was joined by Joe, who looked equally dashing in a tuxedo. Although Tristan wore his like a second skin, Joe appeared less at ease in his.

She couldn't deny she was still attracted to Tristan. But he was with Nancy. Surely she was the one he would be dancing with?

As more guests arrived to take their seats, the women realised they needed to get ready for the fashion show. Beth returned backstage and helped Rhianna and Cathy to get the models into their first outfits. Before long, Anya was knocking on the bedroom door, and asking, "Ready?"

Beth followed Anya out and took her place at the front of the stage, where a seat had been reserved for her. There was a microphone ready.

Among the audience she recognised some Kittiwake Cove locals and regulars at her boutique. Noah, Olly and Rachel were in one row. Poppy and her husband were in another, with the other business owners at The Stables. Tilly, very heavily pregnant with Liam beside her, waved to Beth and gave her an encouraging thumbs-up. Then the music started, and taking a deep calming breath, Beth launched into her prepared speech.

"Ladies — and Gentlemen! — you're in for a real treat!" Beth gave some background about her clothing range and the Paris-based Vivienne Rémy label. "All of the clothes you will see tonight are available to order exclusively from Beth's Boutique. They are not available in any retail shop on the high street. Fifty per cent of the profits raised from the clothing sales will be donated to the Elowen Trust, who we are raising money for tonight. Everybody, if you would like to put your hands together and welcome Nancy, our first model, onto the catwalk…"

The music changed to 'I'm Too Sexy' by Right Said Fred, and Nancy strutted onto the catwalk like a natural, wearing a floaty floral winter dress with a black jacket, which she took off and slung over her shoulder when she reached the end of the runway. She paused to let everyone see what she was wearing while Beth said a little about each of the garments. Next up came Tara, in black trousers and a blouse, wearing the same jacket but in a different colour. Within five minutes, Beth's nerves had dissipated as she realised she did know her stuff. The music changed to Madonna's 'Material Girl', and as each model entered the runway Beth spoke confidently about each item of clothing, what it was suitable for, and what it would go with.

Once it was all over, Tristan took the mic off Beth to say a few words. "Firstly, can we have a huge round of applause for Beth and the models." All the models came out in their final outfit. Nancy grabbed Beth's hand, and all seven of them, holding hands, took a bow like actors doing a curtain call. "I believe you have a sheet in front of you detailing the clothing range. Anya and Cathy will be taking the orders, and Beth will be along shortly to answer questions." He pointed to the other end of the room, where Beth could see Anya waving. "There's no obligation to place an order tonight, but if you wish to do so you will be helping raise more money for the Elowen Trust. Afterwards, if you'd like to gradually make your way out to the marquee, remembering to visit the silent auction on the way, dinner will be served in about forty-five minutes."

There was another round of applause, after which the models and Beth hurried off the catwalk and out of the morning room.

Back in their changing room, Rhianna and Cathy helped the ladies take off their outfits and get back into their glamorous cocktail dresses. Beth gave them all a brief hug, thanking them all hugely for their amazing effort. She could feel a lump forming in her throat, filled with pride at how wonderful her clothing range had looked and the friendship and support each woman had given her. Empowered, she realised, was how she was feeling.

In the sitting room, Anya was at a small desk, taking orders. Cathy and Beth came to join her.

"Ah, there you are, Beth. Could you advise this lady about sizing?" Anya pointed to a middle-aged woman, and Beth made her way over to her. She was then inundated with a steady stream of women asking questions about sizing, price, quality, and appointments. Luckily, Anya had had the good sense to get some business cards off Beth and had them available to give out. Judging by the pile of orders Anya and Cathy had received, it looked as if she was going to have a busy Christmas and New Year.

Beth's brain whirled with ideas and excitement. She tried to calm it. Once she'd crunched numbers and deducted the charity donation from her profits, then she could get excited. She might even be able to afford to hire Trenouth Manor for a fashion show to present her summer range.

Maybe she did owe Tristan that dance. He'd just given her the biggest opportunity to get her business off the ground.

CHAPTER 22: TILLY

It started snowing as the guests made their way from the house to the marquee. Tristan wasn't so sure of its magical allure given the rate it was falling, blanketing the grounds in white. He and Joe had gritted the pathway leading from the house to the marquee. But if the snow continued at its current rate, they would be shovelling guests out of it later.

Tristan hadn't been able to catch Beth before the dinner. He'd seen her caught up with assisting Anya and Cathy with the orders. The fashion show had been a huge success. People didn't mind spending their cash when they knew it raised money for charity. Since bumping into Beth in the kitchen at the beginning of the evening, and seeing how radiant she looked, he hadn't stopped thinking about her. He had snatched a brief second while having their photo taken, even if it were just to feel the heat of her fingertips. How he'd longed to take her hand in his.

Tristan was seated at a table with his mother, Joe and Rhianna, Rose and Charles, and another couple who were friends of Janine's and involved with the Elowen Trust. The falling snow hadn't hindered the smooth running of the three-course dinner. The catering staff had served it to perfection. The charity ball always had a great atmosphere — it was the mix of Christmas cheer and raising money for a good cause that did it. Plus, the wine. Although, to keep his wits about him, Tristan had stuck to one glass.

He smiled as he glanced across at Olly on another table, kissing his wife Rachel under the mistletoe that he held above her head. His mother always insisted on sprigs of mistletoe being placed on each table. They had so much they could collect from the grounds. It gave her such joy to see the love in the room. But watching Olly made him feel he was too far away from Beth. She was at a table with Nancy and her friends. He kicked himself for not placing her on his table when they'd done the seating plans. But Anya had overseen them, and he hadn't wanted to interfere. Besides, requesting that Beth be seated with him would have meant Anya asking him all sorts of awkward questions.

After the dinner had finished and the band had started playing, he was making his way towards Beth's table when Tilly suddenly clutched his arm.

"Oh Tristan, can you help me? I don't feel well," she said, taking his attention away from Beth, who was chatting with Noah and Olly. He grabbed a free chair and made Tilly sit down. He noticed she was holding her enormous belly and appeared anxious. The band was playing, most of the guests were dancing, and the evening was in full swing. He still hadn't managed to talk to Beth.

"Where's Liam?" he said, over the din. He scanned the marquee to see if he could spot him.

"Gone to fetch the camper van." Tilly winced, rubbing her stomach.

"Do you think you're having contractions?"

"No, they're only Braxton Hicks," Tilly said. "I've been having them for weeks."

"Braxton Hicks?"

"They're false labour pains."

"When's your due date?" Tristan frowned.

"I'm overdue. It was Wednesday just gone."

Tristan's heart started racing. Panicking would not be good for Tilly. He needed to remain calm. To his relief, he spotted

Joe close by. "Joe, I need a hand. I think Tilly might be in labour."

"Please don't make a scene," she pleaded. "I'm sure it's nothing." Then she gave a moan. "Oh, God, they've not felt like this before."

Both men stared at one another. Neither of them had any experience of pregnant women, but they both instinctively knew this was no practice run.

"Where the hell is Liam?" Joe asked as he and Tristan helped Tilly out of the marquee.

"He went to get the camper van," she said breathlessly.

"I don't think you'll be going anywhere in that thing in this snow," Joe said, not very reassuringly.

"Shouldn't we take her to the house?" Tristan said more quietly to Joe.

He shook his head. "No, we'll take her to my Range Rover; it's parked by the house. Worst case scenario we drive her to hospital in that, if an ambulance can't get through."

Outside the marquee, the snow was falling steadily, the wind making it drift. One minute they were walking on a couple of inches, the next it was a foot deep. A couple of times they nearly lost their footing.

"When I noticed it was coming down heavy, I thought I'd fetch my vehicle," Joe said. "I think I'll be giving people lifts home." Joe opened the back door of the Range Rover, driver's side, and with Tristan, he helped Tilly in. She slowly backed onto the backseat.

"I'll ring for an ambulance, just in case, and then go and find Liam!" Joe said, pulling his phone out of his pocket. Tristan knew as well as Joe that an ambulance wouldn't be able to get through. "You stay with Tilly! Get her comfy."

"Why me?" Tristan said, looking aghast, then realising how bad that must have sounded, he gave Tilly an apologetic look. She didn't notice. As if in her own bubble, she was concentrating on breathing through the contractions. This was now serious. She was moaning as a contraction came, and it certainly wasn't long between each one.

"You've delivered lambs!" Joe shouted back, heading towards the marquee.

"I was twelve! And just watching. And lambs are very different from human babies!"

Tilly gave another cry and through gritted teeth screamed, "Just get me to the hospital!"

Usually, women took hours to give birth. They had plenty of time to get her to hospital, Tristan reasoned with himself, not wanting to panic.

"It's okay, I'm here, I'm here. Let's get you comfortable." Tilly slowly twisted around, dropping her legs into the footwell behind the driver's seat, puffing and groaning occasionally. "Joe's gone to find Liam, then he'll take you." Tristan forced himself to stay calm, seeing Tilly's distress. She needed him to be strong.

Tristan spotted Nancy making her way from the marquee to the house. He had to shout over the wind and the music. "Nancy! Nancy! Find Anya, get her to grab some towels from the house. And some blankets!" He realised it was very cold.

"Why, what's going on?" She turned towards him, but then seeing the snow, remained on the gritted path. At least the salt was doing its job there.

"Just find Anya! It's urgent."

"Tristan! Tristan…" Tilly was calling him. "I think my waters just broke."

Standing at the back of the marquee, her shoes killing her feet, Beth could see the snow outside falling in more than a flurry. Her attention was then turned to the band stopping abruptly and making way for Joe, who stood in front of the mic.

"Hey, everyone, sorry to disrupt your evening," he said, waving a hand apologetically. "We have a bit of an emergency. Don't panic!" he added quickly, as a few gasps were heard. "However, the ambulance is having problems getting here due to the snow, so is there a doctor or a nurse in the house, or even better, a midwife?" Everyone on the dancefloor stared up at him, most of them shaking their heads or shrugging their shoulders in bewilderment.

Midwife? Beth's heart pounded in alarm.

Then, through one of the marquee windows, she could see Anya battling against the wind and snow, running out of the house with an armful of towels by the looks of things.

Tilly!

"If you're in any way medically trained, please come find me. Right, I'll hand you back to the band. Please don't worry and enjoy the rest of your evening." Joe handed the mic back to the singer and jumped down from the stage. The band started up again.

Without hesitation, Beth ran after Anya, ignoring the cold. "What's happening?"

"Tilly might be in labour. Here, if you don't mind, could you take these to Tristan?" Anya handed her the towels. "I'll go back and fetch the blankets."

"Sure. Where is he?"

She pointed towards a vehicle that Beth recognised as Joe's old Range Rover parked on the driveway outside the front of the house.

As quickly as she could, her heels sinking into the snow, she made her way over to Tristan. At least the cold stopped her thinking about how much her feet were killing her, the freezing snow numbing the pain.

"Hey, here are some towels." She handed them to Tristan. "Aren't you cold?" She noticed he was only in his shirt.

"I'm freezing. I gave Tilly my jacket. If you go through to the kitchen, past the old one, there's a boot room at the very end of the corridor. I think I've got an old thick jacket hanging up in there. Could you fetch it, please?"

"Of course!" Beth rushed towards the house, thinking now would be a good time to ditch her heels.

Tristan shivered as he watched Beth make her way back into the house. He'd wanted to suggest she grabbed a coat too. But that would imply she should stay and help him. And maybe it was best Beth stayed in the warm.

"How are you doing, Tilly?" Tristan asked, leaning in and getting his hand squeezed when she took it. His knuckles being crushed at least made him forget he was shivering.

"Have you found Liam?" she said, then gave a moan as a contraction came and squeezed his hand even tighter.

"Joe's on the case." He hoped! It felt like hours since Joe had left him with Tilly. But it had probably only been about ten minutes. Liam really needed to be the one holding Tilly's hand.

Anya returned with blankets. She placed some over Tilly and wrapped one around Tristan.

"Thank you," he said. "Can you see if you can find Joe? He was supposed to look for Liam."

"He was in the marquee asking for medical assistance."

"Okay, can you go find him, please? We need to get Tilly to the hospital."

Anya nodded and set off in the direction of the marquee. Tristan could hear the band still playing. At least not everyone's night was ruined.

Beth returned, wearing her coat and carrying an old, thick, waterproof jacket that Tristan usually threw on to walk Flash or if he needed to check the grounds. He dreaded to think what it smelt like. He shook off the blanket, placing it around Beth, and put on the old jacket. It was still warm from being in the house.

Tilly was as comfortable as she could be in the back of Joe's Range Rover. Tristan had started the engine to get the heaters blowing.

To his relief, Liam appeared; wet, cold and bedraggled.

"Thank God," Tristan said upon seeing him.

"I can't get the van out."

"It's okay, we can drive her in Joe's Range Rover," Tristan said, grabbing the spare blanket he'd discarded and throwing it around Liam.

"I don't think the Range Rover will get through either," Liam said, shivering. "I checked. The lane leading to the house is blocked. There's no way to get to the main road. The snow drift needs digging out, it's that bad. It'll take too long." He gestured towards Tilly inside the vehicle.

"Oh, shit, that's not good," Tristan said. "Here, take Tilly's hand." Tristan tried getting out of the Range Rover.

Liam shook his head. "I'll get in behind her. You stay there." Tristan was half in, half out of the car, awkwardly positioned, and Tilly was still gripping his hand. Liam opened the other passenger door and slid in behind Tilly to support her, managing to close the door.

"In that case," Tristan said. "I think we need to move her into the house, it's so cold out here."

"Beth, please can you find Anya, and ask her to get the downstairs bedroom ready, the one we used for the fashion show? No one has that booked tonight," Tristan said. "Oh, and tell Anya she might want to warn our guests that they may be snowed in."

Beth nodded. "They'll have to share rooms."

"Just don't tell them yet. Let them enjoy the evening; the night is still young." Tristan glanced at his watch; it was only ten o'clock. Somehow, he couldn't see he and Beth sharing the last dance at this rate.

Beth found Anya in the kitchen, Joe having just hurried out with a woman who was hitching her ballgown up, and who looked as if she was on a mission. Joe must have found some medical assistance. Beth relayed Tristan's thoughts to Anya, but she was already on it. They set off to clear the bedroom for Tilly. Anya had already anticipated the possibility of being snowed in and had informed the partygoers. Beth quickly ditched her heels and found the ballet pumps she'd brought with her.

"Oh, good idea!" Anya said approvingly. "Shame I didn't think to do the same." She ditched her heels and carried on bustling about in her stockings. "We can move the rails of clothes to the billiard room. I think there's enough room, even with all the furniture." She was clearly good at thinking on her feet. Beth followed all her instructions. "There's twelve bedrooms upstairs, but they are all booked."

"If the roads don't clear, people might need to share with other guests."

"I know, I've already thought of that."

"What's going on?" Nancy appeared as they were pushing the second rail down the corridor towards the billiard room. She was holding a glass of wine.

"The paramedics can't get to Tilly yet, so we're making up the bedroom for her," Anya answered.

"Oh, right," Nancy said. "Can I help?"

"Take this rail with Beth," Anya said. "I'll go grab the last one."

Once the bedroom was cleared, and they were happy it was ready for Tilly's arrival, Beth said she would go and tell Tristan. Having warmed up from the exertion of lugging clothes and furniture, she braced herself for the cold again. Wrapping her coat around her, she was relieved to see the snow had stopped, even if the wind hadn't. It stung her face as she rushed across the drive towards the Range Rover.

CHAPTER 23: THE BABY'S ARRIVAL

Shortly after Beth and Anya had left Tristan, Joe appeared, with someone hurrying behind him.

"Hey, how's our patient?" Joe asked, slapping Tristan on the back affectionately.

"Great, only Liam says we're snowed in. The lane is blocked," Tristan replied, relieved to be taking some respite from Tilly. He stood and straightened up to release the kinks in his upper back and neck where he'd been bent awkwardly. Tilly hadn't wanted to let go of his hand, even with Liam present.

"You found him, then?" Joe waved at Liam, who grimaced back. Tilly gave a moan. "Well, I've found a trainee midwife," Joe continued, looking mightily pleased with himself. "This is Sandy."

"Hello!" A jolly-looking woman with a plump, robust figure had appeared by Joe's side. "I was a nurse before deciding to train as a midwife." Like everyone else, she was dressed appropriately for the charity ball. Tristan wasn't sure how her emerald evening gown would go down delivering a baby. She had a carrier bag with her. "And you are the dad?"

"No! I'm Tristan, I own the Trenouth estate," he replied. "Liam — the dad — is in the back, supporting Tilly from behind." Liam gave a wave in between stroking Tilly's hair and talking soothingly to his wife.

Sandy briefly took in the situation while Joe whispered something to Tristan about coming prepared and having raided the kitchen for what she might need, which was why they'd been a bit longer.

"Let me take a look at Tilly," Sandy said. Tristan had had the good sense to pull the front seats forward, so there was more space in the back. Tilly was now lying on her side across the backseat, her head on Liam's lap. Sandy edged inside the Range Rover, Tristan stepping aside but holding onto the passenger door so that it didn't slam into her with the gusts of wind.

Joe mentioned something about gathering some men and getting the tractor out to see if they could clear the road.

"I'll come with you," Tristan said.

"No, you stay here."

"But Liam's here."

"They still might need you. I've got this," Joe said. Before Tristan could argue, Joe had run off. He knew where the keys were kept for the tractor, having helped Tristan many times on the estate.

While the midwife leaned in to see to Tilly, Tristan thought he'd update her with what he knew. "I think her waters broke," he said.

"When was this?" Sandy stood to face him.

Tristan shrugged. He hadn't realised he should be timing this stuff. That's not how it had worked with the lambs. "Ten or fifteen minutes ago." Sandy nodded. "I've sent Anya to set up a bedroom in the house."

Tilly gave another moan and Liam soothed his wife. They were coming more frequently now. She was breathing more heavily too.

"Good idea." Sandy returned her attention to her patient. "Tilly, dear, do you think you could move?"

"I AM NOT MOVING!" Wow, Tilly didn't sound like Tilly. She gave another involuntary moan. As she moved onto her back, Liam now supporting her from behind, she said urgently, "I can feel the head! I can feel the head!" She started puffing.

"Why are you puffing, dear?"

"Because I keep getting the urge to push. And I can't possibly be ready to push," Tilly said breathlessly between moans as contractions hit. "Doesn't labour take hours?"

"Oh, this sounds like things are moving a lot faster than usual for a first-time mother. But it's not unheard of. The fact you want to push means you're probably ready, but let's check how far dilated you are."

Before examining Tilly, Sandy handed Tristan a torch. "Hold this, so that I can see —"

"*Me?*" Tristan wanted to kill Joe.

"Yes, who else, silly? Liam has his hands full with his wife." Sandy stifled a giggle. "Point it there…" She adjusted Tristan's aim. "Perfect, thank you…"

Holding the torch for Sandy, Tristan focused frantically on Tilly's face, even though the torch was not pointing there, and wondered if he'd ever be able to look her in the eye again. Or Liam.

Just think of lambing…

Before Tristan knew it, Sandy was instructing Tilly to push and that's when the hard work really started. Tilly, apart from her earlier outburst about not being moved, had remained calm, and even now, in the throes of giving birth, she wasn't screaming and hurling expletives. Considering she had no pain medication, not even gas and air, she was being incredibly strong and controlled, only letting out guttural breaths as she pushed. Liam supported her, giving calm encouragement. Sandy kept insisting Tristan remained close at hand, pointing the torch, when his instinct was to run away. This was definitely not like lambing.

Eventually, to everyone's relief, there was a baby's cry, and Sandy was working rapidly, cutting the cord and tying each end with cotton.

"It's a boy!" she said, and there were joyous cries inside the vehicle from Liam and Tilly, Liam kissing the top of her head. Then next thing Tristan knew, before he could object, he was being handed a fragile, sticky, wet bundle wrapped in the towels. "Keep him warm while I check mum. Don't worry about cleaning off the waxy, white vernix."

Tristan felt Liam should have been holding the baby, but the Range Rover was cramped, and he still had Tilly in his arms. He hovered behind the door of the Range Rover and kept the baby close to his body. Sandy had swaddled the newborn, so, in the dim light, Tristan could only make out tiny heart-shaped lips, a miniature nose and surprisingly open blue eyes.

As Tristan was shielding the baby from the wind, wrapping him close, Beth arrived.

"Hey, I was just checking if you needed anything else," she said breathlessly. "Oh my God, she's had the baby — already?"

Tristan didn't get time to answer. Sandy was taking the baby back off him and handing the bundle to Tilly for mother and baby bonding.

"Wow, I really didn't see you as…" Beth said hesitantly.

"What?" he asked, frowning.

"You looked like a natural," she said, not quite meeting his gaze.

"See, I told you that you were the best man for the job!" Joe said, approaching them.

"I pulled a lamb from a ewe at the age of twelve as it got into some stress, and the farmer needed a hand, and Joe thought that made me more qualified than him to help Tilly."

"But you did a fine job," Joe said, grinning.

"Yes, you did." The midwife patted Tristan's arm.

"Yeah, I appreciate you staying with Tilly when I wasn't here," Liam said from inside the Range Rover, still cuddling Tilly and his son, and already looking like a proud dad.

"Now, let's get mum and baby settled in that bedroom," Sandy said, clapping her hands together. "The placenta may take a little longer, as normally we'd give her something to induce it. They'll have to take a trip to the hospital tomorrow morning, once the snow's been cleared."

"There's a wheelchair in the kitchen. I'll go fetch it," Beth said.

"Yeah, I've left men clearing the exit," said Joe. "I think Tristan and I in our four-by-fours could get some guests down to the village, but I wouldn't want to risk a trip to the hospital with a newborn."

Tristan nodded. "Okay, let's see who wants to leave early. But first I'll go help Beth with that wheelchair. She's going to have to drag it through the snow."

CHAPTER 24: THE LAST DANCE

Tristan left Tilly, Liam and their new baby to settle in for the night in the downstairs bedroom with Sandy supervising, while he started ferrying guests back to Kittiwake Cove. Between him, Joe and a couple of others who had driven to the event in their four-by-fours, they drove a good number of people home to the village. Rose and Charles offered any free bedrooms at their bed and breakfast. Those who lived further afield were going to need to stay over at the house, but luckily some of those had already booked the bedrooms.

For those staying on, the band played a little longer. Tristan had already agreed the band could load their equipment into their van and leave it onsite, as it wouldn't cope in the snowy conditions, and Joe would run them home.

Entering the marquee, Tristan realised he hadn't managed to dance with Beth. Having been busy taking some of the guests home, he begged the band for one last song. He winced as he saw the time on his watch: 12.10 a.m. The lead singer gave a nod and announced this would be their last song. The beginning of the evening, when he'd asked Beth for a dance, felt lightyears ago with everything that had happened with Tilly. Poor Anya had been run off her feet. Luckily, his mother and Rose had taken over the silent auction and looked after the guests and the running of the event while Anya and Tristan had been preoccupied.

With his tuxedo jacket retrieved from Tilly, fortunately still clean but a little creased, Tristan put it back on, straightened his bow tie, and freshened up with a splash of water in the bathroom, before going in search of Beth. He desperately wanted this last dance with her.

He found her sitting at a table with an exhausted Anya, Nancy and her girlfriends. He gently took the glass flute Beth was holding out of her hand and placed it on the table. Then, taking both her hands in his, he pulled her up onto her feet. She didn't resist but frowned coyly, looking nervously at Nancy.

"Beth, please give me this last dance."

She smiled gently. "Of course."

Joe and Rhianna were on the dancefloor, and so was Seb with his wife, plus some other couples. Tristan led Beth to join them.

They swayed to the music, Tristan edging a little closer with every step. He held one hand, while his other curled around her waist. He noticed her gaze kept darting off, nervous of something, or someone. She couldn't quite relax in his arms. It still felt like they were teenagers at their first school dance, keeping a metre between them.

"Are you okay?" Tristan asked with a frown. Maybe there was someone else here she would rather be with and he'd totally misunderstood the situation. He noticed Noah had taken a seat next to Anya. Noah was single. Although Anya wasn't. Yet. Having convinced Theo that she'd be working during the evening, apparently, the guy had been relieved he didn't have to attend. And so had Anya. She'd let slip she'd enjoy the evening more without Theo. When would Anya realise Theo was no good for her?

"I'm just wondering if I'm the person you should be having the last dance with," she said softly into his ear over the music.

This surprised Tristan. "Who else should I have the last dance with?"

"Er … Nancy?" She glanced nervously in Nancy's direction. She was deep in conversation with her friends around the table, still laughing and drinking wine.

Tristan shook his head. "Nancy and I are just friends. I know once … but that's all in the past."

"But I heard her… She said she was going to give it a proper go…" Beth chewed her lip. "I thought she meant with you…"

Tristan laughed. Relaxing, he hugged Beth a little closer. "That's with Mark. He works at her firm. They've been on and off over the years. But her heart has always been with him. He's now divorced his wife to make a go of it with Nancy. He's older, loves the city life. He's perfect for her."

"Oh, right." She blushed. "Why isn't he here tonight?"

"This event was planned ages ago, and it's only recently they've decided to make a go of it. He couldn't get out of plans for this weekend. I think he's doing something with his kids."

"He has children? But I thought she disliked kids."

Tristan chuckled. "Yes. Don't be too surprised, though. They are in their late teens, so more Nancy's cup of tea. But I get the impression she doesn't want to meet them yet, so they're taking it one step at a time."

"Oh, right."

He dared to hold her even closer now, hoping she would respond. To his relief, she did. "You're the only woman here I want to be dancing with."

She smiled nervously, and then rested her head on his shoulder, tucking it into his neck. His grip tightened. She felt perfect in his arms. He didn't want the song to end, however exhausted he felt, but he knew he'd have to deal with the guests once the night ended.

"You were amazing tonight, with the new baby," she said.

"Why do I hear a hint of surprise?"

"Because I thought you were like Nancy and allergic to children."

"I like kids. I want kids one day."

She pulled away slightly, to look him in the eye. "You do?"

"Yes, don't be so surprised," Tristan said. "I know my mother harps on as if I'll never give her grandchildren, but I've been too busy making this estate profitable again. I've not had the time to think about my personal life, let alone have a relationship." He hugged her closer. "And maybe I hadn't met the right woman."

"Do you think you have now?"

"I might have, if the feeling is mutual?"

"Is she here? Maybe you should be dancing with her?" she replied teasingly.

"I *am* dancing with her."

The band stopped, and everyone on the dancefloor let go of their partners and applauded. Each member of the band gave a bow after a strum or drum of the instrument they played. Tristan, however, did not let go of Beth's hand and returned his attention to her.

He looked up, and she followed his gaze. They were underneath the mistletoe. Slowly, he dipped his head, and brought his mouth down on Beth's for a gentle kiss. He could have so easily got lost in the moment, but he knew he still had work to do. "Don't go home," he whispered, brushing his fingers along her hairline. "Stay with me tonight. Please."

She nodded hesitantly. "Okay."

His mother, having refused to leave early, had been Tristan's last drop-off, together with Anya. Returning, bone-tired, Tristan felt he couldn't head back to his cottage yet, where he so desperately wanted to crash. He needed to see that his remaining guests were settled first.

The twelve bedrooms upstairs were filled, with some guests doubling up. Anya had pulled every blanket and sheet from the storage in the laundry room. Nancy and her friends had been the last to be taken home by Joe. They were staying at Rose's bed and breakfast.

Apparently, Tilly and the baby were doing marvellously in the downstairs bedroom. Sandy had called in on them and updated Tristan.

After the kiss he'd shared with Beth, Tristan had hated tearing himself away from her. Now he found her in the kitchen. She'd been helping with the clearing up, which the catering staff had had to leave as they'd been driven home earlier than intended.

"Hey, you don't need to do that." He gently touched her hand to stop her.

"It's okay. I thought I'd try to help where I could. At least the snow didn't completely ruin the evening. You got most guests home."

"Yes, I should take you home, but I'd really like you to stay..." He brushed her cheek. "Have you called Jason and told him you're safe? I'll take you home tomorrow morning. I'm just desperate for some sleep now. It's been a very long evening."

"I have, but I can stay here."

"Look, don't worry, you can have my bed," Tristan said reassuringly. "I'm happy to sleep in my spare room." With the run up to Christmas, the room was a tip and the bed still needed making up since Nancy's stay. He didn't want Beth thinking he was a slob. At this rate, and how tired he felt, he'd be sleeping on the sofa with Flash.

"Are you sure? I could crash here somewhere..."

"No, I'd like you with me." He tugged her closer, risking another kiss. How good it felt to have Beth in his arms.

He locked up the store cupboards — he did not need anyone helping themselves to leftover booze. He also left a few lights on in the house, just in case anyone needed to walk around. Then, satisfied he could do no more, he escorted Beth to his Range Rover. The snow had stopped now, but the wind was still causing it to drift. He'd worry about what he may have to face in the morning.

CHAPTER 25: THE FIRST NIGHT

At the cottage, they were greeted by Flash, wagging his tail and whining. Tristan let him outside to relieve himself. He quickly threw a couple of logs on the fire and Beth stood next to it, warming herself. The hem of her floor-length, navy blue dress, which sparkled in the light of the flames, was sodden where it had dragged through the snow. Tristan could glimpse her slender legs through the high split in the side.

"You've no Christmas decorations up," she said as he joined her by the fireplace.

He pulled her into his arms. "Seems like there's little point when I'm the only one here, and I'll go to my mother's on Christmas Day," Tristan replied. He reached to touch her hair, stroke her skin.

"But this cottage would look beautiful with a real tree."

"Maybe next year. Unless I steal one out of the house after the wedding," he said with a chuckle.

Beth gave an involuntary yawn, which made Tristan yawn too.

"Come on, let's get you to bed," he said. He placed the guard in front of the fire and led Beth upstairs to his bedroom. He was relieved to find he had made the bed in the morning and the room was tidy.

"This bed is massive," she said. "Look, you need a decent night's sleep. You take the bed, I'll have your spare bed … or…" she said more hesitantly, "you could sleep with me." Her arms curled around his neck. He felt the softness of her body against his own. "But … I'm not sure I'm ready for anything else…" He watched her gaze drop as she blushed.

"Hey, I'm too tired to manage anything else." With his fingertips, he gently raised her chin.

To Tristan's delight, she took his hand and pulled him towards the bed. "Well then, I'm sure I'll be perfectly safe with you in the bed."

Hesitantly, she kissed him. The taste of champagne was still on her lips, reminding him she had drunk more than him. He let Beth set the pace. As she grew more confident, their kiss deepened, and his embrace tightened around her, heat dispersing between them, their tiredness forgotten.

If she continued to kiss him like that, he might find some energy from somewhere…

Coming to his senses, he pulled away, remembering that she might be more inebriated than he realised. She tugged at her dress. "Have you got something I could wear in bed? I can't sleep in this dress."

"Of course." It was probably a little too soon, he decided, to have her sleeping naked beside him. Releasing her, he rummaged through a drawer and found her a T-shirt. "I'll give you some privacy. You can use the bathroom first if you like." He gestured to the room across from the hallway.

"Oh, first, do you mind helping me with my zip?" Beth turned her back on him.

Tristan rubbed his hands to warm them up. He wanted to make so much more of this moment … tender kisses as he slowly lowered the zip… Gaining some control, he brushed her hair aside, and with cautious fingers, he slowly undid the dress. He tried very hard not to think about the soft, pale skin he was exposing, all the way to the base of her spine, or the lacy black underwear revealed, and concentrated on the rustle of the silky fabric. Fortunately for his self-control, before he could gently trail his fingers down her spine, Beth, holding the dress up with her arms at her chest and clutching the T-shirt, waddled into the bathroom.

Swallowing his desire, as soon as the bathroom door shut, Tristan quickly took his own clothes off, flinging them over a chair. The whole tux would need dry cleaning, so there was no point in hanging it up. Sensing it wouldn't quite be proper to share a bed with Beth wearing just his boxers, he found another clean T-shirt and threw that over his head. He sat on the bed, waiting to use the bathroom, and reminded himself of his resolve to be good. Seducing Beth would not be wise. He wanted her to trust him. He really didn't want to screw this up.

The bathroom door opened, and Beth emerged wearing his T-shirt, the dress flung over her arms in front of her, hiding her bare legs.

"Hope you don't mind, I used a bit of your toothpaste to rub over my teeth," she said, nervously approaching.

"Oh, do you want a toothbrush? I've got a spare one."

"I'm so tired." She shook her head. "I'll borrow it in the morning."

"Get under that duvet, while I use the bathroom."

When Tristan came out, the bedroom lights were off except the bedside lamp. Beth looked as if she was sound asleep.

He wondered if he really should do the more honourable thing now, and sleep on the sofa. He gently brushed her hair from her face and reached to turn off the lamp.

"Tristan, you can get into bed," Beth murmured, barely opening her eyes. "I don't mind."

"Are you sure?"

She gave a sleepy nod.

He wanted more than anything to snuggle up to Beth and breathe her in. He went around to the other side of the bed and slid underneath the duvet. He reached over her, gently placing a kiss on her cheek, then switched the bedside lamp off. Tentatively, he spooned her, praying his body wouldn't betray him, fearing his arousal would overcome his tiredness. As he was about to turn over, thinking this would help, Beth grabbed his hand and pulled it into her chest.

"Night, Tristan," she said.

"Night." He tucked in closer to her, cuddling. His breathing fell in with hers and he relished the fading scent of her perfume, the warmth of her body curving into his. "This wasn't exactly how I envisaged our first night together," he whispered, his breath in her hair.

"Oh, so you have thought about it," she replied drowsily.

Yes, he had. He hugged her tighter. He hoped every night could be like this.

Seconds later, he fell into a deep and restful sleep.

Beth awoke to find the bed empty. The room was dark, only some light coming from downstairs and from the landing. She heard the wooden stairs creak and reached out to turn on the bedside lamp. Still in his T-shirt and boxers, Tristan was carrying two mugs.

"Tea or coffee?" he said softly. "I wasn't sure which, so I made both."

"What time is it?" She sat up and rubbed her eyes.

"Five a.m. Damn dog wanted to go out again."

"He's worse than a toddler." That would explain the groggy feeling; they'd only had about four hours of sleep. And she had been drinking last night. One eye open, she reached for a mug. "Tea will do."

Tristan handed it to her. "Ah, good. I prefer coffee in the morning."

"Aren't you getting back into bed?"

"I thought I might make a start on clearing the roads. You can stay in bed." He gently brushed her hair off her forehead, smiling at her.

"Tristan, it's five in the morning. It's pitch black. Nobody will be up yet." She shuffled over, opening the duvet invitingly. Her T-shirt had ridden up, revealing her lacy black underwear. "Get back in. You must be exhausted."

"Actually, you're right. What am I thinking?" He gave a smile. She liked that smile. It usually led to a twinkle in his deep brown eyes. He put his mug next to hers on the bedside cabinet and got in, facing her. He looped his arm under her neck, pulling her closer into a warm embrace. He felt so firm and comforting.

"Sorry, shall we start again?" he said. "Good morning, beautiful." He kissed her, and she let his tongue search out hers, in a soft, sweet, exquisite kiss. She felt his groin harden against her stomach. She didn't know whether to pull away or not. She didn't want to give him the wrong signals. She wasn't sure if she was ready to take it further with Tristan. It had been such a long time since she'd slept with someone.

As if reading her mind, he said reassuringly, "Sorry, I'm not so tired now… At least you know how I feel about you." He kissed her again, but he didn't push for more than a kiss.

She enjoyed resting her head on his chest, listening to the gentle thud of his heart. She wanted this comfort to last forever. His fingers gently stroked her skin, relaxing her further.

"Sorry … I need to take things slowly, Tristan."

"I know, sweetheart. I know."

After an hour spent snoozing, cuddled up to Beth and reluctant to tear himself away, Tristan had left her to sleep while he took Flash out into the early morning darkness to assess the snow levels. They had done a good job the previous evening, getting most people home, but the wind had caused more snow to drift off the fields. Wrapped up warmer than the night before, Tristan quietly returned his dog to the cottage, then drove his Range Rover to where the snow needed clearing. A couple of his groundsmen had made it on foot and had started shovelling snow off the pathways and laying salt grit. They'd cleared what they could in the car park by The Stables, so that the remaining cars would be able to leave that morning. Snow ploughs and gritters had been out on the main road; Tristan just needed to clear the narrow country lane leading to it. Heavy, dark grey clouds meant the morning took a while to get light.

Liam appeared, looking sleep-deprived. "Need a hand?" He'd found an old jumper in the back of his camper van and had thrown that on over his shirt. He was still wearing his tuxedo trousers.

"Shouldn't you be with Tilly?" Tristan raised his eyebrows.

"She's resting with the baby. And Sandy is about. But I feel I need to get her to the hospital and get them both checked over, so I can relax."

Liam did look anxious, in his scruffy, half-asleep state. Tired, yet too wired to sleep. Exactly how Tristan felt. He nodded. The extra pair of hands would be a great help with shovelling snow.

Like Liam, some guests had risen early, wanting to get home. Most needed a change of clothes, and were still dressed in their ballgowns and tuxedos. With the car park now cleared, they were able to get their cars out. Some vehicles occasionally needed a push from Tristan, Liam and the groundsmen to help them over the icier parts of the road.

Confident he'd now be able to move the camper van, Liam headed back to the house to fetch Tilly and his son.

"I'll come with you," Tristan said. He wanted to check on Trenouth Manor.

While Liam saw to his wife and baby, Tristan busied himself in the kitchen, filling and switching on a large electrical catering urn. He laid out mugs, tea, coffee, and sugar so his guests could help themselves to a hot drink.

Once he was satisfied that everything was in order, Tristan made his way back to the cottage, eager to return to Beth. It wasn't ideal having to get up early to attend to the estate on their first night together. The fact that she had agreed to stay over had to be a good sign. But he knew not to rush her into anything, however eager he was to demonstrate how much she meant to him. He understood she had George to think about. The little boy's welfare was just as important to him as Beth's was.

At the cottage, Flash greeted Tristan with a welcoming whine and a wag of his tail. The fire was smouldering in the grate, giving off a comforting warmth. He gave the fire a poke, cleared some of the ash and threw another couple of logs on. He hadn't realised how cold he was.

In the kitchen, Tristan put the filter coffee machine on. Then, as quietly as he could, he padded up the creaky wooden staircase and entered his bedroom. He felt a mix of panic and disappointment when he saw his bed was empty and neatly made.

Had she left? She couldn't have — how would she have got home?

Then to his relief, he heard the flush of the toilet and the running of the bathroom taps. A sleepy-looking Beth emerged.

"Hey," he said first, hoping not to her alarm her, in case she didn't realise he was there.

"Hey," she replied, nervously smiling back. She folded her arms self-consciously across her chest.

Swiftly, he grabbed his indigo blue dressing gown from the hook on the back of the bedroom door and helped her into it. It was unfair that he was fully dressed, while the T-shirt she wore left nothing to his imagination — the fabric resting on the buds of her breasts, highlighting their sexy curves, those slender, smooth legs, delicate ankles... How he wished that he could scoop her up right now and make love to her on that very neat bed...

"How are you feeling? Can you stomach some breakfast?" he asked. He couldn't resist a soft, brief kiss on her lips.

"I'm not too bad now I've had the extra sleep," she said. "My headache is only mild, and I think that's due to sleep deprivation, rather than the alcohol." She let him hold her close.

"Okay, let's go downstairs."

He really needed to stop thinking about how much he wanted to make slow, passionate love to this woman. He could easily forget everything — the estate, the snow — and spend the whole day snuggled in bed with her.

"Do you have a phone charger? I forgot to charge my phone last night. It's dead."

"Yeah, sure, I've a spare one in the kitchen." Tristan brought his thoughts back to reality.

"When I have some battery power, I'll phone Jason. I'm sure he'll be fine with George. He'll probably take him sledging."

"Well, come and have some breakfast and then you can call him."

Down in the kitchen, Beth watched as Tristan gave Flash his breakfast. Her heart had been filled with a new level of admiration for him last night. She was grateful he had lent her his dressing gown. There was a draughty chill typical of old cottages, even with the fire blazing, and she'd been embarrassed to be wearing nothing but a T-shirt and her underwear. She was touched that Tristan had realised this.

With her phone plugged in, she was able to call Jason, who was more than happy spending the morning with George.

"Wait till the roads are clearer," Jason said. "Don't fight your way home in the snow. I'd rather know you're safe at Tristan's." There had been a hint of satisfaction in his voice as he'd said Tristan's name. Jason confirmed he would take George out sledging and would make sure he took plenty of photos.

"So, I have cereal, toast, or I could do some poached eggs … or a fry up?" Tristan said, once she had ended her call with her brother.

"Poached eggs on toast would work."

"Good, because I have eggs, but I've just realised I don't have any bacon." Tristan grinned and combed a hand through his hair.

Beth laughed, trying to reduce the tension. Was he as nervous as she was? They'd spent the night together, although nothing had happened. It had been charming to not have that pressure. They had kissed and been more intimate with each other than ever before. Just remembering his gentle touches sent a fizz of delight through her body. Tristan often spoke before thinking, she realised that now. Maybe he was trying hard too, scared of saying something that might offend her. She needed to reassure him he wouldn't do that. But she had to be reassured too. Sleeping with Tristan, as in having sex, was going to be a big step for her.

He was a good guy, a gentleman. He'd pushed for nothing more than kisses and cuddles in bed. He had shown such tenderness towards her, making her heart swell with affection for him. She knew now that she could trust him.

But it was more than that. If he let her, she could fall in love him. And she'd never fallen in love with anyone before.

"Shall I pour the coffees while you get the poached eggs going?" she suggested, giving herself a mental shake. One night with a man, and she was already thinking about love. It was still too soon.

"Sounds like a plan," he said, oblivious to her internal conflict.

Beth spotted a radio on the windowsill. She switched it on and it burst into life, already tuned into a local Cornish radio station. She kept the volume low, so they could still talk, but she hoped the background noise might ease both of their nerves.

"Beth, if I'm acting strange," Tristan said, putting a saucepan of water on to boil, "it's because I don't want to fu— I mean, muck this up." His dark brown eyes had never looked so sincere. Flash barked, one sharp woof. "See, even Flash agrees," Tristan said, giving the dog an affectionate scratch.

Beth handed Tristan his coffee, and they clinked mugs. "I don't want to muck this up either." She kissed him on the cheek. He hadn't shaved yet, and the dark shadow along his jaw was rough on her lips.

Taking her mug out of her hand and placing it down, he slid his hands around her back, pulling her towards him. Hesitantly at first, his gaze locked on hers, he dipped his head and kissed her gently, then more thoroughly. The roughness of his skin grazed her own, but she didn't care.

The sound of the water bubbling in the saucepan made Tristan release her. After turning the gas ring down so that the water simmered, he said, "Sorry, I couldn't resist doing that."

"I gathered that."

"Maybe I'm worried this is the only opportunity I'm going to get. So I want to make the most of you being here."

"It won't be."

"Good."

By the time the poached eggs were ready, they were starting to relax in one another's company. Over breakfast, they chatted and drank more coffee. Tristan told her about his morning clearing snow and seeing Liam and Tilly off.

Starting to feel more human, her hangover fading, Beth still found herself inquisitive about Nancy. She needed to know she wasn't going to hurt anyone, or get hurt herself. "So, you and Nancy are definitely over?" she asked cautiously.

"Beth, we never were anything." Tristan reached over and took her hand, giving it a squeeze. "She's just a friend." He gave a sigh, as if making up his mind whether to say something or not. Beth remained silent. "Nancy's been the only person I felt I could talk to. This estate, the running of it, my family, I offloaded my grievances onto her."

"Grievances?"

"I used to worry Joe and my other cousins resented me. I'd inherited the bigger piece of the estate compared to them. Rose — their mother, my aunt, my father's sister — only inherited the farmhouse. Yet, this estate was spiralling downhill, and was badly in debt. We were likely to lose it all due to my father's mismanagement, and we didn't really discover how bad it had got until after he died," Tristan said, shaking his head. "At times, I was jealous of my cousins. Only me dealing with this estate, and the mess my father had left behind, and the three of them off doing what they wanted to do. Not that I don't enjoy running this estate, but that's another topic." He smiled, taking her hand again, his thumb circling her palm. "However, I soon learnt that Sam, Joe and Heather didn't feel like this at all. Nancy helped me see this and encouraged me to open up to Joe, who I am closest to. Growing up, they were more like siblings to me, rather than cousins. Families are families, and Rose was more than happy with her farmhouse … and apparently, she'd been financially rewarded by her father to compensate for the lack of the estate."

"I can see how the estate takes up a lot of your time."

"Yes, and now I have it under control — no thanks to my father's mistakes."

"You sound very angry with him."

Tristan shook his head. "He was my father, of course I loved him. And Elowen's death affected both of my parents in different ways. I understand that now." He took a deep breath. "But that's the past and this is the present, and I do need to learn to trust my staff more and delegate. Anya keeps telling me this. And so does Nancy."

"Can you do that?"

"With the right motivation." He winked at her, squeezing her hand. "Look, Nancy and I did have a fling, it's how we met, but I knew from the beginning we were never going to be more than friends, because one day I want children. I know my mother thinks I don't, but deep down, I would love a child… It's time I started looking out for me a bit more. The estate is running profitably. I can loosen my grip on it — especially now I can afford to pay people to manage it for me."

"And if the right woman came along…" Beth said. "It's a bit of a cliché."

"Cliché or not, I think the right woman has come along." He ventured across the table to steal a kiss from her, with mischief in his eyes.

"It's a good job you didn't hit me with your tractor!" she said, laughing.

"Hey, I like to believe that was fate, throwing you in my path." Still holding her hand, he pulled her into his lap and brought his mouth down on hers, making every inch of her feel alive. His hands ventured inside the dressing gown and under her T-shirt, his fingertips stroking her spine.

"Tristan." Her tone sobered. She maintained eye contact as she spoke. "Please can we take this slowly, for George's sake?"

"Of course, I wouldn't have it any other way." Tristan pushed a stray hair off her face and behind her ear. His knuckles lingered, brushing her neck. Every touch, every kiss, sent butterflies fluttering in her stomach. "Look, I really like you, Beth. We can take this as fast or as slow as you like. I'm not going anywhere."

CHAPTER 26: A FAMILIAR FACE

Four days until Christmas

So that Beth didn't have to return home in her party dress, Tristan lent her a pair of jogging bottoms. She'd kept the T-shirt she'd slept in, and he'd given her a thick jumper. If he still fancied her now, he was a keeper!

On arriving home, she had a shower and changed her clothes, and then joined Jason, who had a cup of tea waiting for her in the lounge. George was engrossed in CBeebies and so he slouched next to her on the sofa.

"Well, how did it go?"

"The fashion show was amazing. I've sold loads. On Monday I'll be busy with getting orders ready."

Jason rolled his eyes. "And?" She knew what he really wanted to know about. *Tristan.* She glanced at George. He was watching *Mr Tumble* and appeared totally oblivious to their conversation… However, she knew that as soon as she started talking about something she didn't want him to hear, his ears would prick up.

She kept her voice low. "We slept together." Jason raised an eyebrow. "But we did just that, slept and cuddled. It was adorable."

"Really?" Jason eyed her suspiciously.

"Yes, really! I told him I wanted to take it slowly, because of…" She gestured towards George, and Jason gave an approving nod. "I didn't want to rush into anything."

"And what did he say?"

"That he understood, and that he wasn't going anywhere, so he'd go at my pace."

"So, he's not as big a D. I. C. K. as you thought, then?" Spelling out rude words around George was riskier nowadays, but they both hoped he was so engrossed in the television he wouldn't have picked up the word.

"No. He's actually a really good guy."

"Glad to hear it. You deserve someone who will treat you well." Jason pulled her into a hug. "I was worried I might have to put on the big protective brother act."

"I'm sure I'll be fine, but keep it in reserve, just in case." She patted his arm.

By Monday morning, the snow had been cleared from the roads, making it safe for Beth to drive to The Stables. Driving cautiously and more slowly than usual, she was able to enjoy the views of the hills and some of the fields, still blanketed in pristine white. This added to her happy mood. She couldn't stop thinking about Tristan — his tender kisses and caresses. It filled her with an erotic excitement.

Take it slow, she reminded herself.

George was off school for the Christmas holidays now, so she'd arranged a playdate as she needed to concentrate on processing all the orders from the charity ball before Christmas arrived. She'd dropped him off with a change of clothes, because she imagined he and his friend would be going out to play in the snow today.

Tristan had been texting her regularly, increasing the excitement swirling inside her and making her feel like a teenage girl again. But she reminded herself that she was older and wiser now and needed to tread cautiously.

He'd asked how her Sunday had been and if George was enjoying the snow. He'd apologised for being busy, but promised that once the wedding was over, and his Bridezilla was satisfied, he would come and see her.

The wedding was on Christmas Eve. Three days away. Because it had snowed, Isabella Le Bon now wanted snow on her wedding day. However, getting a snow machine at the last minute was proving tricky for Tristan. And he couldn't guarantee the snow would not thaw.

Most of the workshops were open, still fulfilling Christmas orders. Wrapped up in a scarf, a thick coat and wellies, Seb popped over to Beth's Boutique in the morning, carrying a Christmas gift bag.

"A little something for George," he said, handing it to Beth. She took the ribbon handles and peered in.

"Oh, you didn't have to."

"Oh, I did. I enjoy his company."

There was a present for Beth too. She felt herself blushing, because she hadn't thought about buying gifts for Seb and his family.

"And before you say anything, we don't give to receive," Seb said, as if reading her mind. "You save your money and treat the boy." He winked, squeezing her shoulder affectionately.

"Thank you," she said sincerely. It meant so much to be thought of like this. She couldn't wait to see George open the present.

Once Seb had left, it did make her think. Should she get something for Tristan? But what did you get a man you didn't know very well, and had only been dating a few days...? And were they dating? Is that what she should call it? She had already bought a bone treat for George to give Flash, but maybe she needed to think of a little something for Tristan. She would need to pick Jason's brains tonight.

Tristan called in around lunchtime, his hands behind his back as if he were hiding something. "Hey, you," he said.

"Hey, you, too." She eyed him curiously as she approached, kissing him on the lips. The warmth and the pressure, the brush of his stubble, sent pure delight through her body. Would she ever get used to this sensation?

"Have you eaten?" he said.

"Not yet."

"Good, I thought I'd bring you lunch, and we could eat together." He revealed the paper bag he held behind his back. "I had to pop into Kittiwake Cove, so I passed by the bakery."

She kissed him again. "Want to eat here, or did you have other plans?"

"Here will do. Your sofa is comfy, isn't it?"

They sat down close to one another and Tristan pulled two freshly baked pasties out of the bag.

"I got a traditional Cornish pasty and a steak and stilton." He'd also bought some saffron buns, two bags of crisps and two bottles of fruit smoothie. "I wasn't sure which you'd like. You choose, I'm happy with either."

"I'm happy with the traditional pasty. Not had one in ages, believe it or not."

He laid out napkins on the table to place the pasties on.

"So, have you found a snow machine?" she asked, before taking a bite.

Tristan nodded. "I'll have to go all the way to Truro to fetch it, though."

"Drive carefully, won't you?"

"Concerned about me already?" He nudged her playfully.

She blushed. Sometimes she could curse her red hair and freckles. "Maybe, a little." She decided to change the subject. "This morning I've been going through all the orders. I've totted them up and this is how much we've raised." She showed him the figure on her notepad — over £1,500.

"Wow, that's great. Thank you so much, Beth. I'll let Mum know. Anya manages the charity's social media pages, so Mum will get her to update them with the final amount raised after Christmas."

"Thank you for the chance to promote my business. I've already got loads of appointments in the diary for January."

"Thank you for saving my bacon. Everything had been booked up. I was worried I wouldn't find something to replace the casino. As it happened, the fashion show was a much more lucrative event."

Tristan only stayed for an hour. Like Beth, he was busy. Reluctantly, after a lingering kiss, he said goodbye and promised to see her tomorrow. She left the shop early to pick up George.

Once Jason came home from work, he took over looking after George while Beth dashed out to the shops and braved the last-minute crowds in Wadebridge. Her main aim was to look for something for Tristan. Jason had given her some ideas, but she hoped browsing the shops would give her some inspiration too. While she was out, she decided to pick up some fresh bits and pieces for Christmas, not wanting to leave it too late. Christmas Eve was usually devoted to George, baking mince pies and gingerbread biscuits. She didn't like to spend it shopping.

In the supermarket, her final destination, Beth browsed the alcohol aisle. She decided to grab a bottle of wine for Seb and his family. Even though he had said he didn't expect anything, she wanted to buy a small gift for him. He did, after all, treat George like a grandson. Now, should she get red or white?

As she reached for a bottle in the Australian reds section, oblivious to her surroundings, her trolley suddenly clashed with another and she found herself face to face with a man.

"Oh, I'm sorry," she said.

"My fault, I wasn't looking where I was going," he replied. He looked at her intently for a moment. "Hey, do I know you from somewhere?" he asked. By the looks of him, Beth hoped not. He was scruffily dressed in an old jumper and smelt of drains. But she had to admit his face was vaguely familiar, and not altogether unattractive, even if he was dressed like a tramp. Who was he? "Oh, yes, December, a few years ago, at the club." He clicked his fingers. Blue eyes, familiar blue eyes, searched hers. "Mirage?" It was the trendy bar-cum-club in Wadebridge where she'd spent her eighteenth birthday. "That's what it was called back then. Yes!"

Then it dawned on her. Beth tightened her grip on the bottle of red wine for fear of dropping it. She was looking at George's father.

"Elizabeth?"

Oh Christ, he knew her name. But she couldn't remember his.

"Kenny. But I think I told you George." He smiled.

Now her face was on fire. Had she remembered his name subconsciously, and that's why she'd named her son George?

"Gosh, it's been a long time," he said.

"Seven years," she said, finally regaining the ability to speak. She knew her face was probably flushed pink and betraying her embarrassment. The man needed a shave, and his blond hair was grimy with bits of dust and muck.

Best not mention he has a son in the middle of the Co-Op then. Did she want to tell him? Should she tell him?

"Wow, you have a great memory," he said, chuckling.

"Not really. I remember because it was my eighteenth birthday." *And I got pregnant!*

"Oh, yeah … gosh, you haven't changed. Well, you have… You're even prettier than I remembered."

"Oh, thanks." She really couldn't return the compliment, though. He could be a handsome guy underneath the dirt. He did have a nice smile. It was probably what had attracted her to him in the club. That, and his blue eyes.

"You know, I would have taken your number, seen you again…"

She blushed. They'd gone back to his place. She'd been the one to leave early. One, because she'd feared her mother would have wondered where she was, and two, she'd thought it was only meant to be a one-night stand and hadn't wanted to be around in the morning to face any embarrassment. He'd lived with a couple of other guys at the time. She hadn't known how they'd treat her and hadn't wanted to find out. She'd just panicked and fled.

He reached into the back pocket of his shabby jeans and pulled out his wallet. "Damn it, I gave my last one out. I was going to give you my card. Maybe after the madness of Christmas we could meet up for a coffee, catch up?"

"Er, yes, okay."

"My name's Kenny Penketh — George is my middle name. I was using it that night." He gave a chuckle, shaking his head. "Do you have a pen?" He checked behind his ear, as if he'd have one there.

Beth rummaged in her handbag. She should take his number. This was George's father. She found a pen, and he wrote his name and mobile number on a crumpled piece of paper retrieved from his back pocket.

"Call me, and we'll arrange something." He handed the paper to Beth. She slipped it into her handbag.

She nodded. "Yes, will do." Would she? Should she? Did he have a right to know about George? What if he wasn't good father material? Would she want George to meet him?

"Hey, I promise I scrub up better than this," he said, laughing again. "I've been on a very dirty job today."

God, he'd read the horror on her face as she'd taken the piece of paper from him, hadn't he? "Oh, right, yes, yes…"

"It's great to see you. We'll catch up soon."

Beth watched as he disappeared around the corner of the aisle. Her heart raced. Her throat felt dry as tightness built in her chest. *Breathe, Beth, breathe…* If George's father had been living in the area, how had she not bumped into him before?

Beth was quieter than usual that evening. She wanted to talk to Jason, but knew it needed to wait until her son was sound asleep. When she entered the lounge, Jason was waiting for her with a glass of wine.

"Are you okay?" he said as he handed her the glass. "You've been quiet all evening, as if something's spooked you. Is everything okay with Tristan? He hasn't done something to upset you already?"

She breathed deeply, and looked him in the eye. "I bumped into George's father today."

"What? Where? How?" Jason's eyes widened.

"I was in the supermarket in Wadebridge, choosing a bottle of wine for Seb."

"Did you get his number?"

"Yes, he gave it to me. His name is Kenny Penketh. But his middle name is George. He was using it that night."

"Why?"

"I actually think I remember, now I come to think about it. Him and his mates were playing silly drinking games and they couldn't use their first names, or they'd get fined a drink."

Jason chuckled. "No wonder you look freaked out. So what's troubling that head of yours?"

"I don't know what to do for the best. Should I tell Kenny he has a son? What if he doesn't want to know George? What if he's not suitable Dad material? The man needed a wash, Jason! For all we know he could be a drug addict, living rough, serial killer … anything. I know nothing about this man."

"If he'd been a serial killer, he'd probably have bumped you off that night." Jason already had his mobile out and was tapping on his screen.

"Funny."

"Besides, he was in a supermarket… Did he look like he was stealing?"

"No, he had a trolley like me."

Jason held his phone out to Beth. Staring back at her was Kenny — his Facebook profile. He looked a lot cleaner, and although his account was all locked down so nothing was revealed publicly, except some photos, there was a link to his page.

"He's a plumber?" Beth said, frowning.

"Might explain why he looked like a bum. Maybe he'd come from a job?" Jason said. "I don't always return from the garage smelling of roses, remember."

"He did smell of drains." Beth much preferred the smell of oil on Jason.

Jason did a little bit more digging on the internet, finding a LinkedIn account and Kenny's website: Penketh Plumbing. "Meet him for coffee after Christmas, get to know him a little and then you can tell him," Jason said, rubbing Beth's knee reassuringly with his free hand. "If he wants nothing to do with George, then nothing changes for us, and we won't say anything to the little man."

Jason was right. It could wait until after Christmas.

CHAPTER 27: A BROKEN BOILER

Three days until Christmas

The next day, Beth couldn't shake off her unease. She had gone to bed but hadn't been able to sleep. When she hadn't been staring at the ceiling, she'd whiled away the hours stalking Kenny on social media, trying to grasp what kind of person he was. She didn't want to risk introducing George to a dad who wouldn't be a good father figure.

She really wanted to see Tristan. Saturday night and yesterday's lunch felt so long ago now, with everything that had happened since. Although she was pining for a kiss, a touch or one of his cute smiles that had so grown on her, that wasn't the main reason for wanting to see him. She needed to tell him about Kenny.

Tristan had informed her he was busy first thing. Therefore, after doing some work in the boutique, answering emails, and fulfilling more orders from a delivery she'd received, she headed over to the office at Trenouth Manor at around eleven, eager to find him. In her coat, gloves, and scarf, she looked ready to face a blizzard.

Anya welcomed Beth into the office. She and Cathy were as wrapped up as she was. "Hi! Looking for Tristan?" Anya asked, nudging Beth knowingly. Flash gave a whine and a wag of his tail, but obediently did not leave his bed.

"Yes." Beth blushed, chewing her lip. She went over and scratched Flash under his chin.

"He's a different person to be around now he's seeing you," Anya said.

"Are you talking about Flash or Tristan?"

Anya chuckled. "Tristan, silly! I love it when a romance happens," she said, all starry-eyed. "He's in the house. Try looking for him in the kitchen."

"Thanks."

"You okay, Beth?" Anya asked. "You seem ... quiet..."

"Just got something on my mind. It's nothing really."

"Well, I'm here if you need a chat."

"Thank you."

It wouldn't be fair on Tristan if Beth didn't confide in him first. They needed to be able to talk openly if they were to build a relationship.

Beth made her way over to the house, and around the back to the kitchen. As she entered, a little dazzled at going from the gleaming brightness of sun on snow into the dark corridor, she bumped straight into someone coming the other way.

"Oh, sorry," she said. The wind had whipped her hair up into her face and she was busy clearing it out of her eyes. She focused on the person in front of her and her heart leapt into her mouth.

Shit.

Kenny — looking a lot cleaner and smelling a lot fresher. His blue eyes — George's blue eyes — stared at her, his smile reaching them. "Hey, well, isn't this a small world?"

You are not kidding, she thought. She hadn't seen the man for seven years, and now she'd bumped into him twice in less than twenty-four hours. But at least it confirmed he had a reputable job, even if it meant smelling of drains occasionally. He was ticking a few of her boxes as a suitable father figure for George.

"What are you doing here?" she blurted out. "I mean, sorry, I just wasn't expecting to see *you* here..." She nervously wrung her hands. She could now see why she'd fallen for him back on her eighteenth birthday. Clean and freshly shaven, albeit dressed in grey work trousers with kneepads and plenty of pockets, and a jumper with the Penketh Plumbing logo embroidered on it, he looked very attractive. Blond hair and blue eyes — the complete opposite of Tristan. Even though he had filled out — once scrawny, he was now muscled — he still had a young, boyish smile. At the time, when she'd been turning eighteen, he'd been nineteen. That would make him around twenty-six now.

"Oh, I've been called out on a job. What are you doing here?"

"I have a boutique over in The Stables." She thumbed over her shoulder in the general direction of the courtyard.

"Hey!" Tristan called before Kenny could say more. He came to stand beside Beth, giving her a cheeky wink, but kept his manner professional in front of Kenny.

"Oh, hi, Tristan, all is salvageable. It just needs a part. I'll see if I've got something in my van, otherwise I'll be back in an hour or two," Kenny said.

"Can you believe it? The boiler's playing up in the house," Tristan said to Beth. That would explain why Anya and Cathy were in their coats and scarves in the office.

Beth gave a nervous chuckle.

"Can you believe it? I haven't seen Elizabeth in years, and now I can't stop bumping into her." Kenny turned his attention to Beth, eagerly pushing his hands into one of the side pockets in his work trousers. "I've got a business card on me now. I'll give it to you. Please call me." Kenny handed Beth the card, and she could feel Tristan watching them both. "Let's catch up."

"Yes, of course," she replied quietly, conscious that Tristan was observing it all.

"Well, what was that all about?" Tristan asked once Kenny was out of earshot. "And why would you want to call him?"

"Tristan, there's something I need to tell you."

His eyes narrowed suspiciously. "What?"

Beth didn't want to air her business in the kitchen with groundsmen and various other staff walking in and out, especially when it concerned George. The marquee was being prepared for the wedding; Trenouth Manor was considerably busier than she had thought it would be.

"Can we go somewhere private?" She took his hand.

"You're worrying me now, Beth." He linked his fingers between hers.

"It's nothing for you to worry about, but I need to tell you something."

"Okay, let's grab Flash and go for a walk," he said. "I could do with getting away for a bit. The bride is insisting on changing the colours of the Christmas tree baubles!"

Beth waited outside the office while Tristan fetched Flash, and they set off across the grounds, taking the long way to his cottage. The snow was still thick in places and they walked through areas untrodden by humans, with only a few bird prints and paw prints. She resisted a childish urge to run across the pristine blanket.

"So, what do you need to tell me?" Tristan asked, squeezing her hand. She couldn't feel its warmth as she was wearing her gloves, but she enjoyed the sensation of holding hands. It created a connection, confirmed an intimacy between them.

Beth took a deep breath. It had been far easier to tell Jason. He was her brother and would never reject her. "It's about

Kenny," she said, the words escaping from her mouth before she could stop them.

"Are you seeing him?" Tristan stopped abruptly, turning her to face him, making her look him in the eye.

"No!" Angered by his accusatory tone, she told herself to remain calm. As far as Tristan could see, she was acting guiltily. "You heard it yourself, silly, we've not seen each other in years and then … I bumped into him last night in Wadebridge…"

"Oh. Is he an old school friend?" Tristan was still frowning. She shook her head. "What on earth is the matter, Beth?"

She took a deep breath of cold air. "Tristan, he's George's father."

"Right … right…" Tristan's response was surprisingly calm. Although why Beth feared he'd be angry she had no idea. It was just the shock of running into Kenny after all these years, and not knowing what to do about it. "And he doesn't know?"

"No, he doesn't know. I never saw him again after that night. I didn't even know his full name. I now realise he'd used his middle name that night. He and his mates were playing drinking games, and he'd told me his name was George." Tristan looked at her sharply. "Yes, I know, I must have subconsciously thought of it when I named my son. I named him after his father."

They started walking again, following Flash.

"But I never knew his full name, so I could never search for him," Beth continued. "I was so thrown last night, it's all I've thought about. The implications. It'll change my life, George's life … Kenny's life! And he might not be interested, and then what would I do? Do I keep this big secret from George until he's old enough to understand?" She sighed. "Everything was going so well, and now this. There's too much to think about.

Kenny said to call him after Christmas, so maybe I shouldn't worry about it until then…"

"I don't know, Beth, this is pretty big," Tristan said. "But will you tell George?"

"He's only six! I'm not telling George anything until I've spoken to Kenny," Beth said impatiently.

"Of course."

"And I'm not even sure if I'm going to tell Kenny. I don't know what to do for the best." The second she spoke, she realised these thoughts were probably best kept to herself.

Tristan flushed with anger. He threw Beth's hand away. "Beth! You have to tell Kenny."

"What if he doesn't want to know?"

"If George was my son, I'd want to know!" He glared at her fiercely.

"Tristan!"

"You women never consider the father!" he said, his voice raised. "You're all the same." He called Flash and stormed off, leaving Beth alone in the middle of a snowy path, fighting back tears.

CHAPTER 28: KENNY

Drying her eyes in the quiet confines of her boutique, Beth reflected that Tristan wasn't the best person with whom to discuss her predicament rationally after all.

She realised she needed to give Kenny the choice as to whether to be involved with George or not. She didn't have the right to take that decision away from him. That's why Tristan had reacted so badly. But did she really want to spring this on Kenny before Christmas? It was either going to be the perfect surprise…

"Hey! You're a dad!"

…or his worst Christmas nightmare.

"So, you're a dad…"

Either way, she had to tell him. And then, after that, depending on Kenny's reaction, she would decide what she told George. After all, she couldn't knowingly deprive the child of the chance to get to know his father. And if George found out about him when he was older, would he ever forgive her for keeping this a secret?

She fetched Kenny's business card out of her back pocket. With her mobile in her other hand, her thumb hovered over the numbers to dial. Her throat tightened.

God, what was she doing? She knew he was at work — here at the house. Did she want to have this confrontation now? Should she do this before Christmas? She decided to wait, to think on it some more this evening, and maybe call him then.

Instead, she texted Tristan: *I will tell Kenny. But in my own time.*

Tristan slammed the front door of his cottage shut, stamping snow off his boots onto the doormat. Flash whimpered, making straight for his bed, tail tucked under, ears flat. Tristan, realising Flash was cowering and misunderstanding his anger, went over to stroke him.

"Hey, boy, it's not your fault."

Flash started wagging his tail cautiously, then licked his hand.

When Tristan had seen Kenny hand Beth his card, asking her to call him, all sorts of mixed and irrational emotions had surfaced that he hadn't known were there. Jealousy — another man interested in her. Fear — of losing Beth. His heart had hammered so hard inside his chest, he'd been relieved when she suggested they go somewhere quiet to talk.

He'd had no idea she was going to tell him Kenny was George's father...

And he was angry because Beth had to tell him. She *had* to. Whatever the consequences.

He felt conflicted, though. He wasn't sure if he was happy George's father had arrived on the scene. Why now? What would it mean for them? Their relationship was very new. Fragile, even. It could end as quickly as it had started. Tristan had seen the way Kenny had looked at Beth. What if they decided to make a go of it as a couple — for George's sake?

Don't be ridiculous.

But they could. There had been an initial attraction seven years ago. What if the spark hadn't died?

And now he'd just shouted at Beth and insulted her ... well, he'd given her every reason to do whatever the hell she liked. God, why couldn't he keep his thoughts to himself?

Of course Beth would tell Kenny. She was just thinking of her son first. As she should do.

Tristan combed his shaking hand through his hair. Anger, jealousy, and fear all rose to the top again. It wasn't even lunchtime and he needed a drink. But pouring himself a whisky at this time of day would be stupid, given the amount of work he had to do before the damn wedding and Christmas Day.

Why did Beth get under his skin so much? Why did he care? Why couldn't he stop thinking about her, even when she made him angry? And had he screwed up their relationship before it had even started? Maybe he should just revert back to the old Tristan, the one who only had time for the estate.

Why had Beth come to tell him about Kenny? It wasn't really any of his business … unless she'd wanted his support, to help her through this. Maybe she wanted him there when she told him.

And he'd not even given her the chance to ask, because in true idiot style, he'd jumped to conclusions. He really did know how to mess things up. Three days before Christmas Day too.

His phone beeped. *Beth.*

He didn't know how to reply. It was best he spoke to her face to face, rather than risk having a text message misinterpreted. This was Beth's problem, and he should support her in dealing with it in her own time and in her own way.

But he knew full well he could never be with a woman who would knowingly hide a man's child from him.

Beth had hoped Tristan might be with her when she eventually told Kenny about George. However, she now realised that their relationship — if they even had a relationship — was far too new, and this was something she had to do by herself.

Jason would be willing to come with her, but she needed him to mind George. Besides, she'd got herself into this mess; it was hers to deal with. Beth had never imagined bumping into George's father. She hadn't thought she would recognise him. For the last seven years, his face had been a blank. The only thing that confirmed what had happened on her eighteenth birthday hadn't been a figment of her imagination was George. He was one hundred per cent real and she loved him with all her heart. She would always protect him.

"Are you sure you want to do this before Christmas?" Jason asked, frowning. They'd put George to bed before having this conversation. Their lounge now looked like Santa's grotto, with decorations hanging from the ceiling and Christmas ornaments lining their bookshelves. Tinsel glistened over picture frames and the Christmas tree twinkled with lights and baubles. The only things missing were the presents, but they would arrive on Christmas Eve with Santa. Beth had told Jason about bumping into Kenny this morning, but not about the row she'd had afterwards with Tristan. "I mean, it's been seven years, what's a week or two more?"

"I don't know. I'm not sure I'll be able to relax until I've got it off my chest."

"But it might ruin Christmas," Jason said, concern etched across his face.

"I think I'd rather go into Christmas knowing whether Kenny wants to be a part of George's life or not."

"If he doesn't, I suppose life goes on as before." He shrugged.

"And if he does, then we'll come to some arrangement."

Jason nodded in agreement. "I'll leave you to make the call. I need to have a shower," he said, getting off the sofa. He kissed Beth on the forehead, as he always did. He used to do it to wind her up when she was a little girl, to remind her how much taller he was. Now she knew it was affection. As George's uncle, he too had a protective streak. Maybe Jason feared he'd lose his fatherly connection with George. She wouldn't let that happen either.

But what if Kenny wanted custody?

The longer she left telling Kenny, now they'd been reacquainted, the worse it would look if she failed to tell him about George.

She had to do this now and worry about the consequences afterwards. She could be worrying about nothing, after all. Kenny seemed to be a nice, friendly guy.

Nervously, she keyed Kenny's number into her phone, adding him as a contact. Her finger hovered over the green button to dial. She took a deep breath and pressed. The phone started ringing.

"Hello, you've reached Kenny at Penketh Plumbing, please leave a message and I will call you as soon as convenient."

Damn it. Answerphone.

"Hey, Kenny, it's Beth. I know you said we should catch up after Christmas, but I'm wondering whether you're free tonight, or tomorrow? Call me on this number."

Her phone rang a minute after she'd hung up. It was Kenny.

"Hey, Elizabeth, or do you prefer Beth?"

"Beth's fine."

"Yeah, sorry, I always let the phone go to voicemail after seven o'clock, otherwise I'd never get a break. If it's an emergency, I call them straight back, but the rest can wait until the following day."

"I understand."

"Anyway, yeah, I can do tomorrow night if you like. I'm pretty knackered tonight; it's been a long day. But I'll make sure I cut it short tomorrow."

"Great."

"Did you fancy going out to eat?"

"Oh, er, yes, sure," she replied.

"I'll pick you up. Say seven?"

"Er, no, no, I'll meet you there," she said. They agreed on a location and then, after hanging up, she started to panic. Did Kenny think it was a date? Should she tell Tristan? What was even going on between her and Tristan?

Beth flicked through the TV channels. Jason entered, smelling a lot less like engine oil and much more like Lynx.

"How did it go?" he asked. She was cradling her phone to her chest.

"Okay. We're meeting tomorrow."

Jason nodded, sitting himself down beside her on the sofa. "Hey, I know this might be short notice, but do you mind if Scott joins us on Christmas Day?"

"Absolutely not." She nudged her brother playfully. "We always have plenty of food." Recently, she'd noticed Jason hadn't come home some evenings, staying late at Scott's. Her brother was as entitled to a relationship as she was.

"Great," he said.

"Does this mean he's becoming one of the family?"

"Yes, it does."

Beth had always imagined big family get-togethers, especially at Christmas. It would be a welcome change to have someone new spending Christmas with them. "Jason," Beth said, "do you think I should tell Tristan I'm meeting Kenny tomorrow night?"

Jason shrugged. "I suppose, if it were me, I'd like to know. You did spend a night together; he's clearly interested in you."

Beth looked down at her hands. "I don't know. We had a row this morning."

CHAPTER 29: WISE WORDS

When Tristan's mother walked in, he was sitting in his warm office — now the boiler had been fixed — and on the phone about removing the tinsel from the Christmas trees. Bridezilla didn't want tinsel.

"Hello, darling," she said cheerily, once he'd put the phone down. She was holding a couple of elaborately decorated giftbags. She always treated Cathy and Anya to a Christmas gift. She dropped the bags on Anya's desk and gave both women a hug. Then she took one of the dog treats she always carried out of her pocket and gave it to Flash, who was lying in his bed next to Tristan's desk. The Border Collie wagged his tail appreciatively. "Why such a long face?"

Was his misery over yesterday's row with Beth really that obvious? Cathy and Anya had been quiet with him all morning, giving each other meaningful looks.

"It's nothing."

"It's clearly not nothing." She sat down in the chair opposite Tristan's desk. "Come on, a problem shared and all that? Is it something to do with this wedding?" The wedding was tomorrow. He'd be glad when it was over. Changing Christmas decorations last minute because the bride had changed her mind had not been on the agenda. He'd never known a more awkward customer, and it was causing him way more stress than he needed at this time of year.

"No, nothing we can't handle — as long as the snow doesn't come back."

"Well, what is it, darling?" she said. "I was going to suggest you invite Beth and George over for Christmas."

Tristan must have winced.

"Ah, now we're getting somewhere." Why was his mother so intuitive? "What have you done?" Then, thankfully, realising Anya and Cathy were going about their business in the office, she said, "Let's take a walk, shall we? I have something I wish to discuss with you anyway."

Tristan agreed, knowing Flash never tired of a walk. He took his coat off the back of his chair, and they left to cut across the grounds.

As they walked, Janine said, "Come on, out with it, tell me."

"Beth bumped into the guy who's George's biological father."

"Oh. Wow. That must be some emotional dilemma for her. I assume the man doesn't know about George?"

"No, he doesn't. And then he was here yesterday fixing the boiler."

"What, you mean Kenny?" His mother knew of Penketh Plumbing. She knew the family through her charity work and various clubs she belonged to in the village. "No wonder she's not bumped into him before now. He was living in London. He's returned, tired of the rat race apparently, to take over his dad's business. Seems to be the done thing." She looked at Tristan knowingly. Tristan was here, after all, looking after his late father's business.

They made their way to Elowen's grave. There lay a Christmas wreath. His mother had already visited. The bench near it was still covered in snow, so they remained standing.

"So why have you two fallen out?"

"Mum, I need to tell you something, about me and Kimmie."

She looked at him quizzically. "Shall we continue on to your cottage so you can make me a cup of tea, if there is more to it?"

"Yes, okay."

As they cut across the grounds and made their way over to the cottage, Tristan confessed to his mother about Kimmie and her decision to abort their baby without Tristan's knowledge.

"It's not an easy decision, Tristan. Kimmie must have had her reasons."

"I know. I know. But we could have made that decision together."

"Maybe she was worried you'd talk her out of it," Janine said. "But it's so long ago now, darling. It's all water under the bridge; you need to let that go."

He nodded. "So, when Beth said she wasn't sure about telling Kenny he was a father, I spoke before I thought." *As usual.*

Once they reached the cottage, Tristan made them both a cup of tea in the kitchen.

"You got cross with Beth and stormed off. You're just like your father at times!" She laughed at him.

"But how do I make things better between us?"

"Oh, darling, I'm sure if you apologise, she'll forgive you. And maybe tell her what you've told me about Kimmie. You have to understand, she's just had her world turned upside down. She probably never imagined having to deal with George's father turning up in her life. She's such a sensible woman, with that boy's best interests at heart. It's so much harder for mums these days. They have so much more pressure on them than I did in my day. And it's very hard to let go of that protectiveness you feel for your child. And to lose one is unbearable." She was reflecting on Elowen now. Stillborn. Carried for nine months, Janine's love for her child growing each day. Tristan watched his mother regain her composure. "I am awfully proud of you, you know?" She kissed him on the cheek.

"Thanks, Mum. It's not been easy."

"I know it hasn't, darling. Your dad would be proud."

Tristan took a moment to gather his composure now. He wished his father could see what he'd done to turn the estate around. His thoughts quickly returned to his present troubles. "What if Beth decides to make a go of it with Kenny, George's father?"

"Oh, Tristan, just because they had one night together and produced a child, it doesn't mean they are meant to be together. And if Kenny does want to be a part of George's life — which I am sure he will do — it doesn't mean you can't be too. Beth needs you, maybe more than she realises." Janine patted his arm. "After everything with her parents... Which leads me on to the reason I came to see you. I think I've found them."

"Who?"

"Her parents."

"Oh, Mum, we might be meddling with something even bigger that doesn't concern us." Beth's emotions were already in turmoil over George's father. Would she cope with her parents trying to get back in touch with her, too?

"Maybe. But I can't help thinking there's been a misunderstanding — from both sides — and the sooner it's fixed, the better."

CHAPTER 30: A SURPRISE GIFT

Two days until Christmas

Whether Tristan was avoiding her, or he was just busy, Beth didn't know. She hadn't seen him all day. She assumed that with the wedding tomorrow, he was snowed under. Quite literally. He now had a snow machine to operate.

She closed the boutique early to head home. With no appointments booked in until the beginning of January, and all the orders from the fashion show placed, she was shutting the shop until after the New Year. But with the winter sale in January, and preparing for the arrival of the spring/summer collection in February, there was plenty she could do before then. It would pay to come in for a day or two over the Christmas period and get organised before things got busy with appointments.

With it being the school holidays, she'd brought George in with her today. She had let him walk over with a giftbag for Seb, containing a bottle of red wine. Nervously, she'd watched, worried he might drop the bag, but he'd held it as she'd showed him, keeping one hand underneath. Guessing the fragility of the giftbag's contents, Seb had quickly relieved George of his burden. He had insisted George stay with him to allow Beth to concentrate on her work. Under the twinkling fairy lights in the courtyard, which were on day and night, Seb and George built a little snowman with the remaining snow. It had meant she could finish her work and get home earlier. Anxiety hung over her, like the dark clouds in the sky, knowing she was meeting Kenny that evening.

Since Beth had last texted Tristan, he hadn't texted her back. And now she worried that if she messaged again, she'd appear needy. But he had been the one to storm off yesterday, she reminded herself. So maybe he needed the time to cool off, visit his man cave, as Jason put it, and he'd come out when he was good and ready. There was no point poking the bear while he was still in his cave. Jason's words, not hers.

At home, she served George his tea and left Jason's in the oven. Her stomach fluttered with nerves at the thought of meeting Kenny. What if he took the news badly?

Jason walked through the door, apologising for running late.

"It's okay, I don't have to leave just yet," she said, as he washed his oil-stained hands at the kitchen sink. "George is in the lounge watching television." She'd stuck on a Christmas movie to add to the Christmas magic and George's excitement. "Your dinner is in the oven."

"Have you heard from Tristan?" he asked. He dried his hands, then donning oven gloves, he retrieved his meal of sausages and mash with onion gravy and peas.

"No," she replied.

"He'll come round. You'd better go — look at the time." The kitchen clock read six forty-five. She was meeting Kenny at seven. She kissed her brother on the cheek and headed out.

Despite having to drive cautiously in the remaining snow, Beth made it to The Cormorant pub on time. The car park was full, but she managed to squeeze her small Fiat 500c into one of the last spaces. Before getting out of her car, she texted Kenny to say that she'd arrived. He replied: *I'm already inside.*

Beth walked into the pub to find it noisy with people, the warmth welcoming her in. Of course, leading up to Christmas, with work parties and friends gathering, it would be busy. Christmas songs were playing over the din of chatter. The whole pub was decked out with garlands and tinsel, and a large Christmas tree stood in the corner near the pool table. She recognised Tristan's cousin, Joe, busy behind the bar, pulling pints. He was wearing an elf T-shirt.

Kenny waved her over to a small table near the window.

"Good job I had the foresight to book a table," he said, standing up as Beth approached. He gave her a kiss on the cheek, and then they both sat down. "It's really good to see you," he added eagerly. He was wearing jeans and a long-sleeved shirt. He scrubbed up well, she thought, and his spicy, citrus aftershave was very pleasant. A real transformation from the guy she had bumped into at the supermarket smelling of drains.

"It's good to see you, too," she said. And she meant it. She didn't look back at her one night with Kenny with negative feelings. She couldn't remember it as clearly as she'd have hoped, but she didn't regret it. She had George.

"I suggest we take a look at the menu, and I'll brave the bar to go and order."

While they perused the menu, there was an awkward silence.

Once they had made their choices, Kenny got up from the table, tucking a menu under his arm. Fifteen minutes later, he returned, carrying a pint of Cornish lager and a small glass of white wine for Beth. She decided to have just the one, hoping this would take the edge off her nerves, and give her the courage to tell Kenny about his son. She reached for her purse to pay her share, but he pushed her hand away.

"My treat," he said.

This made her worry that he thought it might be a date, but she smiled her thanks. Before each taking a sip of their drinks, they clinked glasses.

Beth decided to start the conversational ball rolling by asking Kenny what he'd been up to since their brief encounter. She wanted to assess what kind of a guy he was before dropping her bombshell.

"So, I think when I met you, I was about to go travelling," he said. Yes, she remembered now. Hence, they had decided it would be a night of fun with no commitment and she'd sloped off early in the morning for fear of teasing and questions from his housemates. "I did that for a year or so — absolutely loved it — and to cut a long story short, I'd met a girl whilst travelling, as you do, so I moved to London to be with her, and finished my training as a plumber there." He took a sip of his lager. "Then, this summer, after that hadn't worked out, I decided that city life wasn't really for me, so I came home and took over from Dad, who wanted to reduce his workload, take Mum on more holidays and all that." Kenny winked. "So that's why you haven't bumped into me before now. I only moved back a few months ago. I actually live in Kittiwake Cove now."

"Oh right," she said. Gosh, if she had bumped into him again years ago, what a different life she might be leading right now.

The food arrived. Both had ordered the beer-battered cod and chips, deciding they would be eating enough turkey in a couple of days' time. While they tucked into their food, sprinkling salt and vinegar on the chips, there was a silence. Beth couldn't decide if it was awkward or not.

"What about you? Have you been in Kittiwake Cove all this time?"

Beth nodded because she had her mouth full. This was it: she had to confess now, otherwise it would look odd if she left it to the end of the evening. "Yes, yes, I've been here all this time."

"Weren't you going to university after your A-levels?"

Boy, he did have a good memory.

"I didn't go in the end."

"Really? You seemed so keen. What were you going to study?" He clicked his fingers excitedly, as if to recall the memory.

"Fashion Design," she said, helping him out.

"What happened? Why didn't you go?" He frowned at her.

Beth took a deep breath and finished her wine.

"Shall I get you another?" He stood up and went to take her glass, but she shook her head, placing her hand on his.

"Kenny, I have something to tell you. You might want to sit down."

"Is everything okay?" His expression sobered. He sat down, pulling his chair in closer to the table. "Beth?"

"Yes, everything is fine, but I'm not sure how you're going to react to my news."

He frowned some more, taking a sip from his drink. He still had half a pint. "Are you sure you don't want a drink?"

Now she thought about it, her throat was dry. "Just a glass of water will do."

He was off his seat and to the bar. Beth tried to gather her thoughts on how best to tell him. *Get it over and done with.* He returned rather quickly with a tall tumbler filled with water and ice. A slice of lemon floated on the top. She took a sip.

"I don't know how to say this. I don't wish to ruin your Christmas, and I swear I want nothing from you, if you don't want to give it," she said. "That is not why I am here." He looked at her blankly. "That night, seven years ago … I fell pregnant." All the colour drained out of Kenny's face. "I had a son nine months later."

"Shit!" he said. His hands flew to his head and he leaned back in his chair. "But we…?"

She shrugged. "I know." They had used a condom, but something must have gone wrong.

"Are you sure he's mine?"

"I promise you, he's your son, Kenny."

"Shit!" Kenny said again. He lifted his lager to his lips and took several gulps. She remained silent, allowing him to digest this information.

"I couldn't tell you because I didn't have your number, and I couldn't really remember your name. And I didn't realise I was pregnant until weeks later. Then my life did turn to shit for a while." She dropped her gaze for a moment. "My parents didn't support me…"

"What?"

She shook her head. She didn't really want to go into that part of her life. "When I bumped into you at the supermarket, I really didn't know what to do or say, and I thought I'd wait until after Christmas, but then I bumped into you again, yesterday —"

"What's his name?" Kenny burst out, interrupting Beth.

She gave a meek smile. "His name is George. I must have subconsciously remembered your name." Kenny beamed back.

"George. I like that," he said. "So he's … six?" Beth could see Kenny doing his mental arithmetic.

"Yes, he's six. Now in Year One at school." Beth relaxed. Kenny hadn't flown off the handle and thrown a drink in her face. "He really loves school." She proudly told Kenny a little about George, including his birthday.

"Have you got any pictures? Can I see what he looks like?"

Kenny's eagerness put Beth at ease. She fetched her phone out of her handbag. Kenny pulled his chair around to be closer to Beth, resting his arm on the back of her chair, both of them huddled over her phone as they flicked through the photos.

"I don't have many of him as a baby on here. But I think there are loads on my Facebook," she said. "This is him sledging — Jason took this one."

"Jason?"

"He's my brother. We live with him. He took me in. He was there for the birth."

"So, George has had a father figure in his life?"

Beth nodded. For some reason tears were forming, and she wasn't sure why. Relief, maybe, that Kenny was being so receptive about his son.

"Beth?"

She looked up to see a man standing next to their table. He was in silhouette against the light from the bar behind him, so it took Beth a second to realise who it was. "Tristan?"

"You're looking very cosy," he said pointedly. His hands were shoved into his pockets.

Beth frowned. She was about to reply that she was just showing Kenny photos of George, but she stopped herself. It was none of his business. "How did you know I was here?"

"I didn't. I called in to see Joe."

Kenny removed his arm that had been resting on the back of her chair and stood up. It was then that Beth understood Tristan's reaction. She and Kenny had been sitting very close.

"Hey, Tristan, man, Beth and I are just catching up... I didn't realise I was treading on anyone's toes."

"You're not," Beth said sharply. She also got to her feet.

Joe appeared at Tristan's side. "Everything okay?" He was probably sensing hostility coming off Tristan like steam from a dung pile. And it was totally misplaced.

"Tristan, I'm talking to Kenny, and this is very important. Can we talk tomorrow?" He should be happy she was telling Kenny about George.

Oh, Beth thought as the penny dropped. *He's jealous.*

Before she could say anything to reassure him that nothing was happening between her and Kenny, other than her confessing to him that he had a son, Tristan shrugged Joe's arm off and swept out of the pub.

Joe looked askance at Kenny and Beth. Beth chewed her lip, and Joe gave a nonchalant, laidback shrug, as if to say it was none of his business. Satisfied that the calm atmosphere had returned with the disappearance of Tristan, he left them both to it.

"Look, Kenny, I'd best get home. It is getting late."

"Sure, sure." They both fetched their jackets off the back of their chairs and wrapped up warm.

"Thank you for taking it so well," she said. "I was so worried about telling you."

"It feels a bit strange to think I've been a dad all this time. And I feel bad I've not supported you." Kenny walked Beth to her car.

"It wasn't your fault," she said, fumbling for her keys in her handbag.

"I'd like to meet him, if I may?" Kenny said. He shuffled from foot to foot, looking nervous for the first time.

"Yes, of course. But I need to speak to George first."

"Hey, we can take this slow. But I don't want to miss out on any more."

"I understand. But we need to take this one step at a time." Beth had a sudden vision of parting with her son at weekends, so that he could see his dad. But it wouldn't be fair on George to keep him away from his father, especially if his father did want to play a part in his life.

She wouldn't just throw George into the deep end with a complete stranger. Which was what Kenny was until George — and Beth — got to know him a bit more. Kenny would need to have supervised visits with George until everyone was comfortable.

"Hey, that was one hell of a Christmas surprise," Kenny said, smiling, clearly happy about the revelation.

"Maybe we can arrange for you to come over one day over the Christmas holidays, before George goes back to school. What about Boxing Day?"

"Boxing Day would be great!"

They hugged awkwardly, Kenny brushing her cheek with a brief kiss, and agreed to stay in touch. Kenny assured Beth that George's best interests would be their priority.

She drove home, her heart lighter. The anxiety over Kenny had lifted, but she was still troubled by thoughts of Tristan.

CHAPTER 31: MINCE PIES

Christmas Eve

Tristan was bossing everyone around at Trenouth Manor like a bear with a sore head. As he busily organised the last-minute wedding preparations for his most difficult bride to date, all he could think about was finding Beth and Kenny sitting in the pub, and how he'd acted like a jealous fool. Really, he should have been relieved to see Beth talking to Kenny, because it had meant that she was telling him about George. But they had looked so cosy together…

He was angry with himself and therefore taking it out on the staff. He was impatient and irritable with everyone, from the caterers polishing the cutlery to his groundsmen, who he'd left in charge of the snow machine. It was Christmas Eve. He really needed to get into the festive spirit.

He hadn't slept well, tossing and turning with the fear of losing Beth, the green-eyed monster whispering in his ear… What if Kenny and Beth *did* decide to make a go of it for George's sake? What if they found that their initial attraction was still there, several years on? What if his latest screw-up had pushed Beth away from him … and into Kenny's arms?

He'd half hoped George's father would be some layabout loser and wouldn't want anything to do with the boy. He didn't know Kenny well, but he knew his family. Janine certainly did, but she knew everyone in the village, and she said Kenny would not be the sort of man to shirk his responsibility.

"Yes, that there!" Tristan shouted at someone carrying a planter, which contained trailing silk flowers, with red helium balloons rising from it. "In the marquee." So much for delegating.

Actually, no, that's what he should do. He had said as much to Beth on the evening they'd shared together — which felt like a lifetime ago. How had they got so close only to drift so far apart? If he wanted Beth in his life, he needed to prove that he could make time for her. The estate, with the right staff, could run itself well. He didn't need to be watching over Trenouth Manor twenty-four-seven. Not anymore.

He hunted down Anya who, in complete contrast to his current mood, was calmly pointing staff and suppliers in the right direction, checking the flower delivery, and showing where the cake should go, with her habitual ease and organisation. That's why he'd hired her. She wore a headset linked to a walkie-talkie, with a clipboard in her hands and her mobile poking out of her back trouser pocket. He knew Cathy would be in the office supporting Anya, too.

"Are you okay if I pop out? Do you need me?"

Anya shook her head. "No, if you need to go, you go." She had everything under control. She was totally trustworthy. Next year, he'd give her a raise.

"I need to go see Beth."

"Well, go!" She shooed him off.

Seb, who was shutting his workshop, confirmed that Beth wasn't coming in to the boutique today. It was Christmas Eve. There was a note on the door with the date she would be returning after Christmas.

Tristan hurried over to his cottage with Flash, who made straight for his bed, and grabbed the keys to his Range Rover. He wanted to see Beth in person. Thankfully, his mother had given him a good excuse, if turning up to say he was sorry wasn't a good enough one.

"That's it, press the star-shaped cutter into the pastry…" Beth guided George's hand. They were making mince pies. On the kitchen counter, a twelve-hole non-stick cupcake tin contained twelve partly made mince pies with the brandy-fed mincemeat spooned in, and now they were cutting out the tops in star shapes. How George had managed to get flour in his hair and on his nose she would never know. His clothes were only partially protected by an apron. But despite the inevitable mess, she remained as patient as she could. Jason was only working for the morning and would be returning after lunch — then Christmas would officially start.

Much as she loved building her business, Beth treasured this time with her son. George was at the perfect age, when Christmas really was magical. She had to cherish these wonderful moments. There was so much pressure to be the perfect mum, but listening to some of the other mothers at school, Beth knew mums were allowed an off day. She was only human, after all. But today, nothing could dampen her happy mood.

They popped the first tray in the oven and started to make another lot, rolling out the next batch of pastry. The recipe made nearly thirty mince pies, if her memory served her right from last year. Just as George was about to cut the first circle for the base of the mince pies, the doorbell rang. Beth was puzzled. It couldn't be Jason. He had his own key. But she wasn't expecting any visitors.

"Wait there, George… Yes, cut them out, like I showed you. Then we'll spoon the mincemeat in."

Wiping her hands on a tea towel, she opened the front door. *Tristan.*

"Hi," he said, rocking on his heels on the doorstep.

"Hi," she said, frowning.

"Can I come in? Please?"

"Oh, uh, sure." Beth dreaded to think what she looked like. Hair scraped back, possibly as much flour on her face as George had. The pair of them probably looked a right state.

Tristan followed her into the small, square kitchen, which now felt even tinier with his presence, even though he remained in the doorway. "I'm sorry about last night," he said.

Beth ignored him and continued helping George cut out the pastry.

"Did you tell *him* about —?"

"*Shhh…*" She cupped her floury hand over Tristan's mouth and glared at him, before ushering him quickly out of the kitchen. "I've not said anything to George yet." She lowered her voice. "If you must know, we decided he would come over as a friend and get to know George before we reveal the full truth. I didn't want to bombard George with it all at once."

"I wasn't going to say anything in front of George," he hissed back.

"It sounded like you were." She handed him the tea towel. He now had flour on his face. If she'd been in a better mood with him, she'd have laughed. He'd turned up, smartly dressed, and now he was covered with a dusting of white powder. Actually, she couldn't help smirking.

"I'm sorry if I fu— *fudged* this up…" He corrected himself swiftly, seeing George appear in the hallway.

"Mummy, I've finished."

"I'll be there in a sec, George."

The oven beeped.

"Wait a minute, Tristan." She headed back into the kitchen, grabbed the oven gloves, and retrieved the cooked mince pies.

251

"Stand back, sweetheart, please," she said to George, who was eager to see the results.

"Wow, they smell great," Tristan added, following Beth eagerly back into the kitchen.

"Is Flash with you?" George's little voice asked. He looked up at Tristan adoringly.

"Sorry, mate, I left him at the house. Which is a good job, or he'd be pinching the mince pies — like I might have to." He reached over Beth, tantalisingly close, as she was transferring them from the hot tray to a cooling rack.

She smacked his hand. "They're too hot!" She turned, her face inches from his, a magnetic force pulling her close to him. She wanted to kiss him, but the stubbornness inside her fought the impulse. Tristan was looking at her like she was one of the mince pies, as if he could devour her any moment. Beth found her voice. "Why are you here?" She glanced at George to remind Tristan her son was present, and he stepped back. She breathed a little more freely.

"I came here to let you know that Mum has invited you all over on Boxing Day."

"Oh!"

"Can we go, Mummy? Can we?" George tugged at her arm.

"Uh, yes, I think so, but we do have a guest coming over."

"Who?" Tristan frowned, then held his hands up defensively. "Sorry, none of my business."

"My old friend, Kenny, is coming to visit," Beth said as casually as she could.

"Oh." Tristan nodded nonchalantly.

"He's coming for lunch, so would it be okay if we came over in the evening?"

"Is Uncle Jay-Jay invited?" George said.

Tristan crouched down to George's height. "Of course, the more the merrier!"

"And Flash?"

"Yes, Flash will be there." Then, smiling up at Beth, he said, "And that's fine, I'll let Mum know." On his way out, Tristan paused and kissed Beth on the cheek, sending a pulse of heat and excitement down her spine. With his thumb, he rubbed her other cheek tenderly. "I'll see you on Boxing Day. Have a good Christmas."

"You too."

Shutting the front door, Beth wondered if she should have invited him over for Christmas Day. Jason was having Scott over. She pulled open the door to watch the Range Rover drive off. Tristan didn't see her waving frantically as she shouted his name.

She hadn't even shown him the Christmas tree that she, Jason and George, amidst the madness of all the Christmas events, had managed to find the time to decorate. Larger than they would normally buy, it stood proudly in front of the patio doors in their lounge, decked out in fairy lights, tinsel and baubles. There were some presents already wrapped and placed under it. One was for Tristan. The rest Santa would deliver tonight.

CHAPTER 32: FESTIVITIES

Christmas Day

"He's been! He's been!"

George had Jason and Beth up early. No matter how late they put him to bed on Christmas Eve, he was still always up at the crack of dawn. He'd dragged his large stocking, stuffed full of presents, into Beth's bedroom, before running into Jason's room to wake him up, telling him he had to join them. Wrapped in his thick, fluffy dressing gown, Jason was wearily perched on the side of Beth's bed, yawning and rubbing his eyes, and trying to capture George's surprise and delight on video with his phone. Beth remained under the duvet, trying to keep out of the way of the filming, as they watched George's face as he opened the presents in his stocking from Santa. It was wonderful to see the little boy's excitement about even the smallest of gifts.

Once he'd finished emptying his stocking, Jason went down to the kitchen to put the kettle on while Beth supervised George and his huge pile of presents. George had remembered to check on the mince pies, sherry and carrot he'd left out for Santa. Jason had snapped off the carrot, putting it back in the fridge, and then had nibbled the remnants to make it look as if Rudolf had chomped at it. Beth had had one of the mince pies and Jason had eaten the other. He always let her have the sherry. Beth had a taste for it, especially at Christmas.

As their house didn't have a chimney, George left out a special key for Santa. That was now beside the plate with the crumbs from the mince pies and the gnawed end of the carrot.

There was so much to think about before heading to bed the night before Christmas. She didn't dare put the presents or mince pies out too early, in case George woke up. What if he came down because he couldn't sleep and found Jason and Beth eating them? Explain that to a small child. She had never known anything as stressful as Christmas Eve in all her life, keeping the magical secret of Santa to a six-year-old.

But his cute, excited face in the morning was totally worth it.

By the time George had finished unwrapping his presents, there was a huge pile of paper in the middle of the lounge. Beth had found Spiderman-related toys for him, amongst other things, which he was thrilled about. His main present from her and Jason had been a Playmobil pirate ship. It had been at the top of his list to Santa.

Scott arrived at around midday. Beth hadn't properly observed Scott when they had first met. Now she noticed he was similar in height to Jason, but stockier, like he visited the gym regularly, with short blond hair and green eyes. He had both ears pierced and up the left-hand side of his neck Beth spied a tattoo, the main design hidden by the collar of his shirt. Scott came bearing a bottle of prosecco and a bottle of whisky. He had a little gift for George, too, whose expression changed to pure joy as it was handed to him. He eagerly tore open the paper and was thrilled to reveal a Cadbury's selection pack. He thanked Scott with a hug that almost knocked him off balance, then put the gift in a pile with the rest of his hoard. He'd already started building some Lego he'd received and playing with his new Matchbox cars. While Beth concentrated on cooking the Christmas dinner, Scott and Jason helped George put together the Playmobil pirate ship.

With Christmas music playing in the background and a Nigella-inspired mulled cider on the go in the slow cooker, the house smelled of all things Christmas: cinnamon, clementines, pine needles and roast dinner.

They sat down to eat at two o'clock. Scott's initial nerves at being introduced into their family circle had disappeared, and now they were all wearing their paper hats from the crackers they'd pulled and laughing at the bad jokes. The booze was probably helping.

They decided to postpone the lighting of the Christmas pudding until later, as they were all stuffed. All the pigs in blankets had been devoured, and she'd roasted extra! Beth let George leave the table to play with his toys and the three adults remained seated, rubbing their full bellies.

"I was wondering if I should invite Tristan over," Beth said, the prosecco making her voice her thoughts out loud.

"Yeah, go on," Jason said. He turned to Scott. "Tristan owns the Trenouth Estate; you know, where Beth has her boutique. He's sweet on my baby sister."

"Not sure about sweet…" Beth mumbled.

"He came to see you yesterday. He likes you more than you realise."

"I just feel we've left things up in the air," Beth said. She felt so torn. It was Christmas, and perhaps she should forgive Tristan for his outburst the other day. Part of her was still angry with him … but then, yesterday…

"Call him," Jason urged, Scott concurring.

Jason filled Scott in on the situation while Beth fetched her phone. She stepped out to the kitchen and dialled Tristan's number.

"Hello, Beth. Merry Christmas," he answered.

"Merry Christmas… Tristan, I was just thinking, if you weren't doing anything, if you wanted to come over this evening, you'd be more than welcome…"

"Yeah, I'd love to —"

"We usually just watch a film or play a boardgame," she interrupted him, riddled with nerves.

"Beth, but I can't, I'm sorry," he said softly.

"Oh." She could hear laughter and women's voices in the background. Nancy?

"I'm over at my aunt's. All of my cousins are here, and I've probably had a bit too much to drink now to get in a car," he said, "otherwise I would."

"Okay." His sincere tone instantly dispelled Beth's ridiculous thoughts of him being with Nancy.

Tristan continued, "I just thought it might be too early in our relationship, you know, to mention Christmas Day. I knew you'd be busy with George, and I wasn't sure of your plans. The run-up to Christmas became rather fraught at times…"

Why was a lump forming in her throat? She wished more than anything to have Tristan here right now. "I understand," she said, fearing the tremor in her voice might betray her. "We'll see each other tomorrow evening."

"Yes, and I'm really looking forward to that," Tristan said eagerly. "Look, I must go, we're in the middle of playing Monopoly and I'm winning. But my cousins are rather good at cheating."

"Okay, I'll let you go."

"See you tomorrow."

"Yes, see you tomorrow," Beth said. Then, "I love you."

Oh my God! Her hand flew to her mouth. Why had she said that? The words had slipped off her tongue without a thought.

He hadn't responded, so she hoped he'd hung up. Maybe he hadn't heard? She really hoped he hadn't.

CHAPTER 33: A SPECIAL GUEST

Boxing Day

George had allowed Beth a small lie in. But he was still up way too early, considering how late she'd gone to bed.

Scott had stayed over, as they'd ended up opening the bottle of Scotch he'd brought. Once George was in bed, exhausted from the excitement of the day, Beth had joined them for a nightcap, even though whisky wasn't really her thing. Drinking, laughing and joking, and raiding the Quality Street tin, the three of them had played cards. Beth really liked Scott, having spent the day getting to know him, and was impressed by how easily he fitted in with their small, complicated family. He was a builder, which explained the flatbed truck Jason had borrowed to deliver the sofa to her boutique. Apparently, they had met when Scott's truck had broken down and was towed to Jason and Archie's garage. She liked that he was good with George too. Scott's brother had kids, so he wasn't allergic to small children. And it was heart-warming to see her brother so happy. Their old family was lost to them, but she and Jason were steadily building a new family of their own. They might even need a bigger house one day.

Now she was keeping George quiet downstairs. After breakfast, and with a fresh cup of coffee, she snuggled up with him on the sofa to watch *Cars*, one of his favourite films. She imagined Jason and Scott might have sore heads, judging by the almost empty bottle of whisky, but she would have to remind Jason to be ready for Kenny at some point. He was arriving at lunchtime.

She still felt apprehensive about George meeting his father. There were so many unknowns. Would it change the dynamic of their relationship? What if he started demanding unreasonable access?

And then, another thought came to her: what if Kenny was homophobic?

She shook that thought away. *Highly unlikely. One step at a time.*

At around half-past eight, she left George to watch the end of his film while she showered and got dressed. She decided to make a cold buffet for lunch.

Before Kenny was due to arrive, Scott said his goodbyes. He was off to spend Boxing Day with his parents and family. He gave Beth a hug. The man was solid. She could feel his muscles bulging under the seam of his tight cotton shirt.

"Nice to meet you properly," Scott said, smiling at Beth and ruffling George's hair.

"Lovely to finally meet you too," Beth said. "Even if you're a bit of a card shark!" Scott had won a lot of the card games last night. Good job they'd only been playing with pennies.

"Having two older brothers and learning at a young age, I needed a poker face."

"Yeah, my poker face is rubbish."

"You can't lie for toffee, sis," Jason added, laughing. "Way too honest for your own good."

The red hair and the freckles didn't help either.

What was worse, they hadn't even been playing Poker! They'd started off playing things like Cheat and Old Maid, then moved on to playing trickier games like Newmarket for pennies once George had gone to bed.

Beth led George into the lounge so that Jason and Scott could say their goodbyes privately. She had a feeling they would be seeing a lot more of Scott, now he'd been properly introduced.

Kenny arrived on time at twelve noon. Once again, she felt a small jolt of surprise when she saw him freshly shaven, his hair gelled and smelling clean. She really needed to forget that first image she had of him in the supermarket. He was smartly dressed in dark blue denim jeans and was wearing a Christmas jumper over his shirt. He came armed with a couple of Christmas giftbags, which Beth could see George had his eye on.

"Tea or coffee, or something stronger?" Jason asked him, as they sat down in the lounge.

"Tea — milk, one sugar, please," Kenny said. Beth could see he was nervous too, perched awkwardly on the edge of the sofa with the giftbags between his legs.

"George, this is an old friend of mine, Kenny," Beth said, anxious to alleviate any tension.

The small boy held out his hand and Kenny tentatively shook it, a grin spreading over his face. "Hello, George," he said.

They swapped pleasantries about what they had been up to on Christmas Day until Jason appeared with a tray of mugs of tea for everyone.

"I hope you don't mind, but I couldn't come empty-handed," Kenny said. "Is it okay if George has his present now?"

"Can I, Mummy? Please?"

Beth couldn't contain the laughter in her voice. "Yes, I'm sure you can."

Kenny knelt on the carpet to be level with George, who had been playing with his new Spiderman toys while the adults talked. He was completely oblivious to the significance of this meeting with Kenny. Hopefully, it wouldn't be so overwhelming for him if Kenny became a friend first. Kenny handed George the largest of the two giftbags. He'd checked with Beth what George liked, and she'd assured him that he couldn't go wrong with Lego. George tore open the paper eagerly, revealing a Lego *Star Wars* set.

"Wow! Thank you, Kenny," George said, his eyes wide.

"I always wanted something like this as a kid," Kenny said.

Jason was down on the floor too. "So did I!"

Star Wars. That would connect the boys. Jason had been patiently waiting for George to get a bit older before he introduced him to the films.

"Come on, George, open it up. We'll help you build it," Jason said eagerly.

"This is a little something for you," Kenny said, handing Beth the other giftbag.

"Oh, thank you." She prised it open. There were two gifts. One was a posh box of chocolates from Hotel Chocolat and the other was a Christmas jumper.

"It's a tradition in our household to wear Christmas jumpers over the holidays," Kenny said, smiling at her.

Fortunately, it wasn't a tasteless one with a garish elf or reindeer on the front. It was red, with a Christmassy pattern woven into it. Baubles and holly. It was actually quite pretty. Beth pulled it over her head and said, "How do I look?"

Kenny looked up admiringly. "Lovely."

Beth was annoyed to feel a blush rise to her cheeks. "Thank you," she replied primly.

Kenny, as if remembering the real reason for his visit, turned his attention back to George. Satisfied that they were bonding over the Lego, Beth left them to it to prepare lunch. A few minutes later, Jason joined her in the kitchen.

"So, tell me, what do you think of Kenny?" she asked, keeping her voice low, as she pulled a plate of turkey sandwiches out of the fridge.

"Well, you could have slept with worse on your eighteenth," Jason said, smirking. Then, he added reassuringly, "He's a nice guy." He placed a supportive hand on Beth's shoulder. She smiled, feeling her throat tighten and her emotions coming to the surface. Relief, joy, and love for George. Jason pulled her into a hug, rubbing her back. "You don't need to worry. It'll be all right."

Together they laid out the cold buffet on the dining table, which was already adorned with Christmas crackers and candles. As Beth placed a jar of pickled onions down, she made a mental note to lay off them, knowing she had a trip to Tristan's mother's later. Alongside the cheese and biscuits and the sandwiches, there was a bowl of salad, celery sticks, carrot sticks and cherry tomatoes. Just because it was Christmas, they still needed their five-a-day. Or at least, George did!

They returned to the lounge to find George ripping open another present that had been forgotten with the excitement of his *Star Wars* Lego. Kenny had also bought George a Christmas jumper. With Kenny's help, he pulled it over his Spiderman T-shirt. His was more garish than Beth's: dark blue with Rudolf on the front with a flashing red nose. Chuffed with the additional gift, George kept pressing the nose to make it light up.

Around the dining table, they pulled crackers and told the bad jokes. It was like Christmas Day all over again.

Kenny would fit in with their family. Beth could see that with her own eyes. Jason was right; she had nothing to worry about. After lunch, they played a round of Frustration, which George had received in his pile of Christmas goodies.

Before they knew it, it was time for Kenny to leave. They needed to get ready to go to Janine's.

"Will you be seeing my mummy again?" George asked innocently.

"Yes, and I'd like to see more of you," Kenny replied, placing a hand on George's shoulder affectionately. "Would you like that?"

George beamed. "Yes! Next time, we can play Hungry Hippos. I got that last year for Christmas."

"It's a date, buddy."

Beth led Kenny to the front door. As Jason carried him upstairs to get washed, George waved and shouted, "Bye, Kenny!"

"Thanks for today. He's a great kid," Kenny said. "You've done an amazing job on your own."

"I've had Jason. He's been my rock at times."

"Well, now I hope I can be there to support you, too."

Beth nodded. "Yes, perhaps after a couple more meetings, we might be able to tell George the truth."

Kenny stepped closer to Beth and touched her arm. "I'd like that very much. But what I said to George is also true. I'd like to see more of you, Beth."

He was electrifyingly close. Heat rose to her cheeks. All afternoon she had just been seeing Kenny as George's father. Even though it had been fun, she wasn't sure she wanted to revisit what had happened between them seven years ago.

"Just think," he continued, his gaze fixed on hers, "how wonderful it would be for George if we hit it off…"

"Oh." Beth gasped, unable to form any words.

"Hey, I wouldn't expect us to just jump into bed, like the last time. I understand we need to get to know one another, properly," Kenny said, clearly recognising she was in shock.

"Kenny ... I don't know..." Beth said, stuttering. "I think it's important we just remain friends... What if it didn't work out? George would then have two parents who might not like one another. I really want us to be friends." And she wasn't sure she saw Kenny that way anymore. Yes, she could see why she'd had a fling with him. He was handsome, funny, kind ... but something was missing. That spark, that chemistry... If there had been a spark seven years ago, would she have run away so fast in the morning?

"Hey, I understand ... one step at a time, but I do like you Beth..." He tucked her hair behind her left ear, his fingers lingering by her chin.

"It's just — Tristan..." She chewed her bottom lip.

"Oh, right ... well, the offer's there." He winked. He pulled her into a hug, his warmth and strength enveloping her. "Thank you for letting me meet my son." His breath was pleasantly warm on her neck.

When he released her, she said, "He's not at school this week, so if you're not busy, maybe you can come for tea one evening?"

"I'd love that."

"I'll text you tomorrow," she said, slightly relieved when Kenny stepped out the front door, hoping she had made the right decision. If she tried to make a relationship work with Kenny, George would have a complete family. But would it work?

CHAPTER 34: THREE LITTLE WORDS

George insisted on wearing Kenny's Christmas jumper to Janine's, so Beth wore hers too. Considering her initial apprehension about Kenny, she now felt very much at ease with him entering their lives. Any doubts she had been having were ebbing away. But she still wanted to take the introduction to George slowly.

Jason drove to Janine's, saying that his liver needed to recover after the amount of whisky he'd drunk with Scott the night before. They found Janine's house easily enough, situated off a country lane not far from Trenouth Manor. When giving Beth directions, Tristan had mentioned it was a converted barn that had once been a part of the estate. Jason parked beside Tristan's Audi.

"Come in, come in." Janine ushered them in from the cold. It was only four-thirty, but it was almost dark, with dark clouds looming. Beth prayed it didn't snow again. "Oh, I love the jumper," Janine said, helping George off with his coat. Flash greeted him ecstatically, wagging his tail and licking his hand.

Beth had imagined that Janine's house would be as sleek and immaculate as she always appeared, impeccably dressed in her trouser suits. But the converted barn oozed rustic charm with thick wooden beams crisscrossing the walls and ceilings, and exposed stone walls. In the open-plan living area there were bookcases loaded with books, Christmas ornaments, and photographs of friends and family. There were also cheerful lamps, vibrant artwork hanging on the walls, and colourful rugs covering the wood flooring. A roaring fire was blazing in the large fireplace, which was flanked by comfortable leather sofas with cream and red scatter cushions. In one corner, near the patio doors, stood a floor-to-ceiling Christmas tree, so tall that the top of the fairy's head touched the thick beam in the ceiling. It was beautifully decorated in silver and red with white fairy lights. Underneath it lay a pile of unopened presents.

The only area that appeared modern and uncluttered was the large kitchen. But the solid wood units, Cornish slate countertops and flagstone floor were still perfectly in keeping with the rest of the property. Over the island in the middle hung stainless steel saucepans and various kitchen utensils.

Tristan appeared on the solid wooden staircase. The banister had a garland of artificial pine and holly with berries twisted around it. Casually, he jogged down, shaking Jason's hand as he passed and planting a kiss on Beth's cheek.

"Merry Christmas," he said, clearly happy to see her. His smile reached his dark eyes. He led her over to the fire, where he chucked more logs on, sending up orange sparks. "You look pretty. I like the jumper. Is it part of your range?" He rubbed her arm. It was good to feel his touch. She realised how much she'd missed him.

"Thank you. No, Kenny gave it to me. Apparently, it's a tradition to wear Christmas jumpers in his family, so…" Beth was unsure where she was going with this. Did it imply she was a part of Kenny's family now, too?

"Oh, right, it's nice." Tristan's hand dropped.

Beth frowned. Was he jealous? "He bought George one, too. His is a little less tasteful." She pointed at George, who was showing Janine how Rudolf's nose lit up when he pressed it. Janine was in fits of giggles with him. "But it's cute."

"How did they get on?"

"Great. Really great."

"When do you think you'll tell George?"

"Tristan, not now, please." She glanced at George, worried he might hear.

"Yes, sorry, I'm just curious." He squeezed her hand. She hadn't realised he'd taken hold of it. He pulled her closer, cuddling her to him. His breath was hot on her neck, sending goosebumps up her spine, as he murmured, "We'll talk later." Something so innocent, yet it turned her insides to jelly.

"Come on, you two," Janine said, making them jump apart like teenagers caught canoodling. "There are presents to be opened!" Holding George's hand, she led him towards the beautiful Christmas tree.

While everyone took a seat, Tristan ensured they all had a pre-dinner drink. Jason was sticking to orange juice with George, but everyone else had prosecco. Once they were settled by the fire, they began exchanging presents. Janine had bought them each a gift, even Jason. Sitting beside Tristan on one of the sofas, Beth gave out her gifts from them, handing Tristan his last. "I hope you like it," she said. "It was hard to know what to get you."

"Likewise," Tristan said.

They didn't get time to open their gifts from each other. George, so eager to open his and show his mum, climbed on Beth's lap. She remembered when he would do this aged two. At six, and a lot bigger, she realised soon he'd be too big to do this at all. He sat half on Beth's lap and half on Tristan's, showing them what he'd received. Tristan didn't complain. In fact, he looked more than happy to join in the excitement.

Once George had jumped off their laps, they were finally able to open their gifts. There were two parcels for Beth. One was a bottle of perfume: Chanel Coco Mademoiselle — her favourite, which she had been applying more liberally since Jason had bought her a new bottle for her birthday.

"How did you know this is my favourite?" She eyed Tristan suspiciously. He'd never been in her bedroom, hadn't even been upstairs to the bathroom. The scent was floral and not too overpowering, suiting her. It had become her favourite because her mother had bought her this perfume on her eighteenth birthday, before all had turned sour between them. It reminded her of the good times they'd had.

"I went round smelling every perfume over the counter until I found it," Tristan said, laughing. "I really like it on you. Reminds me of you, when I smell it."

"Thank you."

"Open the other one," he said.

Beth eagerly unwrapped the other, larger parcel. She gasped in delight as she held up three hearts, beautifully carved in wood, hanging one below the other.

"I thought it could hang on a wall in your boutique," Tristan said. "It's carved out of driftwood I found on Kittiwake Cove beach, and I asked Seb to make it for me."

"It's so beautiful," she said, giving him a chaste kiss on the lips.

"There's one more," Tristan said.

Inside the giftbag was an envelope that she hadn't spotted. Opening it, she was touched to find it was a gift voucher for the spa at the Kittiwake Cove Hotel.

"I thought you deserved a pamper day," Tristan said.

"Oh, thank you! It's too much, though." Beth blushed. He'd remembered her saying how she couldn't afford such a luxury.

"Nonsense. Not for my favourite person."

"Open yours," she said, nervously. "I hope you like it." She feared she hadn't put as much thought and effort into Tristan's gifts now.

Tristan tore at the paper to reveal a jumper and a small giftbox. She'd bought him a Christmas jumper, not realising Kenny would do the same for her. Unlike hers, his was bright green and gaudy, with an elf's body on the front and back, reading: *Elf and Safety*. "I could have done with this for the wedding," Tristan laughed, holding the jumper up to his chest. "The number of things that bride found to complain about."

"I'm sorry, I couldn't resist. I bought it before Kenny gave me mine. But now we match." She edged closer.

Tristan tugged it over his head. "Not quite. Yours is prettier."

She handed him the other gift box. Inside was a Christmas ornament of Santa delivering presents by a Christmas tree.

"I thought it could be your first Christmas decoration in your cottage," she said. "Considering how bare it looks, especially as you don't even have a tree!" It was an elegant ornament made of glazed bone china.

"It's lovely, and now I have a Christmas tree — of sorts."

He kissed her just below her ear, his breath lingering on her neck, making heat rise to her cheeks. There was the spark she craved. She'd never felt as drawn to anyone as she was to Tristan.

Around six, Janine got them all seated around her large oak dining table. The supper was laid out buffet style on the kitchen counter, so they could help themselves to a selection of cold meats, jacket potatoes and salad. On the table there was an array of cheeses from cheddar to stilton, and different chutneys and pickles to dip into. It looked like Nigella Lawson had visited. Or Marks and Spencer's food hall had been emptied. There was enough food to last for days if they did get snowed in.

"Tristan, I keep meaning to ask you," Janine said, as they all tucked into their food. "Has Tilly named her baby yet?"

"Yes, she has." He put down his knife and fork, patting his lips with a cloth napkin as if about to make a speech. His chest puffed out with pride. "Jacob Tristan Conway."

"Ah, that's lovely," Janine said. "You did help deliver him, after all."

"Oh, that is very special," Beth added, seeing Tristan rather pleased with his announcement.

"Easier or harder than lambing?" Jason joked.

"Have you been speaking to Joe?" Tristan jibbed back, and Jason grinned.

"To Jacob Tristan Conway," Jason raised his glass of non-alcoholic, sparkling Shloer. Everyone followed suit. Even George with his orange juice.

"You never know, one day you might get to deliver one of your own —"

"Mum!" Tristan said, glaring warningly at her. But Janine couldn't hide her expression, clearly enjoying pulling his leg.

Beth felt heat rise to her cheeks and prayed nobody had noticed that she was blushing. She wouldn't say no to more children … but would Tristan be the father of them? Was it too soon to even be considering something like this? Clearly his mother was desperate for a grandchild.

"I've got a couple of classic cars tucked away in my garage, if you'd like to see them later?" Janine said, turning to Jason, thankfully changing the subject. "They belonged to Raymond, Tristan's father. I can't bear to part with them."

"I would love to," Jason said.

After the buffet was devoured and they were all feeling rather full, Janine offered them dessert and coffee. "Beth,

270

please could you give me a hand to clear this first?" she asked, getting up from the table.

Tristan stood up. "I'll do it. You sit down, Mum."

"Thank you, darling, but why don't you take Jason and George out to see the cars?" she said to her son, who frowned. Then, realising she wanted time alone with Beth, he gave a nod. "I'll give you a shout when dessert is ready."

Beth's nerves raced momentarily. Alone with Janine, would this be when she told her she wasn't good enough for her son, or gave her the third degree about whether she wanted more children?

Their coats on, George went happily towards the door between Jason and Tristan, holding their hands. Even the dog followed them all out. Beth helped Janine, chatting idly as they cleared the table, both loading the dishwasher as they went along.

"Two things," Janine said, as soon as the front door was shut and they were alone. "Firstly, if I could arrange a meeting with your mother, would you want it?"

Beth stood blankly. Luckily, she'd just placed the plate she was holding into the dishwasher, otherwise she might have dropped it. "Pardon?"

"Sorry, I'm talking quickly, because, well, you never know when we'll get interrupted." Janine gestured to the front door. "Through the charities and organisations I work with, I know a lot of people. It so happens I know someone who knows your mother…" She looked hesitantly at Beth. "Don't get your hopes up, and if you'd rather I didn't meddle…"

"No, that's fine." Beth gathered her thoughts, taken aback by the revelation. "I'd love her to meet George."

271

"So would I! He is a delightful boy, and she should be proud of what you've achieved; a single mother building up her own business whilst raising a son."

"Jason's helped me so much," Beth couldn't help saying modestly.

"You still took the leap," Janine said, then nodded. "Okay, no promises, I'll see what I can do."

Beth shrugged. What did she have to lose?

"And secondly," Janine said softly, "I understand George met his father today." She continued covering the leftovers and putting them back in the large fridge.

Beth sighed with relief. Janine also wanted to talk about Kenny. Tristan must have told her. "Yes, but he doesn't know Kenny's his father. Not yet." Her panic spiked. Would Janine criticise her for not telling George?

"Of course, one step at a time." Janine gave her a reassuring pat on the shoulder. "But Beth, I just wanted to reassure you; I've known the Penkeths a long time. They're a solid family, Kenny's always been a good lad … and he's grown into a fine man. You have nothing to worry about. He'll treat George well, and will be a good father."

"I did get that impression from how he was around George today, but thank you for putting my mind at rest. He does seem to be a great guy."

As if she could read Beth's mind, and her turmoil over Tristan and Kenny, Janine said, "There's no reason why George can't have two dads. A biological one and a non-biological one."

"I know. It just seems to have all come at once. Tristan is lovely … but I could be depriving George of a happy family."

"You can't be with someone just for the sake of a child either. Kenny is a lovely young man, but don't settle for him if your heart is set on someone else." Janine handed Beth a plate from the fridge: a homemade strawberry cheesecake, which she quickly placed on the counter, out of fear of dropping it. "I know he's my son, so I am biased." Janine took another plate from the fridge and placed it on the counter, next to the cheesecake. "But I by no means feel you should stick with Tristan either, if he's not right for you. But don't let your head rule your heart." Janine gently tapped her own breastbone. Beth's heart was filled with so much admiration for Janine, she could feel a lump forming in her throat. Now was not the time to get teary.

At that point, the front door opened and a gust of cold air whooshed in. Tristan was carrying George, and Flash trotted behind them both. Jason closed the front door quickly to keep out the cold. All three of them were smiling. Just seeing George and Tristan together gave Beth's heart a little tug. She could see Janine watching too, as Tristan patiently helped George out of his coat and shoes, his big hands fumbling with the little zip and George's face, rosy from the cold, smiling up at him.

Janine was right. Though there had once been an attraction between her and Kenny, Beth now knew where her heart truly belonged.

With the way they'd all been ushered out of the house, Tristan knew his mother must have wanted a quiet word with Beth, but about what?

There was only so long a six-year-old could be entertained by a couple of classic American cars. He had let George sit in the driver's seat of the white 1950s Cadillac Fleetwood, which was sometimes hired out for weddings. The boy had happily placed his hands on the large steering wheel, pretending to drive it.

Jason drooled over the striking red 1966 Ford Mustang, which had been Tristan's father's toy, and which Janine occasionally took pleasure in driving now. Tristan had always preferred this car, with the parallel white stripes running over the bonnet and roof. As they talked, Jason appreciatively smoothed his hands over the polished metal.

Leaving Jason with the cars, Tristan took Flash for a swift walk, George coming with him. The little boy enjoyed throwing the stick for Flash to fetch. But it was cold, so Tristan kept the game short, only letting them play for ten minutes before returning to the house, calling out to Jason on their way back. He hoped his mother had got whatever she needed to say off her chest, but at the same time he didn't want to leave it too long in case Beth needed rescuing. His mother could be interfering and opinionated; her directness might be scaring Beth off the premises. And he didn't want that to happen. He needed to talk to Beth — privately.

He'd heard her say those three little words at the end of their phone call on Christmas Day. It had left him speechless, and before he could return the sentiments, Beth had hung up.

For dessert there had been a choice of Christmas pudding, strawberry cheesecake, a pavlova oozing with berries and cream, or profiteroles with a generous helping of chocolate sauce, which George got all around his mouth. Before Beth could reach him, Janine was busy dabbing his face with a napkin.

After the dinner table had been cleared, Janine got out a boardgame for George to play with Jason. Beth was about to join them, when Tristan grabbed her hand, giving it a tug.

"Come with me a minute," he said, in such an urgent whisper it made her stomach flutter. "We need to talk." The fluttering turned to anxiety.

Leading her up the stairs, Tristan kept hold of her hand. His tenderness surely meant he didn't want to end things — although had they really started anything? They'd only shared one night, cuddling.

They entered a room to the left at the top of the stairs. This bedroom was uncluttered and decorated in neutral colours. A double bed with cream embroidered covers stood in the centre, with solid wood furnishings surrounding it. The roof beams were bare, and the ceiling was sloping. Mingled with Tristan's woody scent was a cotton-fresh smell of clean laundry emanating from the bedsheets.

"This is where I'm sleeping tonight," he said. He sat on the end of the bed and patted beside him for Beth to sit down too. They could hear laughter and the drone of voices coming from downstairs. "I've been really worried, with Kenny showing up, and the row we had. I thought I'd blown it with you, so I want to apologise." His hand gently pushed a wisp of hair off her face as he hesitantly kissed her. Closing her eyes briefly, she let herself get swept away by his warmth and tenderness. She opened her eyes to find him gazing at her seriously. "You need to understand why I reacted the way I did."

"I understand."

"No, you don't." Tristan shook his head. "A few years ago, I was in a relationship with someone who I thought was my future." He sighed. She rubbed his hand to encourage him to continue with his confession. "Anyway, to cut a long story short, she fell pregnant with our child, but without telling me she had an abortion."

"Oh."

"And I know it was her right, her choice. It was her body. But it hurt that she'd not confided in me. It hurt that she'd felt she didn't want a child *with* me." Tristan tightened his grip on Beth's hand now. "Obviously, we drifted apart very quickly after that. But that's why I've been oversensitive regarding George not knowing about his father." Beth nodded. It did make sense now. Before she could answer, he continued, "But I would understand if you do want to make a go of it with Kenny. George needs a father. I'd give you space. We can be just friends."

"Oh, Tristan," Beth said, edging even closer. She didn't want to jump to conclusions. It could be too early to mention how she felt about him. He couldn't have heard her as she'd ended the call yesterday. "I know it's early days between us, but, well… If this worked out with us, and Kenny is seeing George, it's not like you can't be there too. There isn't any animosity between Kenny and me, like there would be if we'd had a nasty break-up. I like Kenny, and I want to be *his* friend. It's important for George that we, as his biological parents, both get on. But I want *you*…" She rested a hand on his cheek. He'd shaved and his skin was smooth. And being this close, he smelt divine, igniting their spark. "And I want you in George's life as well. If that's what you want?"

"Oh, what a relief." Tristan's hands cupped her face. "I want that too. I want you." His dark brown eyes were fixed on hers. Without hesitation, his head dipped, and his mouth found hers, their kiss deepening. When he broke away, he said, "I've been dying to get you alone all evening." He kissed her again, hotly and passionately.

Beth felt aroused, heat pooling deep in her core. How easy it would be to fall back onto the bed and make love. She wanted nothing more than to get lost with Tristan in this moment.

She broke away. The sensible part of her brain was kicking in. The bedroom door was still open. "We can't do anything here," she said, mild panic in her voice. However much she would love to fall into bed with Tristan right now, the fact that his mother and her brother and son were downstairs would definitely dampen the romance. Their voices and laughter could still be heard below.

"I know," Tristan said with a sigh of frustration. "We'll pick this up again later." Beth went to stand, but he grabbed her hand and pulled her back into his firm embrace. "Not so fast. I've something else to tell you, something important."

"What?" She frowned.

"Beth…" There was a twinkle in his eye. "I love you too."

Her heart skipped. The telephone call yesterday! "You heard me?"

"Yes, I did." He kissed her and she could feel the smile on his lips. "I want you to be a part of my family."

"And I want you to be part of mine."

CHAPTER 35: NEW YEAR'S EVE PARTY

On the morning of New Years' Eve, Beth awoke first, tangled in Tristan's arms. They were in his bed at the cottage. What a way to wake up on the last day of the year... As she gently came to her senses, Tristan's warm naked body pressing against hers, she remembered the night before. Not for the first time, they'd made love in front of the fire downstairs. Everything slow, sensual, tender; a continual discovery of each other's body.

After the last disastrous time she'd had sex, seven years ago, her fears had dissipated with Tristan's touch. Losing her virginity had been painful, even with Kenny's tenderness all those years ago. Now, sex felt bloody fantastic.

As she pleasantly recalled last night — Tristan's kisses, touches, and the waves of pleasure he had created — she found herself becoming aroused again. She wasn't the only one. Tristan, behind her, started to stir, brushing her hair aside, kissing her neck, pulling her towards him.

"Good morning," he whispered sleepily into her ear. His fingers trailed down her arm, brushing the side of her bare breast.

"Good morning." Slowly, she turned in his arms to face him, kissing his lips.

As he pushed her gently back so he was on top of her, he stopped. "Shit!" he said, bowing his head to his chest. "We used the last condom last night."

A small part of her didn't care. But the sensible side soon took over — she didn't want a repeat performance of her eighteenth birthday. Not yet. She wanted time with Tristan first.

A devilish wickedness passed over Tristan's face as he smiled at her. "I'll just have to improvise." He pulled the duvet over him and tenderly kissed her, trailing from one breast to the other, down the side of her body, around her bellybutton, with his lips and tongue, until his stubble was grazing her inner thigh.

With a moan, she closed her eyes, and relaxed into the tender sensations Tristan was provoking, wondering if this really would sate her passion.

But it did. Like a pebble skimming across the water, making ripples, waves of pleasure surged through her body. Afterwards, she could easily have fallen back asleep, Tristan cuddling into her, but she knew she needed to get up and get back to George. She pulled Tristan into the shower with her, only to find this still slowed them down. This was what love felt like. They couldn't get enough of each other.

Beth had seen Tristan every day since Boxing Day. Her heart ached when she wasn't with him. And every time he looked at her, with that gorgeous smile plastered over his face, his eyes burning with desire, she was filled with so much love, she wasn't sure she could contain it. They'd spent the last few nights — once George was in bed, and Flash exhausted from long walks — getting to know one another more intimately, making love, forging a bond. To create Christmas in his cottage for Beth and George, Tristan had dragged in a tree, no longer required at Trenouth Manor, placing it in his lounge. And her gift to him, the Christmas ornament, stood in pride of place on the mantelpiece over the fire.

Kenny had visited again too, even with Tristan about, so that George was gradually getting to know his father, even if he didn't realise it quite yet. However, Beth felt confident she would be able to tell George soon. There was no doubt in her mind that Kenny was, as Janine had affirmed, a decent guy, and would be a good father. He'd already spoken about George meeting his parents: George's grandparents.

Beth fantasised that George would be spoilt by two sets of grandparents. Janine, his newly adoptive nanny, and Kenny's parents were keen to be a part of his life. Beth would have no problem finding a babysitter now. She didn't care if her mother wanted no part in their lives; there were others prepared to love them for who they were, with no judgement.

With a lingering kiss in his car, Tristan dropped Beth home later that morning, vowing to buy condoms, and promising to return later to pick her and George up. In the evening, they were heading back over to Janine's.

As they pulled up outside Janine's house, the night was cold and clear, and the stars were shining brightly down upon them.

Tristan helped George out of his car seat. Flash jumped from the open boot of the Range Rover, and then Tristan and Beth each took one of George's gloved hands, so that he was between them with the dog trotting behind.

"Mum always holds a party here for friends, family and some of her neighbours," said Tristan.

"I would have thought her neighbours were mainly sheep and cattle," said Beth. Janine's house was in rather a remote part of the valley. "It was lovely of your mum to invite Jason and Scott too."

"Nonsense. He's your brother, they're family too." Tristan lent over George to bury his face in Beth's hair. "My mother has always wanted a large family."

"So have I," Beth said.

Janine greeted them at the front door with a glass of red wine in her hand. She kissed each of them on the cheek. There was the chattering and laughter of guests in the background, over Christmas songs playing on the stereo.

Janine's house looked very much like it had on Boxing Day, although the dining table had been pushed to one side, to make more room for guests. A finger buffet had already been laid out with nibbles. The oven was on, emitting an aroma of warming pastry, and mulled wine simmered in a slow cooker on the side. Bottles of drinks filled a section of the kitchen worktop, and beside them stood a selection of glasses, all gleaming as if Janine had polished every single one. And as with all good parties, everyone seemed to be congregating in the kitchen.

"There's a room next to Tristan's made up for George," Janine said, helping George out of his coat. "In case it gets too much for him. Tristan, darling, take your bags up there now."

"Thank you," Beth said to Janine.

"And I've invited your parents." Janine kept her voice low. As if sensing Beth's panic, she took her hand and squeezed it. "Don't worry. Everything will be fine, Beth."

Beth had already known that Janine was inviting Kenny and his family, so that they could meet George. But she hadn't realised her parents would be coming too. Her heart thudded at the mention of them.

Tristan made his way back downstairs to Beth, relieved of their bags, and made introductions to the few people that had already arrived. Joe and Rhianna couldn't make it. Owning a pub, Joe tended to have his own New Year's Eve party to manage, but Beth recognised Rose and Charles, who had come for the quieter affair.

"The pub gets too noisy for me," Rose said.

One of Janine's neighbours had a little girl, so George and Flash had a playmate. Jason and Scott soon arrived, and Beth felt she should tell him that their parents might make an appearance.

"Better get a drink inside me," Jason responded anxiously with a frown.

Beth looked imploringly at Scott for support.

"It'll be okay," Scott said, giving Jason a firm pat on the back. "I promise not to let him drink too much," he said more quietly to Beth.

Kenny arrived with his parents, and they were subtly introduced to their grandson. Anxious about her own parents, Beth held off drinking too much prosecco. Tristan, obviously sensing her worries, kept close by.

"Beth…" Janine approached her half an hour later. "There's someone here to meet you."

"Oh God."

"Now, don't panic," Janine said reassuringly. "She's as nervous as you about this. But she does want to make amends. So please hear her out."

This was the moment. Beth took a sip from her full glass and joined Janine, who led her to a quiet part of the room, by the fire in the lounge. Her mother was sitting on the leather sofa and stood up when she saw Beth, nervously smoothing her hands down her skirt. She was the same woman; maybe a little thinner, a little greyer, a few more age lines on her face, but she was as Beth remembered her. Now Beth had grown into a woman, she could see their resemblance. Jason had often said they looked alike.

"I'll go grab you that cup of tea, Carol," Janine said tactfully, giving Beth's arm a gentle squeeze as she left them.

"Mum," Beth said, then frowned. "Where's Dad?"

"He couldn't make it. He's not very well," Carol said. Or maybe he couldn't face Beth. "Look, Beth, I think there's a lot to discuss."

"You don't say," Beth snapped. The fear of rejection — again — kept her from moving nearer. But she mustn't make a scene, not at Janine's.

"Tonight might not be the right time to go over the past," Carol said nervously, glancing around. "Janine just felt ... well, she's told me a lot about you." She smiled and sat down on the sofa, gesturing for Beth to do the same.

"Has she?" Beth anxiously glanced over at the crowd of people in the kitchen. "All good, I hope?"

"Of course. You have your own boutique, and you raised money for her charity, didn't you?"

"Yes, yes, at the charity ball held at Trenouth Manor, I put on a fashion show." Beth decided to brave sitting beside her mother, although she kept to the opposite end of the sofa. She wanted a safety gap. "Why didn't you come and find us?" she blurted out angrily.

Carol's gaze dropped to her lap. When she looked up, her eyes were shining as if she was about to cry. "I'm sorry, Beth. Your father and I, well... We felt..."

"You kicked me out."

"We didn't kick you out. You left." Carol chewed her lip before speaking again.

"You kicked Jason out."

"That was different ... and wrong, too."

"I'll say!"

"Look, there's too much to go over. Let's not do it here, Beth." Carol tried to take Beth's hand, but she recoiled. "I'm sorry, we're both sorry. Your father got a promotion, so we had to move away, and then you'd moved. I wasn't sure you'd want us in your life… What matters is that now we are back in touch. We can start over. Please…"

At that moment, George came running in front of the fire with the little girl he was playing with. Her blonde hair was tied in a French plait, although there were a lot of loose strands now and it was not as neat. Flash wasn't with them, so perhaps Tristan had made the dog retire to his bed.

"Mummy!" George automatically cuddled Beth, clambering onto the leather sofa, filling the gap between them.

"Is this…?" Carol asked hesitantly.

Beth nodded. "George, this is my —" she hesitated, wondering whether to make something up, then thought better of it — "mother, your nanny…" She looked at her mother. "Or would you prefer to be called something different…? Grandma?"

"No, Nanny is fine." Carol looked at George and gave him a huge smile. "Hello, George."

George and Carol chatted about the presents he'd received for Christmas. It made Beth's heart swell with pride over her son. George, without hesitation, moved closer to his new nanny, unaware of the past animosity. Out of the corner of her eye, Beth saw Scott giving Jason a little encouraging shove. Jason approached the sofa.

"Mum?" His knuckles were white where he was still holding his pint glass.

"Jason?" Her hands flew to her face as she stood to greet him. "Oh, my, you've changed… You were just a scrawny…" She stopped, obviously realising the last time she'd seen her son was when he'd been a skinny teenager. Maybe they didn't need to drag up that memory too. The air felt thick with awkwardness. "I've missed you both so much." Tears welled in Carol's eyes as she stared at Jason, then Beth.

"This is Scott." Jason beckoned Scott over. Beth held her breath. How would her mother react to Jason's partner?

"Mrs Sterling," Scott said with a nod as he politely shook her hand.

"Call me Carol." She cupped her hand with his, regaining her composure.

There was some apprehension, but between them they made conversation, trying to catch up without raising too much about the past, like strangers at a bus stop. Everyone was aware they were in Janine's home and didn't want to create a scene, so they remained friendly, albeit awkward. Maybe that's why Janine had arranged for Carol to meet them there, on neutral territory. Jason told Carol about his business that he jointly owned with Archie. Tristan joined them, putting a protective arm around Beth's waist, singing her praises to Carol, confirming Beth's support for the charity ball and how well her business was doing.

"There is another thing I should tell Mum," Beth said to Tristan. "Maybe take George away for a bit."

"I'll do it," Jason offered.

"No, you stay," Tristan said. "Come on, George, I think Janine has a treat for you." Tristan took George's hand and led him away for a moment. She saw Tristan have a brief word with Kenny, who was ruffling George's hair.

"Mum, I've recently met George's father." Beth said it quickly, as if removing a plaster. She was grateful to have Jason standing beside her. Scott had gone to fetch more drinks. "Although George has met him, he doesn't yet know Kenny is his father."

"He's a great guy," Jason added, hugging his sister. He had replaced Tristan's protective embrace.

Kenny arrived, joining them by the fireplace, and introduced himself to Carol. He laughed about bumping into Beth at the local supermarket.

"Gosh, I've missed so much, haven't I?" Carol said, her eyes misty with tears. Beth handed her a tissue from a box on the coffee table, and her mother wiped her eyes.

"It's okay, the important thing is you're here now," Beth said, deciding that to confront her mother would not change what had happened in the past. Beth and Kenny related their story, and when they would choose to tell George. Slowly, Carol was welcomed into the fold of the party. There was still plenty to discuss, but tonight wasn't the right time. Maybe now that Jason and Beth were both older and fully mature, they'd be able to discuss things with their parents in a less heated way and reach a place of forgiveness.

There was one burning question, though, and in the end, Beth couldn't hold it in, as Carol said she would have to leave soon.

"Where *is* Dad?" Beth asked, fearing the answer. Maybe he still wanted nothing to do with his children.

Carol bit her lip. "He's not well, love." As she slipped on her thick coat, she looked conflicted about what to share. "He was diagnosed with prostate cancer a few months back."

"Oh, shit!"

"It's okay, we caught it early, the prognosis is good, but the treatment has knocked him for six. When Janine got in touch, he was eager for me to see you."

"Does he want to see me?"

"Yes, yes he does, but when he's stronger." Carol rubbed Beth's arm reassuringly. "This illness has made us both re-evaluate life, and the mistakes we've made." She smiled gently. "I'd best go. I don't like to leave him too long." Carol hugged her daughter and kissed her cheek awkwardly. They still had a bridge of trust to build. She then hugged Jason goodbye too, who had joined them. "I'll be in touch soon."

"Well, that was surreal," Jason said, once Carol had left.

Beth agreed, but now she had a new concern: her father's health. Was this why their mother had agreed to get in touch? But Jason assured her that she shouldn't worry anymore. Whatever their parents chose to do, or not to do, Jason and Beth had each other.

"If I've learnt anything over these past few years, it's that you can't control what others do. You can only control your own behaviour," Jason said, giving his sister a hug.

Jason led her back into the throng of the party, and she decided to take her brother's advice and not dwell on it further. The first steps had been taken to rebuild their relationship with their parents. If they didn't succeed, then she knew she could live without them. She had for the last seven years.

Eventually, Beth caught up with Janine, who'd been run off her feet as the host, although she seemed to be enjoying it, making sure everyone was well fed and had a drink in their hand. "In case I forget to say it — thank you, Janine," Beth said, "for arranging for my mother to come here."

"It turned out well, I hope?"

"Yes, I think it did. We've taken the first steps, so thank you."

"Tristan persuaded me to intervene. You should thank him, too." Janine gave her a hug. "But I'm glad I could help."

This made Beth love Tristan even more.

As midnight approached, party poppers were frantically handed out, drinks poured, and the party listened to the chimes of Big Ben on the radio.

"Happy New Year!" everyone shouted. There were cheers, party poppers banged, and Flash barked.

"I love you," Tristan said, kissing Beth firmly on the lips. "Here's to a great New Year."

"I love you too," Beth said.

They reluctantly let each other go and hugged the rest of their friends and family. Then, everyone formed a circle, arms crossing their bodies as they held hands, and sang 'Auld Lang Syne'.

Beth's throat tightened with joy as she held Tristan's hand and Jason danced beside her, holding George — who was far from tired. Her eyes welled with happy tears. Everyone was singing and laughing, and she was surrounded with her new family. She turned to Tristan. "I never imagined on that autumn day, when my car broke down, that the idiot who almost ran me over would turn out to be the man of my dreams."

"Yeah, well, I'm relieved you gave the idiot a chance to redeem himself." Tristan kissed her tenderly.

EPILOGUE

One year later

It was Christmas Day. To Beth's delight, George was surrounded by the people who loved him. Three sets of grandparents: Tristan's mum, Kenny's parents, and Beth's own parents. The boy was spoilt beyond his wildest dreams.

They were spending Christmas Day at Trenouth Manor. It was the only place large enough to cater for everyone comfortably. Janine was thrilled to be back entertaining in her old home again.

The winter sun shone low through the window of the morning room. They'd moved out of the dining room, leaving the wreckage of their Christmas dinner on the large dining table, to sit by the open fire and exchange gifts.

Flash sat obediently by Janine's legs as she perched on the edge of a sofa by the large Christmas tree. The only one who looked frail was Beth's father, Nigel, who was sitting on another sofa beside Carol. The cancer treatment had taken its toll on his stout, sturdy frame and weakened him. But he was on the mend.

Tristan stood beside Beth, holding her hand, as she watched George sitting in the middle of the floor and opening a gift from Kenny. Scott and Jason were fetching the pot of tea from the kitchen, and no doubt bringing in the tin of Quality Streets.

The past year had been busy and successful. Not long after New Year's Eve, George and Kenny had been properly introduced as father and son. Now Kenny had George to stay on alternate weekends and came to dinner midweek. In the spring, Beth and George had moved in with Tristan at his cottage, allowing Scott to move in with Jason. Her boutique was booming, and she had held another fashion show in the summer.

Her parents had built a renewed bond with their children, Jason's sexuality accepted. That was the toughest thing, actually — her parents understanding that Jason hadn't chosen to be gay, and that he shouldn't feel he had to hide it. But between them, they appeared to be moving forward. Since last New Year's Eve, they had all vowed to make a fresh start.

"Hey, beautiful," Tristan said, kissing Beth on the side of her neck, just behind her ear, knowing full well it sent goosebumps of pleasure down her back.

"Hey." She kissed him back. "I have something to tell you…"

"You do?"

She shook her head. "Later, though… It can wait." However much she loved her extended family, Beth wanted this to remain between her and Tristan for the time being.

"Good." His mouth covered hers as he kissed her passionately. He then called, "Everybody, could I have your attention?" He clapped and waved, pulling Beth into the centre of the room with him. George stopped opening his present. Everyone looked up from their seats, parcels half unwrapped on their laps. Jason and Scott paused in the doorway, holding the trays of teacups. Then, in front of the family and the smouldering fire, Tristan got down on one knee before Beth and presented an open ring box. A large solitaire diamond ring sparkled back at her. "Beth, my darling, will you marry me?" he said, looking up at her, a heartfelt expression on his handsome face.

She fell to her knees beside him. "Oh my, yes, yes." She kissed him, tears welling, then closed her eyes and hugged him.

The whole family were cheering and clapping as they got back on their feet. Janine asked Scott to forget the tea and to fetch champagne from the kitchen. Kenny shook Tristan's hand. The Christmas presents temporarily abandoned, everyone was congratulating them.

With Tristan's ring on her finger, Beth knew she must always be honest with him. The trust between them was strong and needed to remain that way. Once the family had settled down again, she pulled Tristan aside, keeping her mouth close to his ear. "Tristan … we'd better make it a quick wedding," she whispered. He frowned, confused. She smiled and kept her voice low. "Because I'm pregnant."

Tristan's shocked expression changed to a grin. "Is that what you were going to tell me?"

"It might have been."

"And why you haven't drunk your prosecco?"

She nodded.

Tristan kissed her tenderly. Then, cupping Beth's face, with devotion in his eyes, he said, "This has got to be the best Christmas gift ever!"

A NOTE TO THE READER

Dear Reader,

I hope you liked *Mistletoe At The Manor*, and it has given you that escapism we sometimes all need.

If you enjoyed reading this book, the best way to let me know is by leaving a review on **Goodreads** and/or **Amazon**. It's also a great way to share with other readers too! And I will be forever grateful to you.

I love hearing from readers, so please feel free to contact me on any of my social media platforms. I'd love to chat with you. You can follow me here:

Facebook / **Goodreads** / **Amazon** / **BookBub** / **Blog** / **Website** / **Instagram** / **Twitter**.

I also have a monthly newsletter that you can subscribe to **here**. I sometimes run competitions open only to subscribers. You'll get all the gossip there first.

Once again, thank you. You are the reason I love to write romance.

Kind regards,

Teresa

www.teresamorgan.co.uk

Sapere Books is an exciting new publisher of brilliant fiction and popular history.

To find out more about our latest releases and our monthly bargain books visit our website: **saperebooks.com**

Printed in Great Britain
by Amazon